You're My Little Secret 3 (Truths Revealed)

By: Chenell Parker

Acknowledgements

I'll try my best to make this short and sweet. I can't go one step further without giving thanks to God for everything. This writing journey has been an amazing one, and I'm forever grateful. I also have to acknowledge my family. My kids, sisters, brother, aunts, uncles, cousins, nieces, nephews and my many wonderful friends (I didn't name anyone specifically because I always manage to forget somebody). I also thank my publishing Family, Write House Publishing for everything. They have shown me the true meaning of working as a team. Last, but not least, I thank each and every person who has purchased a copy of this book as well as all the others. Without you it would not be possible. Your support is greatly appreciated.

KENNEDI

I'm really starting to get numb to the pain. I'm being calm, but my heart is being ripped apart by the same man who is supposed to love me. Six months into my marriage and my husband tells me that he's fathered another child with the same woman that he cheated on me with before. When I found out that I was pregnant, I was so happy. I ran out and bought some chocolate covered strawberries and wine, thinking Dominic, and I would celebrate the good news. When he walked through the door, I jumped in his arms and kissed him all over his face. I knew that something was wrong just by the way his body stiffened at my touch. Never in a million years would I have thought that he would tell me what he did. I couldn't believe that I would have to go through this heartache all over again, all while carrying a child of my own. It hurt me to my heart to see how upset he looked when I told him that I was having his baby as well.

"Why do you keep doing this to me Dominic?" I wanted to know what I did so wrong to deserve all of this. I tried to be a good girlfriend and an even better wife. Obviously that wasn't enough for him.

"Stop always trying to play like you're the victim Kennedi. We're not happy with each other, and you know it."

"I am happy, so speak for yourself. You never even tried Dominic. You swore that you and Brooklyn were through, but she ends up carrying another one of your kids," I cried. "So how many months is she?"

"She's three months," he replied crushing me once again.

"Wow, so we've been married for six months and she's three months pregnant. So you never did leave her alone like you said," I wondered.

"I tried to do right by you and stay away from Brooklyn. You basically ran me to her with all of your bitching and complaining."

"So I made you cheat on me Dominic? Is that what you're saying?"

"No, I'm saying that we should have never gotten married to begin with. I married you knowing that I was in love with another woman. I bought my baby's mama a gift on my honeymoon Kennedi. Do you know how fucked up that is? This shit was doomed from the start. We weren't even married a good month before I begged Brooklyn to take me back," he yelled.

I was devastated. I knew Dominic had some feelings for Brooklyn, but I never thought that he was in love with her. Then to find out they had been messing around almost as long as we'd been married totally crushed me.

"Well, I'm having your baby too so now what?"

"I'm going to take care of my baby and you of all people should know that," he replied. "That's if you're really even pregnant."

"I have no reason to lie. I can take another test right now if you want me to, but what about us Dominic? I hope you don't think I'm going to sit around and wait until you figure out what you want?"

6

"No, because I already know what I want. I want a divorce," he said like it was that simple.

"So our marriage is over just like that? You fucked up, and I have to suffer for it?" I sobbed uncontrollably.

"You can keep the townhouse. I'll make sure the rent is paid. You know if you need anything all you have to do is call," he said ignoring my cries.

"Please don't do this to me Dominic. I can't go through this pregnancy without you. You know how hard it is for me to carry a baby," I tried to play on his sympathy in hopes of getting him to stay.

"You won't be alone. Like I said, all you have to do is call," he replied pissing me off.

"You're leaving me to go run to that nasty bitch!" I yelled. Just that fast my hurt had turned into anger. I hated Dominic and Brooklyn for what they were doing to me.

"Don't disrespect her like that Kennedi. Not one time have I ever heard her say anything bad about you so chill with the name calling," he said defending that home wrecker.

"You're coming to her rescue, but are you even sure that it's your baby that she's carrying?" I asked him.

"You can miss me with that shit. I'm positive that it's mine, and I don't need a test to prove it. And while we're talking about it, I don't appreciate you running your mouth to Brooklyn about me testing DJ either," he replied making me even madder.

"Fuck her!" I shouted as loud as I could. I knew I was making a fool of myself, but I didn't care. "You're acting like that bitch is somebody special."

"Alright Kennedi, I'm about to grab a few things and I'm out of here. I'm not with this arguing and shit," Dominic announced.

"I know you're not trying to leave tonight!" I screeched. He was filling up an overnight bag with clothes and toiletries. When he started packing his suitcase, I was really freaking out.

"Yes, I am. It doesn't make sense for us to prolong things. I want to be happy, and I'm tired of faking it Kennedi. I can't even be myself around you. You hate everything I do."

"That's because everything you do is so damn hood. All you want to do is hang with your pathetic ass brother and smoke. You're not in the projects anymore, and you need to stop acting like it. I'm not okay with that, and I won't pretend like I am," I said honestly.

"And that's why we need to end this right now. I'm not changing who I am for you or anybody else."

"My mama had you right. You got lucky enough to overcome your circumstances, but mentally you'll never change your ghetto ways," I said angrily.

"You think I give a damn about what your mama says? Four husbands later and her ass is still alone and miserable. You're going to end up just like her if you keep listening to her. I don't blame your daddy for leaving her crazy ass," Dominic barked.

"Dominic, please just think about this before you make a decision. I know we can work this out," I pleaded.

"Kennedi I've been thinking about this for a while. There were so many times that I just wanted to walk away. I put your feelings before my own, so I never did it. I never wanted you to be hurt, so I put my own feelings to the side, but I can't do that anymore. I want to be happy just like everybody else. I just think we got married for the wrong reasons, and I knew it from the start," he confessed.

"Well, I'm not giving you a divorce," I admitted.

"I don't want this to be ugly Kennedi, but that's up to you. We can do this on our own as adults or we can get our lawyers involved."

"No judge on the face of this earth is going to grant you a divorce knowing that I'm carrying your child. My mama has been through this enough for me to know how it works. I'm prepared to fight for my marriage," I warned.

"What are you fighting for Kennedi? There's nothing left between us, but the baby that you're carrying."

"I don't care. I refuse to sit by and let her have you. If I can't get my happily ever after then, neither can she," I seethed.

"Well, I guess I'll see you in court," he said right before walking out the door.

I went to the window and watched as he drove away, taking a part of me with him. I sat on the floor and cried until my eyes started to hurt. Never in a million years did I see this coming. I knew

Dominic, and I had some issues to work on, but him leaving me was never part of the plan. I never imagined myself being a single mother. That was the whole point of me getting married. I'm only four weeks pregnant, but I find it hard to be happy about it. As bad as it sounds, I won't be hurt if I don't go full term with this pregnancy. Without Dominic by my side, I'm not even excited about having a baby anymore.

BROOKLYN

I'm so ready to go to bed, but my house is full of people. My mama, brothers, and cousins are all sitting around my living room acting like they're not going home. I keep telling them that we're alright, but Bryce is acting like a damn detective. He keeps asking us the same questions over and over. The answer will never change, but he just keeps pressing us for info. Dominic had just sent me a text telling me that he's on his way. I'm starving so he's stopping to get me and DJ something to eat. He told me that we needed to talk, and it didn't sound too good. I'm sure that things with him and Kennedi didn't go well. I assume that's why he wants to talk.

I still can't believe that I'm three months pregnant and didn't even know it. Dominic and I have only been back together for five months, so I had to get pregnant in month number two. I don't have morning sickness like I did with DJ, which is great. I gained a little weight, but it all went straight to my ass and hips. I've been sleeping a lot lately, but even that didn't make me suspicious. I guess that explains why I crave ice cream so much now.

"So when are you going to tell everybody that you're pregnant?" Candace asked shaking me from my thoughts. I was in the kitchen drinking some juice when she and Co-Co came in.

"I don't know. Dominic said he would tell them if I was scared to do it. You know my mama is going to have a fit," I said. As far as my mama knew, Dominic and I were no longer together. Even my brothers thought it was over between us. The only people who really knew that we hooked up again was Taylor, my cousins, and David.

"You better stop being so scary. Everybody is here so this is the perfect time. I don't know why anybody would get mad. Dominic takes very good care of you and DJ. Nobody has to do anything for y'all," Candace fussed.

"That boy got some potent sperm. He popping those babies in you left and right," Co-Co said.

"Shut up Co-Co," I said laughing.

"Kennedi is going to die, but that's good for her ass," Candace said.

"He left her," I said.

"Girl wait, who left who?" Co-Co asked dramatically.

"Dominic left Kennedi. He's on his way over here now," I answered.

"What! That's so good for her. After the way she did my friend, I don't feel sorry for her ass. Karma is a bitch," Candace declared.

"Have you talked to Nadia lately?" I asked.

"No, not really. She's always telling me she'll call me back, but she never does. I'm still trying to see what's up with her hanging with Shannon's ratchet ass all of a sudden," Candace replied.

Just the mention of Shannon had me thinking about Kevin. Usually he would be here with the rest of the family, but that was a thing of the past. I really did miss our friendship, but I knew that it was over.

My cousins and I returned to the living room to join the rest of the family. DJ ran around full of energy while my nieces sat around watching TV.

"I'm surprised DJ is home," my mama said. "Usually he's with Dominic whenever I call."

Candace was nudging me slightly trying to get me to say something. This is the perfect time since I have everybody together, but I'm just not in the mood to hear the negative comments that I'm sure are going to come. Dominic is right, he takes care of me and my son, so there is no need for anybody else to be upset. Co-Co is staring at me and nodding his head towards my mother. I'm shaking my head no, but he's very persistent. Even though he's trying to be discreet about what he's doing, my mama still saw him.

"Why are you sitting over there looking like you're catching a spasm?" She asked him laughing.

"I'm good, but Brooklyn has something to say," he blurted out.

I wanted to jump up from this sofa and punch him in his big ass mouth. I hate when he does shit like that. If I wasn't ready to talk, he should have respected my wishes.

"Co-Co you are so wrong for that," Candace said angrily.

"What? She needed a push, so I pushed her ass," he replied like he didn't do anything wrong.

"What's wrong Brooklyn?" My mother asked with concern dripping from her voice.

"Nothing is wrong, Co-Co is just being stupid," I replied trying to brush her off. I rolled my eyes at him and focused on the TV.

"That's bullshit, I know you well enough to know when you're lying. So what's up?" She asked again.

13

Candace looked at me and nodded her head as if she was telling me to go ahead and come clean.

"I'm pregnant," I blurted out loud enough for everyone to hear.

"Aww, shit! Do you even try to use protection Baby? Who are you pregnant by now?" Jaden yelled angrily.

"What the hell do mean who am I pregnant by now? The same person I was pregnant by before," I answered smartly.

"Oh my God Brooklyn! Dominic is a married man. I thought you were done with him. After all the talks we've had about you not being his mistress, you turn around and do just that. You act like you're happy being the woman on the side," my mama spat angrily.

My feelings were hurt by what she said, but I didn't expect her to understand the situation. Dominic never makes me feel like the woman on the side. He treats and respects me as if I'm the only woman in his life.

"It's not even like that. We didn't deal with each for months before he got married, but at the same time I can't help how I feel about him. After tonight, he and Kennedi are no longer together anyway," I explained.

"Dominic is my boy, and I love him like a brother, but I really hope you don't believe that shit," Bryce spoke up.

"I really don't expect y'all to understand and I'm not asking for anybody's approval. I'm three months pregnant and my baby will be here in six months whether y'all like it or not," I said.

"Honestly, I don't like that you're having all of these damn babies so young. But at the same time, Dominic handles his business with you and his son. Besides him getting you this apartment and your truck, he makes sure that you and DJ are straight," Jaden said.

I couldn't believe how calm my brothers are now compared to the way they behaved the first time they found out that I was pregnant.

"Wait, so Dominic got you that truck? You told me that you got that with your school money," my mama said in shock.

"I know, I just didn't want you to know that we were messing around again," I confessed.

"I mean Dominic does do what he's supposed to do for you and DJ. I just don't want you to end up getting hurt in the end. You know how many men claim to be leaving their wives and never actually do it? That's how it goes Brooklyn. They say whatever you want to hear just to keep you around," my mama told me.

"I've already made it clear to him that I don't want him to leave his wife. Dominic and Kennedi's problems go back much further than just me. He's leaving because that's what he wants to do," I explained.

"That man is not leaving his wife, Brooklyn. Now, I do believe that he'll take care of you and your kids, but don't get your hopes up high thinking that y'all are going to be together," Caleb said.

Right when he finished talking I heard a key turning in the lock. Dominic walked through the front door and paused when he saw everybody sitting around my huge living room.

"Hey, y'all," he spoke before handing me our food. Everybody spoke back as he walked back out the front door. A few seconds later he returned with a huge duffle bag and a suitcase. Everybody looked on in stunned silence as he walked down the hall and straight into my bedroom, followed by DJ.

"Well, I guess he made y'all out of some liars. Looks like he's here to stay," Candace commented.

"Daddy's home," Co-Co said loudly singing one of Usher's songs.

"Shut your crazy ass up boy," my mama fused at him. "I'm happy he's here so we can get some things straight."

"Wait a minute, just in case everybody forgot, I'm grown, and this is my house that y'all are sitting in. Nobody needs to get anything straight with Dominic. He doesn't owe anybody in here an explanation. I just told y'all the situation, but it's really nobody's business," I said.

"You might be grown, but you're still my baby. Don't get mad at me for worrying about you. I just know how these situations can turn out. I'm not saying that Dominic is going to do you dirty. I just want you to be prepared for whatever happens," my mama replied.

Dominic walked back in holding DJ and took a seat next to me.

"I know that you'll always look at me as your baby, but I have babies of my own now. In six months, I'll be the mother of two kids," I replied.

"You told them?" Dominic asked looking at me in surprise.

"Yeah they know," I answered.

"I'm not trying to get in your business or anything. I just want to make sure that Brooklyn is alright. Technically, you're still a married man, and I don't condone cheating. You might wake up one morning and decide to go back to your wife. Then where does that leave her and my grandkids?" My mama said voicing her concerns.

"Kennedi and I are officially over. I asked her for a divorce tonight. She knows that Brooklyn is pregnant, and she knows that this is who I want to be with. I haven't lied to Kennedi or Brooklyn about anything. So far as Brooklyn being alright, she's been good since before DJ came along. Besides a ride to school, Brooklyn hasn't had to ask anybody for anything. Now that she has her own ride she won't even need that anymore. I've always made sure that she was straight even when she broke up with me," Dominic answered truthfully.

"He told y'all. Good answer Dominic," Co-Co applauded. My mama gave him one of her famous looks, and he quickly shut up.

"Yeah alright, but don't make me have to hurt you and your wife behind my baby," she threatened. "I'm going home. Brooklyn you need to call Dr. Martin and make an appointment."

"I'm tired, so it's time for everybody to go home," I told them.

"Bitch, you are so fake for that. Dominic walks in and now you're tired all of a sudden," Co-Co said while turning up his nose at me.

17

Dominic and DJ walked downstairs with my brothers while Taylor and I saw my mama and my cousins out. They all wanted to hook up the following weekend, and I agreed. When Bryce came back upstairs, Taylor and my nieces went home with him. Dominic and DJ came back inside right after they left.

"Sit down and eat baby. I'm going to give him a bath and put him to sleep so we can talk," he said.

I sat down and started eating my food, but I really didn't have much of an appetite anymore. I was nervous about whatever Dominic had to say. I already knew it had something to do with Kennedi, but I didn't know what. She's not going to just sit back and let Dominic get away from her. I have to prepare myself for the drama that I know is sure to come. As much as I love Dominic, I'm not putting up with the foolishness.

DOMINIC

When I got to Brooklyn's apartment, I didn't expect to find her entire family there. They were looking at me like I was trespassing, even though, the place is in my name. I was happy to hear that Brooklyn had already told them that she was pregnant, but I didn't have a problem telling them myself. It felt good to let them know where I stood as far as Brooklyn and my children are concerned. Brooklyn can have ten kids, and I would make sure that she and each and every one of our kids are well taken care of. I also have to think about the baby that I'm having with Kennedi. I'm nervous about telling Brooklyn because I don't know how she's going to react. I'm praying that she doesn't go crazy and try to leave me.

Aside from the baby that Kennedi is carrying, I don't want to have anything else to do with her. Brooklyn never has to worry about me going back that way again. There's no reason to. Most times men cheat for sex, and that damn sure isn't happening with Kennedi. I didn't want that boring shit when I was with her. I have a feeling that she's going to make this divorce difficult for me, so I have to get prepared. I just don't want it to tear Brooklyn and me apart in the process. I was so deep in thought that I never realized DJ had already fallen asleep. I had him on my chest while I rubbed his back, and he was dead to the world. I got up and put him in his bed and then went to look for Brooklyn. I'm dreading this conversation, but it has to be done. If she finds out any other way about Kennedi being pregnant she'll leave me for sure.

That's a chance that I'm not willing to take. I walked into the living room and found Brooklyn stretched out on the sofa sleeping. I hated to wake her up, but I need to get this over with.

"Brook," I whispered while shaking her lightly. She stirred a little before opening her eyes. When she focused and saw me standing over her, she sat up and motioned for me to sit down.

"What's up Dominic?" She asked while turning to face me. It's like she knows that I'm about to give her some bad news, and she's ready for it.

"We need to talk. Just promise that you won't leave me after I say what I have to say," I begged.

"I'll never promise you anything like that. If you say some shit to make me leave you then I'm out of here," she replied seriously.

Hearing her say that only made my heart beat a little faster.

"I didn't do anything wrong, but you're still not going to like what I have to say."

"Just say it Dominic," she sighed impatiently.

"Kennedi is pregnant," I said while looking directly at her. Just like Kennedi was earlier, Brooklyn was too calm for my liking. I expected her to wild out or something, but she just sat there quietly.

"Baby, I'm sorry. Please don't let this break us up," I pleaded.

"What are you sorry for Dominic? Kennedi is your wife. You don't have to apologize to me for getting your wife pregnant. I won't lie this shit is embarrassing as hell. Me and your wife walking around pregnant at the same time is just something else for people to talk about," she replied.

"I don't care about what people say Brook. People talk whether you're doing good or bad, so that's the least of my concerns."

"I'm letting you know now I'm not doing the back and forth dance with you and Kennedi. If this is not where you want to be just let me know, so I can be on my way. The first time you try to play games with me I'm done with you," she threatened.

"I'm here to stay, but I am going to take care of my baby. You don't ever have to worry about me playing games with Kennedi and anybody else. I'm filing for divorce bright and early tomorrow morning," I said honestly.

"I know you're going to take care of your baby. I wouldn't have it any other way. The baby doesn't have anything to do with what's going on with you and Kennedi," she replied.

I couldn't help the smile that crept up on my face. Brooklyn could be so sweet at times. Kennedi hates her so much, but she still never has anything bad to say about her. I laid down on the sofa and pulled her in front of me, just like always. I rubbed her stomach, even though, there's nothing there for me to rub yet. We laid on the sofa and talked until we both ended up falling asleep.

When I woke up the next morning, Brooklyn wasn't on the sofa anymore. I heard her talking to somebody. I looked at the time on the cable box and saw that it was almost noon. I must have been really tired to sleep through my alarm. It's a Monday morning, and I would usually be in the office no later than nine. That's one of the good things about being my own boss I never have to answer to anyone.

"Good morning," Brooklyn said when I walked into the kitchen. DJ is in his high chair reaching for me, and she's standing at the stove cooking something.

"Good morning," I replied while giving her a kiss. I grabbed my son and went to the bathroom to complete my morning hygiene. When I got back to the kitchen, Brooklyn had my food on the table waiting for me. Not even twenty-four hours in and I was already happy with the move I'd made.

"David just called for you. He said that he would handle everything if you don't feel like coming in. Your mama and Kennedi called a few times too, but I didn't answer the phone," Brooklyn informed me.

"Okay, but you can answer my phone anytime you want to. I'm not trying to keep our relationship a secret from anybody," I replied.

"I made my doctor's appointment for Thursday morning," Brooklyn said changing the subject. Before I had a chance to respond,, my phone was going off again. I blew out a breath of frustration when I saw my mother's number come up.

"Good morning ma," I said when I answered the phone.

"This is not your mama," my daddy bellowed.

"Oh, what's up pops?"

"I need to see you later on when you get off from work," he demanded in his usual stern tone. I knew right then that my mama put him up on what's going on. There's no need for me to make up an excuse not to go because he's not having it. No matter how old I am, I still know not to play with him.

"Alright," was my simple response before he hung up.

"What's wrong?" Brooklyn asked, taking note of my facial expression.

"That was my daddy. He wants me to come over there later. I knew that it was coming eventually. Dress DJ for me, I'm going to the office for a little while."

"Okay, come on baby," Brook said taking my son to his room.

I sent David a text telling him that I would be there in a little while. I ate my breakfast and took a shower right after. Once I was dressed, I got DJ and headed to my office. When I pulled up, Scott was outside talking on his phone. He ended his conversation when he saw me walking up.

"What's up boss?" He asked when I approached him. "I see you got your twin with you."

"Yeah, you know I can't really go nowhere without him," I replied.

"Come holler at your uncle DJ," David said when I stepped inside the office. My son wiggled out of my hold and ran over to my brother.

"Daddy called and said he wants to see me later on," I told my brother.

"You already know he's going off on you as soon as you get there. I wouldn't miss this for the world so you know I'm in the building," David said laughing.

"I don't even care anymore. I'm not going back to Kennedi no matter what he says."

"That's what's up. He can't make you be with somebody that you don't want to be with," David replied.

"I swear I should have listened to you when you told me not to go through with that shit. You were right about everything you said. I got married for all the wrong reasons, and now her ass is pregnant."

"Wait, Kennedi is pregnant too?" He yelled a little louder than he needed to.

"Yeah man, she told me last night right after I told her about Brooklyn," I confessed.

"Damn lil brother. So what are you going to do now?"

"I told her that I want a divorce. I left last night, and I'm not going back. I'll take care of my baby, but our marriage is over. It's all about me and Brooklyn now, and I really don't care who has a problem with it."

"You already know I don't have a problem with it. Brooklyn is my girl. I always wanted y'all to be together. Now I know why Kennedi's ass has been calling here all morning," he said.

"She can call all she wants, my mind is made up. I'm about to call Cal right now and see who he can refer me to about this divorce."

Calvin "Cal" Anderson is a good friend of my parents. He's also an attorney with a lot of pull in the New Orleans and surrounding areas. He knows a lot of other good attorneys, and I'm in need of one right now. After looking for his number online, I called him at his office. When I didn't get an answer, I left a voicemail asking him to call me back. I need to get the ball rolling on this divorce as soon as possible.

*****

Later on that evening, DJ and I pulled up to my parents' house with David pulling up right behind us.

"Maw-Maw," DJ yelled excitedly when we walked through the front door. He loves to come to my parents' house because they always gave him his way. My little brother and sister also have him spoiled rotten.

"Hey baby," Nyla screamed when she came downstairs followed by Ivan. She grabbed DJ from my arms and walked down the hall with him. I heard my mama and daddy's voices coming from the sitting room. They always got loud whenever my baby came around.

"You might as well go get this over with," David said while shaking his head.

We walked down the hall to the sitting room and took a seat on the sofa. My daddy sat in his recliner playing with DJ while everybody else sat around and watched. He was being his usual spoiled self and enjoying all the attention. They ignored me and my brother like we weren't even in the room, but that was fine with me.

"Can he stay here tonight Dominic?" Nyla asked me. "We already have everything here for him."

"I don't know. I have to make sure it's cool with Brooklyn first," I replied.

"Nyla, you and Ivan take DJ upstairs for a minute," my father instructed.

This is the moment I've been dreading since I walked in a few minutes ago. He's ready to get in my shit. My brother and sister got up, taking my son out of the room. My father started up soon after.

"So it wasn't bad enough that you made a baby on the girl before the wedding, but you went and did the same shit after you married her," he said. He paused, but I knew better than to say anything. He doesn't like to be interrupted when he's speaking.

"What I don't understand is why you got married to begin with. Kennedi would be a damn fool to stay with your ass after this," he fussed.

"I don't want her to stay with me," I confessed.

"What is that supposed to mean?" My mama asked.

"I'm filing for divorce," I answered.

"You just got married boy!" My father yelled in disbelief.

"I know, but I shouldn't have. I'm not happy with Kennedi and I haven't been happy for a while."

"You should have said that before your stupid ass walked down that aisle. You lucky I didn't put up any money towards that shit. I'd be beating your ass until I felt like I was paid in full," he barked.

"I told him not to do it," David chimed in. I don't know why he just couldn't keep his mouth closed.

"Why are you even here David? I know for a fact I didn't invite you, and I don't have a problem putting your ass out," he yelled.

I wanted to laugh, but now was not the time. I could see David smirking, but he knew better too.

"So now what Dominic? Where are you going to live?" My mother asked me.

"You damn sure can't come here with all this drama you got going on," my daddy said.

"I don't want to come here. I'm staying with Brooklyn and my son."

"If this ain't some soap opera bullshit, I don't know what is. Now you want to be with your baby's mama," my daddy continued going off.

"That's who I've always wanted to be with."

"Well, why didn't you drag her ass down the aisle then?" He fumed. "You keep putting all these babies up in her like she's your wife anyway."

"He's not just putting babies in her," David mumbled to me. I elbowed him hard in his side to shut him up.

"No, don't try to tell him to shut up now. What did you say David?" My mama asked.

"I didn't say anything. I'm just messing with him," he replied with a chuckle.

"Boy please, you never could whisper. You just said he's not just putting babies in her. What does that mean?" She asked.

I'm a grown ass man sitting here like a little ass boy who's afraid to speak up for himself. My mama and daddy have a way of doing that to me.

"Y'all are pissing me off, so somebody better say something," my daddy yelled.

"Kennedi is pregnant," I said hurriedly trying to get it over with. I waited for the fireworks to start, but to my surprise, they never did.

"Y'all get out. Leave my grandson here. I'll call and tell Brooklyn that we have him. I'm not about to stress myself into an early grave behind this shit. I never thought I'd see the day where you start acting just like David," my daddy said calmly.

"I'm good, I'm a one woman man now," David said with a smirk.

"You don't believe that shit yourself. Get y'all asses out before I drag y'all out," my daddy replied sternly.

David and I stood up and walked out of the room. As soon as we got outside that clown fell out laughing.

"That nigga straight put us out," he laughed.

"I know, that's a first," I laughed with him.

No matter how mad my daddy got, he never put us out before. I guess I went too far this time. Things with him actually went better than I thought they would. David got fussed at because of me just like he always did. My phone started ringing right when I got to my truck. I got happy when I saw that it was Cal calling me back. If all went well, I would be a divorced man before Brooklyn had our baby.

BRYCE

Two weeks had passed since Taylor and Baby were in the car accident. My car is still in the repair shop, so I'm driving around in a rental. Jaden and I kept trying to figure out who would want to hurt Taylor or our sister and for what reason. They both kept saying that whoever it was drove a black pick-up truck, and only one person came to mind. Larry drives an all-black F-150. He's also the only one who has a problem with any of them. He probably saw Taylor in my car and decided to get her back for what we did to him. I'm really pissed because my daughters and my nephew were in the car too. Things could have gone far worse than they did. Then to find out that Baby was pregnant when it happened really had us heated. Baby being pregnant came as a shock to me, but not as much as the first time.

When she got pregnant with DJ, I really thought that we would be the ones to take care of the baby. Besides a baby shower gift, I've never had to do anything for her or my nephew. Dominic stepped up and handled his business just like he said he would. He'd officially moved in with Brook since he found out that she was pregnant. Jaden and I went with him to get the rest of his things from Kennedi's house. She was acting a fool when we got there, but Dominic just ignored her. He's serious about being with Brooklyn, and he really did file for a divorce. Kennedi is really going to go crazy when she gets those papers.

"Bryce I don't know about this," Taylor said nervously from the passenger's seat. It was Sunday

29

night, and we were in route to Larry's house to confront him once again. I just need Taylor to knock on the door, and we'll take it from there. Besides her, I have all three of my brothers riding with me. I don't know if he's alone or not and I need to be prepared.

"Taylor I just need him to see that it's you so he'll open the door. You know I would never do anything that might put you at risk," I assured her.

"Once he opens the door we'll take it from there," Jaden said. He lives for this kind of shit, and he's ready for battle.

"We don't even know if it was him who ran us off the road," she said. She was getting on my nerves with all of this whining.

"Taylor, just do what I told you to do and stop being so damn scary," I snapped. I made a mistake talking crazy to her, and I knew it.

"Nigga. you asked for my help," she said pointing to herself and snaking her neck. "Don't act like you're doing me no damn favors!"

"Alright, I'm sorry. Just knock on the door, and you can come back and sit in the car if you want to," I said apologetically.

"I don't give a damn who does what just as long as I can get to his ass," Jaden said.

Caleb and Brian were quiet, but they're down for whatever. Jaden is always the rowdy and most vocal out of us all. When we pulled up to Larry's house, I expected to see the truck parked in his driveway or in front of his door. Instead, there was a newer model silver Avalanche in its place. It's been a while since we paid him a visit, so it's possible that he doesn't even live here anymore. The only way for us to know for sure is to let Taylor knock on the front door.

"You think he moved?" Jaden asked me.

"I was thinking the same thing," I replied.

"That's not his truck. Somebody else probably lives here," Taylor said.

"Maybe he just got a new truck. He probably fucked his old one up when he ran y'all off the road," Brian observed.

"You might be right Brian. Let's get out and see what's up," I instructed. I backed my rental car up to the side of the house where it wouldn't be seen. It's positioned for us to hop in and peel off fast if we need to. Taylor walked up the steps, but my brothers and I jumped across the side railing so we wouldn't be seen once the door was opened. Jaden was the first one by the door. He wanted to pull him out if or when he opened the door. Taylor looks so nervous. I hate to put her in the middle of this, but I really didn't have a choice.

"Alright Taylor, knock on the door," Jaden instructed.

Taylor knocked, but it was too soft for anybody to hear it. We're standing right here, and I barely heard anything.

"Knock harder than that Taylor," I whispered harshly. She rolled her eyes at me and started pounding on the door with her fist. A few seconds passed without anything happening. I motioned with my hand for her to do it again. She knocked again, and I heard Larry's voice on the other side of the door.

"I'm coming," he yelled right before snatching the door open. He didn't even ask who it was before he opened it. He paused when he saw Taylor standing there, but he quickly got upset.

"Bitch…." was all he was able to get out before Jaden punched him in his face. When he went stumbling to the floor, my brothers and I rushed into his house and closed the door behind us. Taylor was supposed to be sitting in the car, but she came inside with us. Larry was trying to get up, but Jaden stopped him before he did.

"Stay your punk ass on that floor and don't move," he yelled. "Why would your stupid ass open the door without seeing who it was first?"

"I thought y'all was the pizza man," Larry mumbled while holding his mouth as the blood poured from it like water.

"Stupid moves like that will get you killed, but I guess you know that now," Jaden said.

"Man, what's going on? I don't need any more problems from y'all," he said still holding his bloody mouth.

"You're really not in the position to be talking shit right now," I told him.

"Man, I didn't do anything. I stayed away from Taylor just like I said I would."

"Well, two weeks ago a black truck that looks just like yours ran my girl and my sister of the road. My daughters and my nephew were in the car with them," I raged.

"What! Man, that wasn't me. I don't even have that truck anymore," he screeched.

"Nigga, you probably don't have it anymore since you used it to run them off the road," Jaden yelled.

"Man, I swear that wasn't me. I haven't had that truck in over six months. I traded it in for the one you see in my driveway. I have the paperwork to prove it," he swore.

"Get up and go get it," Jaden ordered. "And I'm coming with you so you better not be on no bullshit."

Larry jumped up and walked to the back of his house with Jaden and Brian hot on his heels. It took them a few minutes, but all three of them came back in at the same time. Larry had a wet towel covering his mouth while Jaden looked over the paperwork in his hands.

"That nigga is telling the truth," Jaden said with a frown. He was ready for war, but it seems that it would have to wait. Now I was really confused as to who came after my family. Taylor stood up and walked to the door with Larry watching her the entire time. Just then, something came to me that I didn't address before. I walked over to him and quickly delivered two punches that had him on the floor once again.

"That's for calling my girl a bitch," I said before walking away. I grabbed Taylor's hand and headed for the door.

"And next time see who's at your door before you open it up dumb ass," Jaden said laughing.

We hopped in the car and pulled off right as the pizza delivery car pulled up.

"What the hell made you deal with that lame ass nigga?" I asked Taylor. "His ass can't even fight,"

"The same thing that made you deal with Tiffany. That bitch can't fight either," she shot back.

We rode the rest of the way in silence. I was deep in thought trying to figure out who could have been behind the attack on my family. The streets talked, so we were bound to find out eventually. Until then I just had to keep a close eye on my loved ones.

CANDACE

"Damn," I breathed heavily as I dropped down to the floor. I was at David's house, and we had been sexing each other all day. I was about to leave when he pulled me back and blew my back out right in his front room. My legs felt like noodles, and I couldn't stand up anymore.

"Stop talking that shit, I told you that you couldn't hang with me," David bragged. He stood up naked in all his magnificent glory and walked to the back of his house. David looked great in clothes, but the view is even better when he was naked. We had been kicking it for a few months, but we still weren't a couple. I'm feeling him, and I know he feels the same. Fear is the only thing that keeps me from telling him. I wouldn't mind being with only him, but I was too scared to make the first move. Co-Co keeps telling me to do it before it's too late, but I just couldn't. As of right now, we are only friends with benefits.

"Open up so I can freshen up Ms. Kitty," David said smiling. He kneeled down in front of me with a warm soapy towel and cleaned me up. He does this every time we have sex, and I love it. When he was done, I got up from the floor and put my clothes back on. I sat on the sofa and looked for something to watch on TV.

"You want me to order us something to eat?" David asked when he came back into the room. I couldn't help but stare at him when he walked in wearing nothing but his boxers.

"No, I'm leaving in a little while. I'll get something to eat before I go home," I replied.

"You don't have to leave. Spend the night with me."

"I would, but I didn't bring any extra clothes with me."

"I told you before that you could leave some stuff over here if you want to," he offered.

"That's funny because Brook and Dominic said that you didn't like females leaving things at your house."

"Usually I don't, but this is different," he admitted.

"What makes this any different than before?" I asked.

"I'm really feeling you. I like how we interact with each other. It's not forced. It just feels natural," he replied.

"I'm really feeling you too," I finally admitted.

"Good, so now we need to make it official."

"Official?" I asked with raised eyebrows.

"Yeah, like me and you together in a relationship," he explained.

I felt butterflies in my stomach, and I don't quite know why. This isn't the first time a man has asked me to be in a relationship, but this time it feels different. I've actually been considering the exact same thing.

"I don't know David. You and I are so much alike until it's scary. I have a crazy past, and I know you do too."

"I know that, but that's the past just like you said. It's been a minute since I've vibed with somebody the way I'm vibing with you. I can't lie, I'm kind of nervous about being in a relationship, but I'm willing to try if you are. I'm getting too old to be running through females like I do. I'm ready to chill with one woman, and I want you to be the one."

"I'm willing to try this with you, but I'm not one for the games. I don't have a problem walking away. And please tell all of your hoes that you're off the market. I would hate to have to beat you and one of them bitches down," I said seriously.

"Damn, you threatening me already," he said laughing. "But you have some loose ends to tie up as well. You need to let all your niggas know that the kitty has officially been locked down."

"That's not a problem," I replied.

"That's what's up. Now let me go get dressed so we can go get you some clothes from your house," he said standing to his feet.

I was so excited that I couldn't stop smiling. I can't wait to tell Co-Co and Brooklyn that I'm officially in a relationship. It will take some time for me to get used to having a boyfriend.

NADIA

After avoiding Candace for months, I'd finally agreed to hook up with her for lunch. I have plans to help Shannon pack later in the day, so I'm meeting with Candace early. I don't know what the hell Kevin and Kyle are into, but they're moving once again. Kyle and I haven't been getting along too well, and I know it's only a matter of time before we break up for good. I know for a fact that he's still dealing with Tiffany even though he lied to my face. I started checking his phone just like Shannon does with Kevin. Most times when he's not with me that's who he's spending all of his time with. Every time I confront him about it, we always end up fighting. I haven't saw or talked to him for the past two days, so he's probably with Tiffany now. He was pissed with me because I refused to go through with one of his check scams. He wanted Shannon and me to go to a local store to cash two phony checks that someone printed up for him. I had no problem doing it until I got to the store and recognized one of the clerks who works there. She and I aren't friends, but we did graduate from high school together, so she knows my name. Shannon went through with the plan, but I left and waited outside until she was done. When we got back to the house and told Kyle what happened, he was furious. He punched me in my mouth and split my bottom lip open. He left soon after and I hadn't heard from him since then.

"Hey stranger," Candace spoke when she walked up to the table. We agreed to meet at the Cheesecake Factory for lunch. I was a few minutes early, so I grabbed us a table and waited for her to get there.

"Hey girl," I spoke back as I stood up to give her a hug. Before we could say anything else, the waitress came over to take our orders. After placing orders for drinks and appetizers, she was on her way again.

"So what's been going on with you?" She asked.

"Nothing much, just work, and school," I lied. I'm no longer working, and I haven't been to school all semester. Kyle and my illegal activities keep me too busy for anything else.

"Where are you working at now? I called your old job, and they said that you no longer worked there," she inquired.

"Oh yeah, I work for another phone company now. They're not local, so you've probably never heard of them."

"Damn, it feels like we're strangers now. I don't know anything about you anymore," she said.

"We're not strangers. It's just how life is sometimes," I shrugged.

"I do want to know one thing though," she said while looking at me.

I already knew what she wanted to ask, and I had my lie prepared. "Okay," I replied.

"What were you doing with Shannon and how do y'all know each other? She's not the type of person that you would normally hang out with," she observed.

"She and I work together. She doesn't have any family here, so we clicked immediately. I was surprised when I found out that she was Kevin's girlfriend. She's cool though."

"Girl please, that bitch is crazy. You better not trust her. She's known for carrying a blade, and she doesn't have a problem using it."

"Well, she doesn't have a reason to use it on me. But what's new with you?" I asked trying to change the subject.

"So much has happened since I last talked to you. For one, your girl is in a relationship now," she said smiling hard.

"Whaaat," I laughed. "Who locked your fast ass down?" I asked.

"Girl it's somebody that you know, but you'll never guess who," she giggled.

"Well, I know it's not Kyle," I chuckled while fishing for info at the same time.

"You got that right. I haven't talked to his dog ass in a minute. I'm with David now," she informed me.

"What David"? I asked hoping it wasn't who I thought it was.

"Dominic's brother David. It's still new, but it's been all good so far," she smiled.

"Wow. You're right I never would have guessed that. I've never known David to have a girlfriend or even want one," I said honestly.

"Well, you could say the same for me at one time, but people change. I'm happy, and he seems to be happy too."

"That's good. So how is everybody else doing?" I asked her.

"Everybody is fine. Taylor and Brooklyn got into a car accident not too long ago. Somebody ran them off of the road and messed up Bryce's car."

"Damn, I hope nobody got hurt."

"Taylor had a few bumps and bruises, but they were fine other than that. We also found out that Brooklyn is pregnant again," she said. I almost choked on the drink that the waitress had just sat in front of me when she said that.

"Who is she pregnant by?" I inquired.

"Girl, Dominic put another baby up in her ass," she replied.

"But he's married now, right? And I thought him and Brooklyn had broken up," I questioned. I knew for a fact that she was messing with Kevin at one point because Shannon almost lost her mind behind it.

"They did break up for a while, but his ass couldn't stay away. She was dealing with Kevin for a minute, but thankfully that didn't last long either. She and Dominic are living together now. He filed for a divorce and everything," she said like it was no big deal.

I was truly at a loss for words. What the hell could Brooklyn have done to make him want her so bad? He hadn't even been married a year, and he left his wife to be with her. That shit had me sick to my stomach, and my appetite is gone.

"He is such a dog. Brooklyn better be careful with his ass."

"Girl, he's so in love I don't think she has anything to worry about. He got her an Audi truck, and he's talking about buying a house as soon as his divorce is finalized. It always takes that one woman to make a man do right," she replied.

I know she didn't mean to, but she hurt my feelings with her last comment. I loved Dominic with all of my heart, but I couldn't make him love me the same way. I guess I wasn't the kind of woman that could make a man like him do right. I just hate that a younger more inexperienced woman came along and did what I never could.

KENNEDI

I hadn't been out of my house since I received the divorce papers in the mail three days ago. I laid in my bed in the dark and stared at the ceiling for three days straight. I don't remember sleeping or eating. Hell, I don't even remember going to the bathroom. My mama and Tiffany were both calling me like crazy because I wasn't showing up for work. They tried coming to my house, but they couldn't get in even with a key. I had the security chain on, and I refused to take it off. My mama was threatening to call the police, but I knew that she never would. She almost made me think that she had something to hide because she never got the police involved no matter what.

I'm now two months pregnant, and Brooklyn is four. I knew everything that went on with her and my husband because I damn near stalked them on social media. Dominic tried calling me a few times to ask about my doctors' appointments. I really wanted him to be there, but my mama quickly put a stop to it. She called and told him that my baby and I didn't need him, but that was the furthest thing from the truth. I need him like I need air to breath, and she doesn't understand that. My mother-in-law tried to reach out to me, but my mama started an argument with her as well. It's like she wants me to suffer, and I don't know why. Once again, my phone is ringing along with loud banging on my front door.

"Kennedi," I heard my mother yelling from downstairs. She could scream all she wanted to, but

I'm not letting her in. I need some more time to myself, and she would only make matters worse.

"Kennedi Elise Henry you open this door, or I'll have someone here to break it down," she warned. If I was in the mood to yell, I would have told her that my last name is Roberts. She refused to acknowledge that since I got married.

"Kennedi it's me, please come open the door for us. We're worried about you," Tiffany pleaded. I still didn't move, and I had no plans to do so.

After a few minutes, it got quiet again, and I was happy that they left. I turned over to my side to get more comfortable when I heard a loud crash coming from downstairs. I jumped up and grabbed my phone right before I ran into my closet. My heart was beating out of my chest as I tried to dial the police on my phone.

"Kennedi where are you?" I heard my mother yell.

I couldn't believe her crazy ass. She threatened to break my door down, but I didn't think she would actually do it. I came out of the closet and headed downstairs. I ran to my front door and saw it barely hanging from the hinges.

"Are you crazy?" I yelled at my mother. She was standing there texting on her phone like she didn't do anything wrong.

"I warned you, you should have let us in," she shrugged.

"So you break down my fucking door because I wouldn't let you in?" I roared.

"You watch your mouth. The maintenance man is about to repair it. After all, he's the one who broke it down."

"I can't believe you," I fussed with my hand on my hips.

"And just look at you. When was the last time you combed your hair or took a shower for that matter? Have you even eaten anything lately Kennedi?"

"No, and I don't plan to do anything until I'm good and ready," I flippantly replied.

"You're pregnant Kennedi or did you forget. I know you don't want another miscarriage now do you?"

"At this point, I really don't care if I have this baby or not. I'll be raising it by myself anyway."

"Don't be stupid. This baby is a guaranteed check every month and Dominic is definitely going to pay. You'll probably never have to work again when we're done with his ass," Tiffany and I both looked at her like she was crazy. Money is really all that matters to her. She can't even be here for me during my time of need without trying to benefit financially.

"You need to fix yourself up and get out of this house. I can put a few curls in your hair if you want me to," Tiffany offered.

"I don't want to leave out of here. I'm fine," I said trying hard to convince them.

"You are not fine, but you were a few days ago. What happened to put you in such a bad place all of a sudden?" My mother asked.

I wanted to answer, but the lump in my throat wouldn't allow me to. I broke down crying before I could utter a word. Tiffany rushed to my side while my mother stood there with her usual cold blank stare.

"It's okay Kennedi. What happened?" Tiffany asked me. I wiped my tears and walked over to the island in my kitchen. I picked up the big brown envelope and handed it to my cousin. My mother snatched it from her grip before she even had a chance to look at it.

"That bastard," my mother yelled angrily when she read over everything. "So he filed for divorce and he's the one that cheated on you?"

"I can't believe he's treating you like this," Tiffany said with a look of pity on her face.

"I hope he's prepared to sign away half of his company because that's the only way you'll be signing anything," my mother swore.

"I don't want half of his company or his money, I want my husband," I sobbed.

"You sound like a damn fool. You are not about to beg him to be with you. He's the one who went fishing in the gutter and came up with a rat. Let that hood rat bitch have him. All you need is for him to take care of you financially," my mama fussed.

"And what about my baby? He or she deserves to have a father."

"He'll come around to see his baby and you know he will. You'll have the upper hand, so you make him dance to your music," she replied.

"You know how much Dominic loves kids. He'll take care of his baby, and you know that," Tiffany reassured me.

"Clean yourself up and let's get out of here. We'll continue this discussion over lunch," my mother instructed.

"Come on Kennedi, I'll help you," Tiffany offered again.

This time, I let her lead me upstairs. We fished around in my closet until I found something suitable to wear. After taking a shower and getting dressed, Tiffany used my wand to put some loose curls in my hair. I looked at my reflection in the mirror and was satisfied with the end result.

"I'm spending the night with you so we can give this house a good cleaning. This is really not like you Kennedi," Tiffany said.

I didn't reply because she was right. My house was filthy and in need of a good cleaning. Dirty clothes are everywhere because I haven't washed them or taken them to the cleaners. I've been too miserable to really do much of anything lately. When we got back downstairs, the maintenance man was done repairing my door. He probably would have been gone if my mother would have stopped flirting with him so hard. He doesn't seem like he's interested, but that didn't stop her. If she loves money, so much she's surely barking up the wrong tree with him. I know for a fact that he doesn't even own a car.

"I'm ready," I announced after watching her make a damn fool out of herself.

"How about we get us a good shrimp salad?" Tiffany suggested. We all agreed right before walking out the door and getting into my mother's truck. I noticed that she was still holding the divorce papers that Dominic sent to me, but I didn't say anything. We ended up going on the Lakefront to New Orleans Food and Sprits where they sell some of the best seafood salads in town.

"I hope we don't have to wait, I'm starving," I complained as we pulled up. Sometimes the wait to be seated is an hour or more, and I just wasn't for it. I've been starving myself for the last few days, and it's starting to get to me. When we got out of the truck, I almost ran to the entrance I was so hungry. I quickly slowed my pace and looked on in disgust when I saw Brooklyn and her two cousins walking out along with Taylor.

"Look at these ghetto bitches," Tiffany mumbled when she saw them.

"Don't you two dare embarrass me out here," my mother warned us as she looked up from her phone.

They were all talking and smiling until they saw us headed in their direction. My eyes instantly traveled to Brooklyn's stomach area, but just like me, she really isn't showing very much. I looked in her face and instantly became angry. I just didn't understand what was so special about her that made my husband leave our marriage for her. Taylor looked at Tiffany and smirked while Brooklyn's cousins flat out laughed in our faces. I was about to let it go, but I just couldn't hold my anger or my tongue any longer.

"Is something funny?" I question with a scowl on my face.

"Well, since you mentioned it, that weave is a hot ass mess. Take my card and hit me up. I'll even give you the family discount if money is an issue," Brooklyn's cousin said as he handed me his card.

"As if I would ever let you touch my hair," I scoffed as I slapped it out of his hand and watched it fall to the ground.

"Girl, you better be happy that you're pregnant. That's the only thing keeping me from knocking you on your ass right now. You need to let somebody touch that hair and that makeup up. Walking around here looking two-toned in the face. Bitch blend it or don't wear it at all," he advised referring to the foundation that I had on.

"Let's go Co-Co, it's not even that serious," Brooklyn said. Just the sound of her voice was enough to send me over the edge.

"Bitch shut up and go tend to that ugly ass little boy of yours!" I yelled angrily. I knew right then and there that I made a huge mistake by talking about her son. As if on cue, Brooklyn rushed over to me and grabbed me by my hair. She started pummeling my face with her fist like we were in a boxing ring, and the bell sounded. I'm not a fighter, but I tried my best to keep up with her wild ass. She delivered blows to my face that would make a grown man cry. It felt like I was swinging at the wind because none of my licks landed.

"I wish you would put your hands on her," Taylor said when Tiffany tried to step in.

"This doesn't have anything to do with you Taylor," Tiffany yelled.

"Anything that involves my sister-in-law has everything to do with me. And like I just said, I wish you would put your hands on her," Taylor repeated.

"Get your hands off of my daughter!" My mother screamed while walking over to us.

"Don't make me put my hands on you out here lady. Please don't make me do it," Candace warned, stopping my mother from intervening.

I swung like crazy trying to get one of my licks to land anywhere on Brooklyn's body, but it never happened. She punched me in my face and pulled my hair, all at the same time. My tracks are sewn in, but it felt like she was ripping the stitches right from my scalp.

Against Taylor's warning, Tiffany stepped in and tried to pull Brooklyn off of me. It only took a second for Taylor to grab her shirt and sling her to the ground. Before my cousin could get up, she pounced on her and started swinging.

"Kennedi stop this. You are pregnant or do you even care about that," my mother screamed frantically. It's like a light bulb clicked in Candace's head, and she quickly moved in and broke us apart.

"Let her go Brooklyn. Dominic will kill us if something happens to you and his baby," she said pissing me off.

Taylor was still beating Tiffany half to death until Co-Co pulled her off of my cousin. Tiffany laid on the ground with blood dripping from various parts of her face. I knew that I had to have scratches because my face was burning and stinging like crazy. I could taste the blood in my mouth, but I needed a mirror to see the full extent of the damage that she done.

"I owe you much more than that, and best believe we're going to finish this," Taylor promised Tiffany.

"That's all you low life tricks know how to do is fight. I bet you can barely read and write, but you know how to throw a punch," my mother said.

"Bitch, if you don't go sit down somewhere with that outdated lace front on. Looking like Al Sharpton," Co-Co roared.

"Let's go Kennedi," my mother said as we helped Tiffany up from the ground. I watched as all four of them piled into the Audi truck that my husband paid for with Brooklyn getting behind the wheel.

"That was so embarrassing. I hope and pray that nobody in that restaurant knows me," my mother complained.

"Is that all you're worried about? We just got our asses handed to us by my husband's mistress and her family. I don't give a damn if somebody saw you or not," I cried. Tiffany poured some bottled water on some paper towels and handed them to me. We both nursed our wounds as my mother continuously fussed and worried about being seen.

"Look at my face," Tiffany said when she looked at herself in the mirror.

"They're a bunch of wild animals. It looks like a cat got a hold of you rather than a human being," my mother observed.

"Let me see your mirror Tiffany," I requested. She handed it to me, and I gasped when I saw the deep cuts and bruises in my face. Brooklyn's nails dug into my flesh so deep that the skin was completely gone in some places.

This is not supposed to be my life right now. Dominic and I are supposed to be happily married newlyweds enjoying our new house. Instead, I was out in the streets fighting with his other woman while we're both expecting his children.

"I can't believe that this is happening to me," I wailed in the back of my mother's truck.

"Dominic is wrong for this shit. Karma is going to bite him in the ass for the way he's treating you," Tiffany said.

"Well, my name is not karma, but I'm damn sure about to do some biting. Fix yourself up Kennedi. We're about to pay your no good ass husband a visit," my mother replied angrily.

I wanted to protest, but the look in her eyes told me to leave it alone. I took my brush from my purse and fixed my hair as best as I could. I'm not looking forward to seeing Dominic, but right now I really don't have a choice.

DOMINIC

"Brooklyn calm down, I can't even understand what you're saying," I told her for the second time. We've been on the phone for about five minutes, and I still didn't know what she was trying to say. I know she's upset about something, but it's hard for me to hear her with everybody yelling in the background. She's trying to talk, along with Candace, Co-Co, and Taylor, making it impossible for me to understand.

"Baby, you need to tell them to be quiet so I can understand what you're saying," I requested.

"Y'all be quiet for a minute. He can't even hear me," Brooklyn yelled.

"Okay, now what were you saying?" I asked once it got quiet.

"I said that Taylor and I just beat the breaks off of your wife and her cousin."

"What!" I yelled. "Why the hell are you always fighting while you're pregnant Brooklyn?"

"They started it…"

"I don't give a fuck who started it," I yelled cutting her off mid-sentence. "You shouldn't be out here fighting period."

"You getting mad with me, but I didn't even do shit," she yelled.

"You should have walked away Brooklyn. You put both of my unborn kids in danger with that bullshit."

"You know what? Fuck you and that bitch. I'm trying to tell you what happened, and you're taking her side. You need to move back home with her ass then," she said going off on me.

Brooklyn has really been in her feelings with this pregnancy. My mama said it was her hormones, and I hope she's right. She's always ready to pop off for every little thing. I'm really not use to her being like this because usually she's always so sweet and calm. I didn't even get a chance to respond before Kennedi and her mama burst through the door with Tiffany trailing behind them.

"What the hell is going on around here?" David inquired. He and Scott were sitting in the office with me when everybody came in.

"You need to keep your dog on a leash Dominic," Kennedi yelled as soon as she saw me.

"I know that hoe did not just call me a dog," Brooklyn yelled. "Tell that bitch that I'm on my way over there."

"Baby no, just let me handle this," I begged, but it was too late. Brooklyn had already hung up on me.

"Baby?" Kennedi repeated with her face screwed up.

"First of all, don't call my girl a dog," I told Kennedi.

"And don't come busting y'all asses up in here like y'all own the place either," David chimed in while walking over to me.

"That little ghetto bitch and her friends just attacked my daughter and niece. This is all your fault Dominic. If you had kept your dick in your pants none of this would be happening," Karen said.

"You mind your business with your lonely pathetic ass. And get the fuck out of my place of business with all this bullshit," I shouted.

"Don't talk to my mama like that," Kennedi yelled in her mother's defense.

"Well, you get the hell out with her old funny built ass then," David replied.

"Fuck you David!" Kennedi retorted.

"You couldn't fuck me even if you wanted to. That's why my brother left your dried up boring ass."

"Really Dominic? So you're talking outside of our bedroom now?" Kennedi asked me.

"Shit, there wasn't all that much to discuss. Lying flat on your back is nothing to brag about."

"I guess that's why you ran to that slut."

"That's exactly why I ran to her," I said honestly with no hesitation.

"You are even more pitiful than I thought, but you can get ready to pay up if you want a divorce from her," Karen said.

"It's all about a dollar with y'all. I'm taking care of my baby, and that's all. Your daughter ain't getting shit from me other than that. That's the whole problem now. Kennedi is too stupid to think for herself, so she lets you do all the thinking for her," I snapped.

"Does she really deserve this kind of treatment Dominic? She is still your wife, and she's carrying your child," Tiffany spoke up. It wasn't until I looked at her that I saw how fucked up both of them were. Taylor did a number on Tiffany, but Kennedi was even worse. Her weave was barely hanging in there, and her face was all scratched and bruised up.

"Look, whatever is going on with me and Kennedi is nobody's business. But since she put y'all in it she needs to tell y'all the truth. We've been having problems long before I even met Brooklyn. I dealt with her bullshit for as long as I could, but I got tired of it," I confessed.

"That's a lie! That's just your excuse for cheating on me. What problems did we have Dominic?" Kennedi yelled.

"You can't be serious right now. Just leave it alone Kennedi."

"I'm very serious. I want to know what problems we had before you met Brooklyn. She's been our only issue."

"So you gon' make me say it in front of everybody?"

"Yeah, go ahead and say it," she urged.

"Okay. Your sex is whack and boring as hell. I have to fake like I'm cumming just to get it over with. You don't suck dick and when you do it's just as bad as the sex if not worse. If it wasn't for my mama and Brooklyn, I would probably starve to death because your ass can't cook. You're too damn money hungry, and you can't even take a piss without your mama's permission. I can keep going if you want me to, but I think you get my point," I rambled. I hated to put her on blast like that, but she asked for it. She should have left it alone like I asked her to.

"Well damn," David said as he fell out laughing. Scott just shook his head like he felt sorry for her.

"So why did you marry me Dominic?" She asked with watery eyes.

"I've been asking myself that question ever since I said "I do," I replied.

Right, when I finished talking Brooklyn swung the door open and rushed over to Kennedi. Taylor, Co-Co, and Candace were right behind her.

"Who are you calling a dog you money hungry bitch?" Brooklyn yelled. I grabbed her before she could get to Kennedi.

"Baby calm down and stop stressing yourself out," I begged.

"Let me go! I don't have shit to say to you," she said trying to push me away.

"What the hell did I do? You need to chill out before you hurt my baby."

"I don't give a damn. You're taking this bitch's side without even listening to what I have to say."

"No, I'm not Brook, but I don't want you out here fighting while you're pregnant with my baby either."

"What did you expect? He's my husband so of course he's going to take my side," Kennedi taunted.

"Baby girl you can have this nigga. Trust me when I say it's not that serious for me. Me and my kids will be fine either way. I ain't doing no trippin' behind a man. Here you go, take him," Brooklyn said while pushing me towards Kennedi.

"Girl, you better stop pushing me. You know I'm not going anywhere," I replied while trying to keep from laughing. She was really trying to give me back to Kennedi like I was a toy or something.

"See, I'm trying to give him back to you. It ain't my fault that he doesn't want you anymore," Brooklyn said.

"Brooklyn you really need to stop acting like this," I pleaded as I held her around her waist.

"I can't believe that you're actually standing here begging this hood rat to act right," Kennedi said.

"You talk a lot of shit when I can't get to your scary ass," Brooklyn said while trying to break free from me again.

"David come get her man," I told my brother.

"Don't tell him to come get me, I'm leaving," Brooklyn yelled.

"You're not going anywhere. I told you to calm your ass down," I replied angrily.

"Come on sis, chill out," David said as he sat her in a chair at my desk.

"Y'all need to leave. Y'all are upsetting my girl, and I don't need all this drama at my place of business."

"It won't be your place of business for long. I'm going to make sure that Kennedi gets half of everything you got when this is all over with. And you don't ever have to worry about her baby because it won't even know who you are if I can help it," Karen said.

"This is my last time telling you to get the fuck out!" I yelled as I rushed over to her. Scott had grabbed me before I had a chance to get too close to her. I've been fed up with her for a long time, and I'm ready to knock that ugly bitch out. She's always saying or doing something to piss somebody off, and I'm tired of it.

"And this is the man that you're shedding tears over Kennedi? A man that doesn't even respect your mother," Karen spat while walking away.

"I'll never respect you. You're one of the main reasons why I left her ass in the first place," I replied to her departing back.

"You good boss man?" Scott asked before letting me go.

"Yeah, I'm alright," I replied calmly. I walked over to Brooklyn, but she jumped up and tried to walk past me when I did.

"Come here Brooklyn," I said while pulling her back.

"No, I'm done talking to you. It's not like you were listening to me anyway," she snapped while breaking free from my hold. She walked out of the front door with Taylor and her cousins rushing out behind her. I'm happy that they were calm when everything went down just a minute ago. It would have been too hard trying to control all of them.

"Man, this damn girl is about to make me lose my mind. I'm leaving for the day, just call me if you need me," I told my brother. I grabbed my car keys from my desk drawer and headed for the door.

"Nah, you call if you need me. You the one with all the drama going on," David replied.

I hopped in my truck and peeled out of the parking lot. I needed to get home and straighten things out with Brooklyn as soon as possible. Kennedi just needs to sign the damn divorce papers and go on about her business. I would make sure her bills were paid, and my baby would be well taken care of. I never neglected DJ when I was with her, and I would treat my baby with her the same way. When I pulled up to our apartments, I saw Bryce and Taylor standing out front talking. Co-Co and Candace were already gone, but Brooklyn was nowhere to be found. I saw her truck, so I knew that she was home.

"What's up man?" Bryce asked giving me dap.

I sighed. "Man, I don't even know where to start."

"I heard about them out there fighting like some damn fools. Baby knows she shouldn't be out there with all that foolishness."

"She always waits until she gets pregnant to turn into Mike Tyson and shit," I complained.

"They started with us. We were leaving when Kennedi started running her mouth," Taylor said.

"It really doesn't matter who started it. Both of them are pregnant. My kids will probably come out all fucked up messing with them," I fumed.

"Well, your baby's mama is up there talking about she's leaving," Bryce said with a smirk.

"Her ass ain't going nowhere. She better go sit down and chill out," I frowned.

"I got something to smoke and drink upstairs if you need to talk," he laughed.

He was joking, but I'll probably be taking him up on that offer sooner than he thinks. I left them and walked up the stairs to our apartment. I had taken a deep breath before I entered, preparing for a long night. I'm happy that DJ is at Brooklyn's parents' house, so he doesn't have to see all the drama unfold. It was dark and quiet when I walked through the front door, but I saw the light on in our bedroom. I had turned on a few lights before I made way down the hall to see what she was doing.

"You might as well put all that shit right back," I said referring to the clothes that she was stuffing into her duffel bag.

"No, I'm not, I'm leaving. I'm going to my mama's for a while," she pouted.

"I promise you are not walking out that door. Fuck with me if want to," I replied.

"You need some time to figure out what you want or who you want. You seem kind of confused to me."

"I'm confused, but I filed for divorce and moved out to be with you. You sound stupid right now. You are always running around here telling everybody that you're grown, but you still doing lil girl shit. You can't run back to your mama every time we have a problem."

"We didn't have a problem. You didn't even give me a chance to tell you what happened before you went off. Then you taking up for her ass like I was wrong, and she was the one that started it."

"Exactly how did I take Kennedi's side? I never said who was right or wrong because I really didn't care. The only thing I said was you shouldn't have been out there fighting. Don't try to twist my words. And like I just said, you are not walking out that door," I told her.

She ignored me and continued to fill up her bag. Unfortunately for her, there was only one door to get in and out of our apartment aside from the sliding glass door on the balcony. We were on the top floor so that one was of no use to her. I walked off and sat on the sofa so I could see her when she came out. After turning the TV to one of the sports channels, I chilled out and waited to see what Brooklyn was going to do. I didn't have to wait long because she came out of the room about ten minutes later struggling with her bag. I jumped up from the sofa and pushed it in front of the door before lying down on it again.

"You better drink some red bull and hope it gives you wings. The only way you are leaving out of here is if you fly off of the balcony," I said while focusing on the TV.

"You can't make me stay here if I don't want to, that's kidnapping."

"Well, call the police then," I shrugged.

"Okay, I will," she threatened as she stormed off to the bedroom, slamming the door behind her.

I laughed because she's really doing too much right now. There is no way in hell I'm letting her leave this house, and she knows that. Brooklyn is spoiled rotten, but I don't give in to her all the time like her family does. She gets her way with me most of the time, but today is not that day. Her ass is wrong, and I don't have a problem telling her. Of course, I was going to go kiss ass and make up in a little while, but I wanted to give her a little time to calm down first.

I looked down at my ringing phone and rushed to answer it when I saw that it was the divorce lawyer calling me. He's a beast with speedy divorces and Cal recommended him to me personally. I'd spoken to him several times over the past few weeks, so he knew my situation. I know it doesn't look good on my end with Brooklyn being pregnant, but he assured me that he could work it out for me.

"What's up Marcus?" I answered on the second ring.

"Hey Dominic, how's it going?" He asked.

"I can't complain, but I hope you have some good news for me."

"Well, I haven't heard anything from your wife yet, so I really don't have any news. I just wanted to run a few things by you and give you some advice for when we go to court," he said.

"Okay, I'm listening," I said giving him my undivided attention.

"I just want you to be prepared for the fight that I know she's going to put up. She's definitely going to bring up your pregnant girlfriend, but that's her word against yours. Since you've only been married for six months, I'm pushing to get an annulment. The only thing that could possibly stand in our way is your wife's pregnancy. Y'all don't have any other kids together so that might not be a problem. You also need to think about how much you're willing to pay in child support because that's going to come up as well," he rambled.

"I'll pay whatever I have to pay to support my baby. Money is not an issue for my kids. I just don't want to be supporting Kennedi's ass for the rest of my life," I replied honestly.

"After only six months of marriage I doubt if she's even eligible for spousal support. That's not enough time to have invested into it. Y'all still have separate accounts, so that's a good thing too."

"True, but she still has access to view all of my account information. I don't want her going to court showing them that I'm supporting Brooklyn before we even get divorced. That's not a good look."

"That's another thing I wanted to talk to you about. Until this is settled, you need to start using your business account for all of your purchases. She can view your deposits and balance, but she can't view any of your purchases on your business account unless she has an actual statement from the bank. Whatever you spend from your business account just write a check from your personal one to cover it. That way everything will still balance out."

"Damn, that's a good idea. I should have been thought of that," I replied impressed with his work already.

"I told you I got you. That's what you're paying me for," he chuckled.

After talking to Marcus for about thirty minutes, I got up to go check on Brooklyn. I smelled her liquid soap as soon as I opened the door so she must have just taken a shower. I found her sprawled out across the bed wearing nothing but a t-shirt and underwear. I stood there for a few minutes watching her sleep while debating if I wanted to wake her up or not. When she turned her back to me, and I caught a glimpse of her ass, the decision was easy. I stripped down to my boxers and climbed into bed with her.

"Wake up," I whispered in her ear. She stirred a little, but she still didn't get up. When I started pulling at her underwear, her eyes popped open immediately. I climbed on top of her to make sure she didn't go anywhere.

"Move Dominic, I'm not doing nothing with you," she said trying to push me away. I ignored her and held her arms over her head and looked her in the eyes.

"You really want to leave me?" I asked even though I already knew the answer. She turned her head to the side, but she didn't answer me.

"Look at me and answer my question. Do you really want to leave me?" I asked again while turning her head to face me. She shook her head no, and I was satisfied with her answer.

"Well, make that your last time saying some shit like that, or we're going to have a problem," I warned her. Breaking up was not an option as far as I was concerned. Things weren't always going to be easy, and she needed to know that.

"You know I love you right?" I said while staring into her eyes.

"I love you too, but I'm scared," she replied.

"Scared of what Brooklyn?"

"I'm scared of us being together, and I'm scared to have another baby when I barely know what to do with the first one," she confessed with tears threating to fall from her eyes.

I laid down on my side and pulled her close to me. I hated to hear the sadness in her voice. She always doubted herself when it came to being a good mother to our son, and I had to take some of

65

the blame for that. I was so excited when DJ was born that I didn't give her a chance to do much. I stepped in and did everything even when she wanted to do it. He's the first grandson of her parents and the only grandson of mine. Everybody had him so much that he was never really with her.

"You don't have anything to be scared of Brooklyn. We'll get through all of this just like we got through everything else. I just want us to be together, nothing else matters to me more than that," I replied.

After talking for most of the night, she seemed to feel a little better. We drifted off into a peaceful night's sleep soon after that.

BROOKLYN

I'm now five months pregnant, and my stomach is really starting to fill out. A few weeks ago it wasn't very noticeable, but it's as clear as day now. Kennedi is three months pregnant, and she's been driving Dominic crazy. She's still refusing to sign the divorce papers and it's stressing him out. That and the fact that she won't let him be involved in the baby's life. She refuses to let him go with her to the doctor, and she never gives him any updates on her pregnancy. He had to practically beg Tiffany to tell him her due date. They're going back to court next month, and I'm hoping that he gets some good news. I hate to see what all of this is doing to him. He's in a good mood right now because today is the day that we find out what I'm having. Besides me and Dominic, his mother is the only one coming with us this time. My parents are on a four-day cruise with DJ and my nieces so they won't find out until they come back. My mama is still in her feelings about me being pregnant at the same time as his wife, but she'll just have to get over it.

"Dominic I want to tell you something that I've been thinking about," I told him as he drove to Dr. Martin's office.

"What's wrong?" He asked with his voice laced with concern.

"Nothing is wrong, but I don't want to know what we're having. I want us to be surprised,"

"I can't do that Brook. That's all I've been thinking about since I found out that you were pregnant. I can't go four more months without knowing," he replied.

"But I want to be surprised in the delivery room. Don't you think that would be nice?" I whined.

"You can be surprised all you want to. When they tell me I'll be sure to keep it from you," he said seriously.

"That's crazy. I'll know once you start buying stuff. If we don't find out, we can do everything in neutral colors."

"Just don't look at whatever I buy and that shouldn't be a problem. I don't care what you say, I'm finding out the sex of my baby today," he said with finality.

"Okay fine, but I still don't want to know," I pouted.

Mrs. Liz was already standing out front when we made it to the clinic. She was on the phone, and she seemed to be upset about something.

"What's wrong Ma?" Dominic asked when we walked up to her.

"That's Karen with her evil ass. I called to check on Kennedi, and that bitch grabbed the phone. I hate to say it, but that's one grandchild that I'm not going to be close to. It's not that I don't want to, but I can't deal with Kennedi and her mama's attitude," she argued.

"It's all good. If I have to take them to court to be in my baby's life, then that's what I'll do. I'm not about to play games with them over mine," Dominic said.

"I'm sorry Brooklyn, how you doing baby?" She said giving me a hug.

"She trippin' today too," Dominic answered before I could.

"I'm fine Mrs. Liz and I am not trippin'. I just told him that I didn't want to know the sex of the baby. I want it to be a surprise," I replied.

"Y'all please don't do this to me. Nyla and I are ready to start shopping again," she said looking at us with pleading eyes.

"We're going to find out, she just doesn't want to know yet," Dominic assured her.

"Oh okay, I'm cool with that. Nyla would die if she had to wait," she said as we got on the elevator.

Once the doctor was done with my checkup, it was time for my sonogram. There was a different tech doing it this time, and I was told that she was the best. Dominic had already informed her that I didn't want to know, and she was fine with that.

"Okay, you can get dressed now Brooklyn," she told me when she finished. I sat up and put on my clothes while she sat at the small desk in the corner. After a few minutes, she handed Dominic an envelope and walked out of the room. He had whispered something to his mother before he opened the envelope that was given to him. Both of them looked at the paper that was inside before he folded it up and put it in his back pocket. I tried to see their reaction to what they'd read, but neither of them gave me and clues. Their facial expression remained the same the entire time. "Did she tell you what we're having?" I asked Dominic.

"Yeah, she told me. Come on so we can get your next appointment from the front desk," he replied. After getting my appointment, we saw his mother off before we got in his truck and left.

"So is the sex of the baby what you want it to be?" I asked him.

"A healthy baby is what I want it to be. I told you that the sex didn't matter."

"So is your mama happy?" I asked fishing for clues.

"You know she's happy anytime she has a grandbaby," he replied.

"You're starting to piss me off with these vague answers," I snapped.

"Don't get mad at me. You said you didn't want to know," he laughed.

"I mean y'all facial expressions didn't change so it must be another boy. If it was a girl y'all would have been smiling or something."

"No, I just told her to keep a straight face no matter what. She did better than I thought," he smiled.

"You make me sick. I knew you had to tell her something. Are you going to tell everybody else?"

"Yeah, I'll tell them if they want to know. If you change your mind, let me know. I'll be happy to tell you too," he offered.

"No, I haven't changed my mind. I still don't want to know."

"Alright cool, let's go get something to eat," he replied.

I looked down at my phone at yet another text message from Kevin. He's been texting me from all kinds of crazy numbers trying to apologize. At first I brushed him off, but he started wearing me down after a while. There could never be anything romantic between us, but I was starting to miss our friendship. I knew that we could never be best friends again, but I at least wanted us to be cordial. He tried to cross the line a few times, but I always shut him down. When I told him that I was pregnant, he said that he wished he was the father like I would ever let that happen. I hadn't had sex for months before I got back with Dominic, and I still didn't get pregnant right away. Kevin has also been begging me to spend some time with him, but that will never happen either. I kept telling him that we would do lunch just to shut him up. I forgave him, but I will never forget that he put his hands on me no matter how many times he apologized, and I let that be known. I also couldn't let Dominic find out that we were still talking. He would go crazy if he knew. He still doesn't know about Kevin hitting me, and I pray that he or my brothers never find out.

"You hear me talking to you Brooklyn?" Dominic asked pulling me from my thoughts.

"No, what did you say?"

"I asked if you will marry me," he said.

"You must be trying to go to jail. Being married to two women is against the law in Louisiana," I laughed.

"No, I'm talking about once my divorce is finalized," he replied.

"I don't know Dominic. That's kind of rushing it, don't you think?"

"I don't think we're rushing anything. I can't see myself being with anybody else. I swear I thought about you the whole time during my wedding and the honeymoon. I don't even know why I went through with that shit knowing how I felt about you. I don't want to be with anybody else, and I'm not letting you be with anybody else either. You might as well marry me because you're damn sure stuck with me," he rambled.

"I guess we'll cross that bridge when we come to it. You're still married, so I don't even want to talk about that right now."

"So what if I get divorced like next month or the month after. Would you marry me before the baby comes?" He asked.

"In a heartbeat," I replied honestly.

"That's what's up," he said as he leaned over to give me a kiss. "Girl you about to make me put a gun to Kennedi's head and make her ass sign them papers."

I laughed, but I could tell he was serious. Dominic was my first everything, so it's only right that he be my first and only husband one day.

NADIA

"What the hell happened to Kevin's truck?" I asked Shannon when I walked into the house. Kevin had just traded in his old truck for a black on black Harley Davidson F-150. I hadn't been over in a few weeks, but it was fine when I saw it before. Now the bumper is dented, and both of the headlights are cracked.

"I don't know, and he gets mad every time I ask him about it," Shannon shrugged.

"Where's Kyle?" I asked. He called and begged me to come over, and I want to know why. I've been putting him off for the past two days, but I couldn't hold him off any longer.

"They're upstairs talking. Kevin made me come down here, so there's no telling what's going on."

Without making too much noise, I made my way upstairs hoping to surprise my man. I told him that I wasn't coming until tomorrow, and I was anxious to see the look on his face.

"I thought it was Bryce at first until I saw her and Taylor sitting at the table with the kids," I heard Kevin say.

"You sure they didn't see you?" Kyle asked him.

"No, they didn't, but I need to get my truck fixed before somebody figures it out. She hurt me, but I don't know what made me do some stupid shit like that," Kevin said.

"Man, fuck her. She tried to play you for that nigga and you sitting here feeling bad about getting back at her. She's alive, and nobody really got hurt.

73

The bitch should be happy that I wasn't the one behind the wheel," Kyle said angrily.

"I was mad, but I wasn't thinking clearly. They had kids in the car man," Kevin said arguing his point.

It didn't take long for me to realize what they were talking about. The damages to his truck made sense to me now. He's the one who ran Brooklyn and Taylor off the road. If any of Brooklyn's brothers or Dominic found out about any of this Kyle and Kevin were both dead men. Jaden's crazy ass would see to that all by himself. I eased back down the stairs just as quietly as I had come up. I rejoined Shannon on the sofa and sent Kyle a text letting him know that I was downstairs. A few minutes later, he and Kevin were joining us in the living room.

"What's up wifey?" Kyle asked while taking a seat next to me. He gave me a peck on the lips and held my hand in his.

"Who me?" I asked while pointing to myself.

"Yeah you, who else would I be talking to?" He asked with a frown.

"I don't know. Maybe Tiffany is around here somewhere because you've never called me wifey before," I replied.

"I keep telling you that I don't mess with that damn girl. We're cool, but that's about all there is to it. It's all about us," he said smiling.

I knew he wanted something just by the way he was acting. Kyle wasn't really the affectionate type unless he wanted sex. He was doing a damn good job trying to butter me up, so it had to be about more than that.

"Okay, so what's up? You've been calling me like crazy to come over here. I'm here now so tell me what's going on," I said getting right to the point.

He looked from me to Shannon and then back to me again. I assumed that Shannon knew what was going on judging by the look on her face.

"Damn, you just come right out with it, huh? But listen, I got some government checks that my boy printed up for me that I needed you and Shannon to handle. It's a lot of them so y'all will have to hit up a few places to cash them all," Kyle said.

I knew there was a reason for him begging me to come over here, but this nigga really had me fucked up. It was one thing to play around with the little paychecks that they printed up, but I was not dealing with any government checks.

"Y'all can count me out. I'm not trying to end up in the feds messing with the government. I'm trying to find me another job so I can stop doing this shit altogether. A one-time thing has turned into months," I replied.

"Girl that's not even a federal crime. If you do this, I can promise that you won't have to look for a job for at least six months. We can all walk away with a nice stash when it's all over with," Kyle informed me.

"Yeah, but Shannon and I are taking all the risk while you and your brother get paid the same amount as we do. I don't know about her, but I'm done playing the fool," I said standing to my feet. A lot of things have weighed heavily on my mind lately, and my friendship with Candace is one of them. I'm taking my anger and hurt out on her just because the man I love is in love with her cousin. I know in my heart that Candace would never do me wrong. She even came to me like a woman and let me know what was going on before I heard it from anyone else. She had no control over Dominic, and I'm dead wrong for doing some of the things that I'm doing, especially fucking with Kyle.

"Come upstairs and let me talk to you for a minute," Kyle said while trying to pull me towards the stairs.

"No, I have somewhere else to be," I lied. I knew what kind of talking Kyle wanted to do. I'll be butt ass naked with his face between my thighs as soon as the door closed. He knows how to make me change my mind and it works every time.

"Come talk to me," Kyle begged while practically dragging me upstairs. As soon as we got in the room, he closed and locked the door behind us. "I'm not changing my mind so you can save the sex session," I insisted.

"I just didn't want to talk in front of Shannon. If you do this for me, I'll give you more than just the usual half. You keep seventy-five percent of what you make and give me the rest," he requested.

"How about I keep all of it since I'm risking my freedom for it?"

"That's not an option. Without me, you wouldn't even have the checks to cash. I'm doing something for you that I'm not even doing for

Shannon, and she's been down with us from day one," he replied in a low tone.

"I don't care. I'm not feeling this anymore Kyle. If you wouldn't gamble so damn much, you could chill out too." Kyle has a terrible gambling habit that he refuses to own up to. He would stay and play all day and night whenever he went to the casino.

"Please baby, I promise this is the last time," he said while walking over to me. When he slipped his hand underneath my dress, the words that I wanted to say were lodged in my throat. He worked his fingers in and out of me until I almost felt like I was too weak to stand.

"Stop," I weakly protested even though I didn't want him to. In one quick motion, Kyle had my underwear off with my leg resting comfortably in the crook of his arm. I gasped from shock and pleasure when I felt him dip his tongue inside my moist opening. He was licking and sucking so fast that I lost my balance and ended up falling to the floor. Kyle never stopped licking, and he went down to the floor right along with me.

"Are you going to help me out?" Kyle asked when he finally came up for air. I didn't answer so he flipped me over and positioned me on all fours.

"Answer me," he instructed as he slipped inside of me and started stroking me slowly. I wanted to answer, but he was hitting my spot just the way I liked it.

"Answer me," he said again, but this time with more force and harder strokes. He had a hand full of my hair pulling me back into him with force.

"Yes!" I screamed out in pleasure with just the right amount of pain. At this moment, I would have said anything just for him to keep going.

"I love you," Kyle admitted right before he released his load and collapsed on top of me. I don't know if he meant it, but it felt good to hear.

****

Two days later Shannon and I were on our mission. We'd already hit up four check cashing spots in New Orleans, and we were on our third one not too far from their house in Slidell. Kevin and Kyle met us to collect the money after each transaction just in case something went wrong. I've been keeping up with how much money I'm supposed to have and it's almost up to twenty-five thousand dollars. After this last stop, I would walk away with thirty thousand dollars, and I'm done.

"Alright, let's do this. We have one more after this and then we're done," Shannon said while getting out of the car.

"I thought this was our last one," I said with a frown on my face.

"No, Kyle said he wants us to go to the one in the strip mall near the house," she informed me. She's been texting with Kevin, and he tells her whatever moves Kyle wants us to make next. Kyle is a greedy bastard, and he's never satisfied with anything that he has. He has enough money to chill out for a while, but he still wants more. I've been over there for the past few days, and we've been getting along great. He's been paying me so much attention until he's almost suffocating me. I love the

78

affection, but it's times like these that he makes me sick.

"Well, I don't care what Kyle says, I'm done after this," I swore.

"Please just do one more for me. I don't want Kevin to get pissed off. You know how he is when he's mad," Shannon said pitifully.

I really felt sorry for her because she doesn't have anyone else in her corner. Kevin is all that she knows, and he treats her like shit. If Brooklyn had wanted him, he would have left Shannon a long time ago.

"I don't know Shannon. We should just leave it alone after this and try again in a few days. Kyle is being too greedy," I told her.

"Please Nadia, just do this for me," she begged.

"Alright, but I'm only doing this because I don't want to be the cause of Kevin putting his hands on you," I admitted.

"Let's do these last two and be done with it," she replied.

After getting the cash from the first spot, we handed the men the cash and went to our last stop for the day. The place is fairly new so no one will know or recognize us here. That's a good thing and made our task that much easier. The clerk is a very young white girl so it would be like taking candy from a baby. After checking our identification, which was fake, she smiled and politely started counting out the cash. I'm happy that we're almost done and more than ready to go home. Shannon and I were all smiles until two uniformed cops walked through the doors a few minutes later. I looked outside and spotted a total of three police cars in the parking lot along with my car, but Kyle and Kevin were nowhere to be found. They followed us here, and now they're gone.

"Just be cool," Shannon whispered to me. My heart was beating fast, and my palms were sweating like crazy. I'd never been to jail a day in my life, and I don't want to go now.

"Good afternoon ladies, we need to speak with you for a minute," one of the officers said. The tears were rolling down my cheeks before I even turned around to face them.

"What's the problem officer?" Shannon asked.

"We need to see some valid identification for both of you," one of the officers said. Shannon and I just looked at each other because we knew that we were busted.

The young clerk put the money away and smirked as she folded her arms across her chest. I had underestimated her, and I was about to pay for such a stupid mistake. She spotted our fake ID's and hit the silent alarm alerting the police. Kevin and Kyle must have left once they saw what was going on. My first mind was telling me not to come here, but like a fool I didn't listen. After not being able to produce a valid form of identification, Shannon and I were handcuffed and placed in the back of the patrol car. She seemed to be fine, but I was a nervous wreck when they read us our rights. I have no family here, and I'm hoping that Kyle will come to my rescue since I did all of this for him. If not, Candace is the next best thing to family that I have.

She had no idea that I had betrayed her, and I could never let her find out after this.

KENNEDI

Dominic and I are scheduled to go to court tomorrow morning, and I'm mentally preparing myself for that drama. The lawyer that my mother hired seems to not care if I stay married or not. She's just like my mother and is encouraging me to sign the divorce papers if the price is right. I'm now four months pregnant and doing well considering my past mishaps. I've been seeing a high-risk doctor twice a month because of my previous miscarriages. My doctor was baffled, wondering why I'd never gone to a high-risk doctor before considering all that I'd been through. It's just my luck to be having a successful pregnancy, but no husband to share it with. I'm even beginning to form a little baby bump that I could do without. Dominic and his mother want to be here for me, but I'm too angry and hurt to allow them to. My mother would die before she let that happen, so that stopped me as well. She's determined to keep them out of my baby's life no matter how she goes about doing it. Tiffany ended up telling my father about my pregnancy when she ran into him a few weeks ago. He called me a few days later, but I never answered for him. He said that Dominic would leave me one day, and I didn't want to give him the satisfaction of knowing that he was right. Besides, I still hadn't forgiven him for telling Dominic all of my business. Because of him I almost lost him before we even got married.

"So how are you going to say you got all of this information?" Scott asked me. We were sitting in my living room on my sofa watching TV and eating Chinese food.

He gave me some information that would hopefully work in my favor when we go to court. Dominic is a slick bastard, but he's not slick enough. He's been using his business account for all of his purchases and repaying it with his personal account. If it wasn't for Scott putting me down on what he was doing, I would have never known.

"I don't know, but I promise that your name will never come up," I assured him. I looked over the statement again and smiled to myself. I couldn't wait to show the judge how he's been supporting his side bitch while we're still married. He had purchases from MAC, Victoria Secret, and a million other places that only a female would frequent.

"It's messed up how he's letting another woman come in and break up his marriage. You really don't deserve that. You should have given me a chance when I asked," Scott smirked.

Scott is and always has been a sweetheart, but he's just not the one for me. I actually met him a few months before I met Dominic, and we went out a few times. Nothing ever came of it and probably never will. I was shocked to learn that he and Dominic were friends, and he worked for his company. I never even told Dominic about me knowing him and neither did Scott. It was crazy for him to think that I would pass up the boss to date one of the employees. Scott's money isn't nearly enough for me to live off of and be happy. I would never hurt his feelings by telling him that though.

"You know I appreciate you Scott, but we can't go there," I replied. Even if I wanted to go there, it wouldn't be with his broke ass.

"I don't see why not. Dominic is doing him. He's in love with Brooklyn and everybody can see that," he said. He's trying to get to me, but I'm trying hard to keep my cool.

"I don't care what he does he's still my husband and you bad mouthing him doesn't change the way I feel. I'm in love with my husband and I'm sorry if that hurts your feelings," I said honestly.

"It's all good. I just wanted to let you know what was up. When I heard him talking to David about it, I felt that it was only right to tell you."

"And I can't thank you enough," I said sincerely.

"Good luck in court tomorrow. Call me if you need me," Scott said as he prepared to leave. I walked him to the door and locked it behind him. I picked up all the paperwork I needed for court and went upstairs to bed.

The next morning I arrived at court thirty minutes before I was scheduled to arrive. My nerves were on edge and my mother was not helping at all.

"Don't sign anything until he agrees to pay what you're asking and don't you dare agree to a lower amount," she instructed. My lawyer, Ms. Iverson, nodded her head as if she agreed with her.

"I just hope the judge doesn't look at the amount of time you've been married as a way for him not to pay anything. Six months really isn't long enough to have invested into a marriage," she spoke up.

"I don't care about any of that. I'm praying that Dominic will have a change of heart and call this entire divorce off," I admitted.

"I don't know where I went wrong with you. Why would you want to be with somebody who clearly doesn't want to be with you? You're better than him, so it wouldn't have lasted anyway. Get whatever you can get from him and move on," my mama snapped.

Silent tears fell from my eyes as she continued to talk, but that didn't stop her. In her mind, Dominic was nothing, but a come up for me and my baby and nothing more.

"Here comes his no good ass now," she hissed.

I looked up and saw Dominic, David, and their parents coming our way. I unintentionally licked my lips as I eyed my husband. He's even more handsome than I remember. His hair is freshly cut, and the Ralph Lauren pants suit he had on complimented him well. It didn't surprise me that David is here with him, but I'm a little hurt to see that his parents accompanied him as well. I was kind of hoping that they would try to talk some sense into him.

"Good morning," Dominic's parents greeted us. Me and Ms. Iverson returned the greeting while my mother turned her head.

"How are you and my grandbaby doing Kennedi?" My mother-in-law asked me.

"We're doing fine. I should find out what I'm having soon," I smiled.

"You make sure you let us know when you find out," Dominic's father said.

"I don't think so. Let's go Kennedi," my mother interrupted. She stood up and walked away followed by my lawyer. Dominic shook his head as I stood there embarrassed by her once again.

"Look, I know that you and my son aren't together anymore, but that don't have nothing to do with us. Now we want to be in our grandchild's life, but I'm not about to kiss your mama's ass to do it. We'll be back in court if that's going to be a problem," Dominic's father said.

"She's upset and she has every reason to be. Your son did cheat and made two babies on me you know," I reminded him.

"Him cheating is why we're here today, but that has nothing to do with the baby that you're carrying," he replied.

"No, we're here today because your son wants a divorce. That's not what I want," I clarified.

"Man, all that shit is irrelevant. We're talking about the fact that you're allowing your mama to keep me and my family out of my baby's life," Dominic said.

"Come on Kennedi," my mother yelled before I had a chance to respond. I slowly walked away and rejoined her.

****

"So you're asking for twenty-five thousand dollars a month even though you've only been married for six months?" The freckled face judge asked me with raised brows. I was happy when we walked into the small room and saw that a woman

86

would be presiding over the case. I assumed that she would be compassionate towards another woman, but she proved me wrong. This witch that sat before us is a pit bull in a long black robe. It also didn't help that no one else was allowed in the room but me, Dominic and our lawyers. My mother had to wait outside along with his family. She prepped my lawyer on what to say, but it's not the same as having her here to talk for me.

"Yes, your honor. My client is asking for a small amount compared to what her husband makes," my lawyer spoke up.

"Five hundred is too much for only six months of marriage," the judge replied sarcastically. I saw Dominic smirk, but I have something for his ass.

"Can I say something please," I asked. The judge nodded her head giving me the green light to speak.

"My husband is very well off financially. He made a baby on me before we even got married, and he still supports that child and the child's mother. He's been trying to hide it by doing everything from his business account and replacing the funds with his personal account. He purchased her a car, and he pays her bills faithfully every month. She's also expecting a second baby with him that he's going to support as well," I rambled.

Dominic's lawyer jumped up and started talking to the judge in his defense. Dominic had a look of shock on his face. I'm sure he's wondering how I know all that I know, but I'll never tell him.

"Okay I need everyone to calm down and listen," the judge ordered. "Mrs. Roberts are you contesting this divorce and if so under what grounds?"

"I'm contesting it because I'm not ready to end my marriage. We've never even tried to work it out, no counseling or nothing. I thought we were supposed to take steps to save a marriage before just deciding to call it quits," I replied.

"While I do feel bad for you none of those are valid reasons to contest a divorce. You said he made a baby on you, but you still married him. Clearly you've had problems long before now. How long have you two been separated?"

"It's been three months ma'am," Dominic spoke up.

"Louisiana law requires you to be separated for at least one hundred eighty days if no children are involved."

"But I'm pregnant right now," I blurted out.

"Please don't interrupt me when I'm speaking. The baby that you're carrying does not count. You have no kids in the home right now. Now you have one of two choices Mrs. Roberts. You can sign the papers now and be a free woman in three months or you can take this to trial and fight it out. But let me caution you before you decide. Taking this to trial can end up costing you money that you may or may not have for absolutely nothing. He will be granted the divorce eventually because you cannot force someone to stay married to you. Either way it goes you will walk away with nothing because six months is not long enough for you to even be eligible for anything. From what I've read you two didn't share a bank account or any other community property items. This is not a family court, but you might want to go to one to discuss child support when the baby comes unless both of you can work it out on your own. I'll give you both a few minutes to speak with your attorneys before we proceed," she said standing to her feet.

"You are a no good bastard. I can't believe you're doing this to me. After everything, I've done for your ungrateful ass. It'll be a cold day in hell before you see this baby," I shouted at Dominic as soon as the judge was gone. He just looked at me with that stupid ass smirk on his face as if he didn't have a care in the world.

"I guess we'll be back in court then," he smiled.

"Fuck you!" I screeched.

"Nope, you tried, but you can't," he chuckled.

"Kennedi calm down. Don't start anything in here. It won't be pretty if you do," my lawyer warned.

"So what do we do now?" I asked her calmly.

"We really don't have a choice, but to sign. I told you that it was a possibility that you could walk away with nothing. You guys haven't been married long, and you've been separated for months. We're fighting a losing battle by taking this to trial. She basically just told you that it would be a waste of money because you wouldn't get anything. Just sign and be done with it," she urged.

When she pulled the papers from her briefcase and handed me a pen, my entire body started to shake. I can't believe that after only six months of marriage I'm already signing divorce papers.

"It'll be okay Kennedi," my lawyer consoled me as tears rapidly ran down my face.

My hand shook so bad that my handwriting didn't even look like my own. I slid the signed papers back to my attorney as I buried my face in my palms and cried. My mother is going to be livid when she finds out that I walked away with nothing. This meeting definitely didn't go as I wanted it to. Instead of possibly reconciling with my husband, I'd just signed him over to be with Brooklyn permanently.

DOMINIC

"Man that shit just don't sound right to me," I complained as David and I sat in our office. It's been three days since Kennedi and I went before the judge, and I still have more questions than answers. I'm happy with the outcome, but I'm still confused about a lot of things. Like how Kennedi was able to get her hands on my business account bank statement. There's no way that kind information was accessible to her. That only meant one thing. Somebody is in my business and giving up info that only employees could get their hands on. Besides David, Scott and I, we have a total of twelve employees. None of them gave me the impression of being a snake, but I wouldn't put my life on it. I thought about each and every man that works for us, and nobody stood out.

"Man, somebody is on some foul shit. You know she couldn't have gotten her hands on nothing like that without help. Ain't no other way to explain it. Her crazy ass probably paid somebody for some info," David said.

"I don't know, but it's been on my mind for the past few days. I don't need any snakes working with me or for me. Too many niggas out here looking for work for me to play games with anybody up in here. I don't mind signing a pink slip, and I'm dead ass serious about that," I threatened.

"I feel you, but you can fire nobody if you don't know who it is. It shouldn't be too hard to find out though."

91

"How can I do that? It's not like they gon' be honest if I ask. Nobody is that stupid. At least I hope not."

"No, but Kennedi is. You know she still got mad love for you. All you have to do is say some shit that she wants to hear. Make her think it's all good for a minute. She'll be telling you her bank account number and everything else," David replied.

"You must be crazy. Brooklyn already beat her down. Ain't no telling what she'll do to her if she finds that out. She'll be trying to leave my ass for real this time. I'm not trying to have another falling out with her. We just got back on track. Nah bruh, I can't even go there."

"Nigga, stop being so damn scary. Let me find out that Brooklyn is putting her hands on you when nobody is around. You all shook up and paranoid and shit," David said.

"I'm just not trying to do nothing to piss her off. She's been on some rowdy shit since she's been pregnant," I confessed.

"Man, Brooklyn is not going to find out. Now, I'm not telling you to go to the bitch's house or nothing like that. You need to take her out to eat or something. You know wine and dine her. Then when you get the info, leave and stick her ass with the bill," David suggested.

"Dude you really are stupid," I laughed, but I was really thinking about what he was saying. Kennedi still loves me, and I know that for sure. She'll tell me what I want to know if I tell her what she wants to hear. I'm not an actor, so I hope I'm convincing enough to make her believe me.

"Just call her and ask her out on a date," David snickered.

"Don't play with me man. If I do call her it damn sure won't be for a date. I'm very happy at home."

"You better be. My lil sis don't play that shit with you. Call and put her on speakerphone. I want to hear when she gets her hopes up high," David chuckled.

"Man, I don't know, I got a bad feeling about this," I admitted.

"Brooklyn's longest day at school is on Mondays right?" David asked. I nodded my head letting him know that he was right.

"Alright, so she won't be able to call you if she's in class and you won't have to lie about where you are. Take Kennedi somewhere far out where you don't know anybody and talk to her," he suggested.

"When you say far out, how far are you talking? I don't want to be around her ass that long."

"Well, not far, but somewhere that you know Brooklyn or nobody we know will see you."

"Man, New Orleans is small as fuck. Ain't too many places we can go."

"Nigga do you want the info or not?" David asked me.

"Yeah, I want it. I need to find out who she's been talking to so I can handle their ass. I can't stand snakes," I fumed.

"Alright, well call her," David said eagerly. He pulled a chair up to my desk like he was about to watch a good movie or something. This clown lives for drama, and I've been keeping him very entertained lately. I picked up the phone and dialed Kennedi's number before pressing the speakerphone button.

"You must have dialed the wrong number because I know you didn't mean to call me," she snapped as soon as she picked up. I'm so happy that we aren't face to face, or she wouldn't have missed the scowl on my face just from hearing her voice.

"Stop acting like that. I'm just calling to check on you and my baby," I replied. I'm shocked that she answered and didn't send me to voicemail. Usually, she would always do that whenever her mother was around.

"We're fine and goodbye," she said.

"Wait," I said trying to keep her from hanging up. "I wanted to know if I could take you out so we can talk."

"Now I know you dialed the wrong number. This is Kennedi, not Brooklyn," she snapped.

"So that's how you doing me now?"

"That's how you wanted it, so I guess I am," I've been ready to hang up, but David keeps encouraging me to keep talking.

"Well, maybe I don't want it like that anymore," I replied with a frown. It's killing me to even fake it with her ass.

"So what are you saying Dominic?"

"If you let me take you out we can talk about it," I suggested.

"Take me out when and where?" She asked. David gave me the thumbs up, and I gave him my middle finger.

"I'm free Monday and I'll tell you the place as soon as I decide," I answered.

"Okay, but you better be saying something that I want to hear," she warned.

"You'll love what I have to say, I promise. I'll let you go, but I'll text you the info on where we can meet for lunch," I promised right before disconnecting our call.

"Now was that hard?" David asked.

"Hell yeah, it was hard. I'm going home to my girl and my son after that shit," I said as I grabbed my keys and walked out. As bad as I wanted to know what was up, I didn't want to be around Kennedi at all.

"Brook," I yelled when I walked into our apartment about thirty minutes later. I knew she had to be in the kitchen because I smelled the food as soon as I walked in.

"Yeah," she replied.

"Daddy," DJ yelled excitedly as he ran up to me. I picked him up and went to see what Brooklyn was cooking.

"Get your dirty hands off of my pots," she fussed while pushing me away from the stove.

"Girl, that stomach is popping out of nowhere," I said taking notice of the bulge that she carried around. I rubbed her belly and put DJ down so that he could do the same. He basically wants to do everything that I do. I try to be careful whenever he's around.

"Go wash y'all hands so we can eat," Brooklyn instructed.

After we ate and cleaned up the kitchen, I gave DJ a bath while Brooklyn took her shower. Once I took my shower, I joined both of them on the sofa to watch the Disney channel. Brooklyn was playing on her phone while I watched SpongeBob with my son.

"I'm going to get me and DJ some ice cream. You want some?" Brooklyn asked me. My son was wide awake which means he must have taken a long nap today.

"No, I'm good, but bring me some water," I replied to her departing back. Soon after she got up, I heard a buzzing noise alerting me to an incoming text message. When I picked up my phone, I didn't see any messages, but I still heard the buzzing. I looked at the spot where Brooklyn sat and saw her phone lighting up. I picked it up, and my heart dropped when I read the messages. It had to be a nigga because he was begging to see her. She didn't have the number saved, but I still scrolled through all of their messages.

"What the fuck," I said a little too loud.

"What the fuck," DJ repeated clearly. He's just like a sponge and soaks up everything he hears. He's almost two and talking like he's three already thanks to Brooklyn.

"Don't say that DJ. That's a bad word," I chastised even though he was repeating what I said. I continued to look through the messages and got more and more heated with each passing second. It didn't take a genius to figure out that it was Kevin, but I can't believe that Brooklyn is even entertaining that clown. I left DJ watching TV while I went to the kitchen and confronted Brooklyn.

"What kind of fucking games are you playing?" I yelled as I grabbed her by the collar of her night shirt.

"What are you talking about?" She replied nervously.

"This is what I'm talking about," I replied while shoving the phone in her face. "I never put my fucking hands on you, but you still talking to this nigga even after he hit your stupid ass. You never even told me about that shit. And then you're trying to meet up with him too?"

"No," she cried.

"Well, that's not what your messages say. If that's what you want let me know now and I can go on about my business. I'm not doing this stupid shit with you Brooklyn," I swore. I would never leave her, but I had to make her think that I would.

"No, that's not what I want. I blocked all the numbers that he called from, but he kept calling," she said with tears pouring from her eyes.

"That's because you keep entertaining his ass. If you really didn't want to talk you would have changed your number or something. Don't stand here and play dumb with me."

"Okay, I'll change my number."

"Don't do it just because I told you to. Obviously you like talking to him. And since y'all texting each other and shit tell his bitch ass it's on whenever I see him," I yelled. I walked back into the living room and picked DJ up from the sofa. Brooklyn started panicking when she saw me going to the front door.

"Where are you going? I said I'm sorry," she cried.

"Don't say anything else to me. I don't even want to look at you right now," I said right before walking out on her. I heard her crying, but I'm too mad to even care. She knew that I wasn't going far without my car keys. Plus, DJ and I were still in our pajamas. I only went downstairs to talk to Bryce for a while. I wasn't there a good twenty minutes before Brook sent me a text with her new phone number. I'm happy that she changed it, but I shouldn't have had to make her do it. I know I have to talk her, but it's not going to be tonight.

*****

Monday came faster than I needed it to, but I'm ready to get it over with. Kennedi and I are meeting at Oceana Grill in the French Quarters. It's still kind of early and many people are either at school or work with the exception of a few tourists. This area usually doesn't get crowded until night time, and I would be long gone by then. I came a few minutes early just to try to get a table away from everybody else. I doubt I would see anybody I knew, but I'm not taking any chances. When I walked into the restaurant, I was shocked to see that Kennedi was already there. Then to make matters worse, she's already seated at a table that sat right in the middle of the restaurant. Her face lit up when she saw me, and I had to remind myself to keep smiling.

"What's up Ma?" I asked when I walked up to the table. I sat down in a hurry before she could even attempt to hug me.

"Hey boo," she smiled while looking into my eyes.

"Why didn't you get a seat by the window? I don't like this spot," I told her.

Within a matter of minutes, she flagged down a waiter who moved us near the window. I felt a little better since we were moved out of the spotlight.

"So let's talk. What is it that you wanted to say to me?" She asked.

"Damn, can we order something to eat first?" I laughed while trying to break the ice. She's looking at me like I'm a piece of meat, and I need a distraction. The same waiter who moved us came back to take our orders. I ordered a shot of patron to help me get through being here. It's probably the first of many if I have to stay here for a while.

"So does this lunch date mean that you've had a change of heart about us getting a divorce?" She asked while sipping her sweet tea.

"You tell me. What do you want to do?"

"You know I never wanted a divorce to begin with," she replied.

"Tell me what's going to be different if we get back together?" I asked.

"What happened with you and Brooklyn? She must have dropped you, huh?" She asked ignoring the question that I asked her.

"I didn't come here to talk about Brooklyn and I'm sure you didn't either."

"No, but something must have happened within the last few days or you wouldn't be here."

I just shrugged, but I didn't reply to what she was saying.

"I know for a fact that you're still taking care of her. The bank statements that I showed the judge proved that," she rambled on. I'm so happy that she mentioned it before I did. She made everything that much easier for me.

"Yeah and speaking of that, exactly how did you get my company bank statements anyway?" I asked.

"Wouldn't you like to know?" She taunted. When our food came, we ate in silence until I mentioned the account information again.

"So how are we supposed to be getting back together if you're keeping secrets from me?"

"I'm not keeping anything from you Dominic."

"Yes, you are. You always keep secrets when it's about money. That was one of our biggest problems," I reminded her.

"No, Brooklyn was our biggest problem," she stated.

"Stop bringing her up. I'm talking about us. And like I said, money was our biggest problem. If you can't even answer a simple question, I'm wasting my time being here. Nothing has changed, and we can't move forward by telling lies. Call me when you're ready to stop playing games," I said as I reached for my wallet. I'm playing on her emotions, and I'm hoping that it works.

"Dominic wait, don't leave. It's not that I'm hiding anything from you. I'm just not trying to involve anybody else in our mess."

"So basically somebody is out to get me and you're helping them. What makes it worse is that I know it's somebody that works for me. I got somebody smiling in my face that don't mean me no good and you're okay with that?" I said laying it on thick.

"No, I'm not baby, but I know you. You'll be trying to take somebody's job," she replied making me cringe when she called me baby.

"I'm about to go. Let me know when you're serious about us being together," I said standing to my feet.

"Wait, okay I'll tell you," she said hurriedly. I sat back down and looked at her waiting for her to continue.

"Oh okay, so this is how we're doing it now Dominic?" A familiar voice said from behind me. I wanted to die when I turned around and locked eyes with Co-Co.

"What's up Co-Co?" I asked nervously. I wanted to tell him what was up, but I'm too close to getting what I need from Kennedi.

"Yeah, whatever nigga. And what's going on with this?" He asked while pointing at me and Kennedi.

"We're having lunch is what's going on. You seem to have forgotten that this is my husband," Kennedi snapped at him. I really wish that she would have kept her mouth closed. Co-Co lives for drama, and he's known for going off at the mouth.

"Was I talking to this human blow up doll?" He asked looking at me. "Bitch don't make me get a stick pen and deflate your artificial ass. Oh, and I don't want you to wonder if I'm going to tell my cousin Dominic. I'm letting you know to your face that I'm going to tell her so don't act surprised when I do. Now y'all enjoy your meals and have a good day," he said as he walked away with a group of women. I saw them walk out of the restaurant, and I'm grateful for that much.

"So you and Brooklyn are still together?" Kennedi asked as soon as they left.

"I wouldn't be here with you if we were," I lied. "So finish saying what you were about to say."

"And then what? You go back home to Brooklyn, and I go home alone?" She assumed.

"Man fuck this, I'm leaving," I'm wasting my time if she's not giving up any info. I'm about to go home and have it out with my girl for nothing. We're already on bad terms because of the situation with Kevin, and this will only add fuel to an already burning fire.

"It was Scott," Kennedi blurted out. I looked at her to see if she would crack a smile, but she never did. She's sitting here telling me that my childhood best friend and most trusted employee had done me wrong. Even though I didn't want to believe it, it made perfect sense. That's how she knew about Brooklyn coming to the office, the car and everything else, but something still didn't make sense to me. Why would Scott help her to hurt me? What's in it for him?

"Are you fucking him or something?" I asked.

102

"What! Hell no I'm not fucking him. I'm not like you. I took my vows very seriously," she screeched.

"So he's helping you just because?" I asked skeptically.

"Maybe he didn't like how you were treating me. Did you ever think about that?"

"You can miss me with the sad stories and guilt trips. I'm really not trying to hear that right now."

"I would never do that to you and you know it. I've never cheated on you and I never will," she promised.

"I really don't care what you do. If Scott wants you, he can have you."

"What is that supposed to mean?" She asked angrily.

"Thanks for the info, but I need to get home to my girl," I said standing to my feet once again.

"Oh, so she's your girl now? You were just begging me to take your pathetic ass back a few minutes ago," she yelled.

"Begging? You don't believe that shit yourself. A little over two months left and it's officially over. Why would I beg you to take me back? I mark my calendar every day because I can't wait to get rid of your ass," I laughed.

"Fuck you! I'm happy we're not together anymore. You like hood rats, and that's why you chose one over me."

"You be good and take care of my baby," I said as I tossed a few bills on the table to cover the check.

"You'll never see it, so don't worry about my baby," she yelled after me making people look at her strange. I went to the lot where I parked my car and got in. As soon as I pulled off I got a call from David. He's off today, but I needed to get up with him soon.

"Yeah bruh," I answered.

"Bryce wants us to come to the house later on to play some spades. You down?" He asked.

"Yeah, but I'm on my way to the office to do some paperwork right now. We need to talk," I informed him. I know Co-Co hadn't called Brooklyn yet because she's still in school. I'm hoping that he doesn't text her so I can at least explain myself first. She knew all about what went down in court, so I hope like hell that she believes me.

It was a little after seven when I got home since I stopped to get us some drinks. David had just pulled up, but he took the drinks and went straight to Bryce's house. Brooklyn had to have been home for a while, but I still hadn't heard from her. It's all good since no news is good news to me. When I walked into the house, it was dark and quiet. I turned on the front room light, but nothing seemed out of place.

"Brooklyn," I called out while making my way down the hall. I didn't hear anything, but I got my answer when I walked into our bedroom. The closet was partially opened, and I noticed that most of the things on Brooklyn's side were gone. I went to DJ's room, and it was the same thing there. Some of his clothes were missing as well.

"I can't catch a fucking break," I mumbled to myself when I pulled my phone from my pocket. I was about to call Brooklyn's phone when a text came through from David telling me that her and my son were at Bryce's house. I didn't hesitate to lock the door and walk down to Bryce's apartment. I rang the bell, but I heard the loud talking before I even entered the apartment. When Taylor opened the door, it looked like one big family reunion. Besides her, Tiana, Co-Co, Candace, Bryce, and David were all sitting around the living room talking. I didn't see Brook or my son, but I knew they were there. Knowing her, she's probably in one of the back rooms.

"Co-Co you are messy as hell. I can't believe you did me like that," I fussed.

"Uh, did I not tell you that I was telling my cousin? I know you didn't think I was playing. I wasn't about to let you play her," he argued.

"It wasn't even like that," I replied.

"Well, I know that now since David explained everything. But hold up, by now everybody in here should know not to do or say anything around me. I'm straight ratting your ass out, and I'm not hiding the fact that I did it. And no, I'm not apologizing once it's done," Co-Co said honestly. I just let it go because that's a losing battle to argue with him.

"My friend is so mad at you," Tiana said. David is sitting there shaking his head like he didn't have anything to do with it.

"What the fuck are you shaking your head for? Listening to you is what started all this shit in the first place," I snapped.

"Nigga don't get mad at me. I told your stupid ass not to get caught. It's not my fault that your dumb ass went to one of the most popular restaurants in New Orleans," he replied.

"Man whatever! Where's Brooklyn?" I asked.

"She's in the room back," Taylor answered.

"You not gon' tell me what happened?" David asked. We still hadn't discussed what Kennedi told me and I wasn't in the mood right now.

"Hell no and stop talking to me," I barked as I made my way down the hall. I had to try and get things straight with my girl before things got too far out of hand.

"My daddy," DJ yelled when I opened the door. Brooklyn was sitting on the bed playing with her phone. I picked my son up and sat down next to her. I was just sitting there staring at her for a few minutes, but she refused to raise her head up to look at me.

"So you just gon' sit there and not say nothing to me?" I asked her.

"I don't have anything to say except, it's over," she replied calmly.

"So you would leave me just like that? You didn't even give me a chance to explain myself. And it ain't never over so you can get that shit out of your head," I said seriously.

"My cousin just saw you at a restaurant wining and dining your wife and you don't think it's over. You must be crazy."

"If you let me explain I can tell you why."

"There's nothing to explain. I told you that I wasn't going back and forth with you and her. I'm not letting you play these games with me."

"What are you talking about? I told you what happened when we went to court. I was only trying to find out how she got ahold of all of my company banking information. I'm not playing with you, and you should know that. I'm sorry for not telling you what I planned to do, but I knew you wouldn't have agreed if I did."

"You don't know that so don't speak for me."

"Baby I'm sorry, but we're not breaking up over something so stupid. That shit didn't even mean anything to me. I'm just waiting for this divorce to be finalized. I'm where I want to be, and nothing is going to change that," I promised.

"Why should I believe anything that you say? This is just a pattern with you. You cheated on Nadia with Kennedi, and you cheated on Kennedi with me. I don't even know why I'm surprised right now. It was only a matter of time before you did it to me too," she replied.

"You're sitting here acting like you were innocent in all of this. You didn't come into this shit blind. You knew what was up when we first got together. Two babies later and now you want to start complaining. You should have said all of this before I fell in love with your ass." I'm pissed that she's even sitting here comparing our relationship to the ones that I had with Nadia and Kennedi. I love her more than I loved the both of them put together. This is the first time that I can actually say I'm happy and really mean it.

"You're still legally her husband, so I don't even know why I'm mad. Y'all can have each other. Obviously, you like all that weave and silicon. I hope she makes you happy," she snapped. I wanted to laugh at her last comment, but I was too mad.

"Whatever Brooklyn, your solution to every problem we have is to run from it. I didn't leave you when I found out that you were still talking to Kevin's punk ass, but you want to leave me behind some bullshit. I'm getting tired of always begging you to be with me. If this is where you want to be, then cool. Me and my son are going home."

"Bye," she said like it was a done deal. I picked DJ up and left out of the room.

"You leaving?" David asked as I bypassed everyone in the living room.

"What it look like?" I replied with an attitude. He got up and followed me to my apartment. I'm happy that he did because I really needed someone to talk to.

****

The next morning David and I were at work before the sun even came up. After having the locks changed throughout the office, we called up the security company to have all of the passwords changed on our computers. We also had the codes to the alarm system reset. Anything that Scott knew would be of no use to him now. He usually came in before anyone else, and that's our reason for getting it done so early. David wants to get rid of him early just in case he decides to make a scene in front of the other employees. Just like me, my brother is hurt that one of our closest friends would do me wrong like that. And just like me, he wanted to know why.

"I hope this dude don't make me knock him out up in here. He can say one thing I don't like, and that's just what's going down," I told David.

"You won't get any complaints from me. I still can't believe he did some hoe shit like that. I told you it had to be somebody close," he replied.

We sat around in silence for a while waiting for Scott to show up. David had the office door locked so that he would know that his keys no longer work. He's playing a game on his computer while I'm texting back and forth with Brooklyn. I took DJ to her at Bryce's house earlier, and he refused to go back to sleep. He's hyped, and she had to stay up and deal with him. I would have taken him with me, but I don't know how everything is going to play out. I can't have my son in the line of fire like that.

"Here comes that white devil now," David said making me laugh. I looked up just in time to see Scott exit his white Camaro. He'd just gotten the car a few months ago and would probably have to send it back since he's about to be unemployed. He walked up to the door and fumbled with his keys before trying to insert one into the lock. When he saw that he couldn't do it, he knocked on the side window. David and I jumped up and walked over to the door at the same time.

"Damn, I'm glad y'all are here early today. My damn key is not working," Scott commented. He had his lunch bag and was headed for the break room until I stopped him.

"How long have we known each other Scott?" I asked.

"We've known each other since elementary. Y'all were the only ones who wanted to be friends with the white boy in the projects. Nobody else wanted to be bothered with me," he laughed.

"That's why I don't understand why you felt the need to go behind my back and do me dirty like you did. We looked out for you when your own family didn't want to be bothered with your ass," I said getting madder as I spoke.

"What are you talking about? I appreciate everything that y'all have done for me. I would never do you or David dirty."

"So you running to Kennedi like a lil bitch is not doing me dirty? You told her everything you knew about me and Brooklyn. And if that wasn't bad enough, you gave her the paperwork to back it up. You're already fired so do yourself a favor and just keep it real. She already told me everything. I just don't understand why you did it."

"Despite what you think everything is not always about you. Yeah, you threw me a few crumbs, but so what. I damn near started this company with y'all, but it was like fuck me once it got off the ground. It was supposed to be the three of us running shit when we planned it. All of that changed once it actually happened," he complained with fire in his eyes.

"You should be happy that we hired your ass at all. You're a fucking alcoholic. We held you down even after your own family turned their backs on you. We would be some damn fools to let you fuck up what we worked so hard to build," David barked.

"Your ass was in AA when we started this shit so don't act like we owe you something. And you didn't help us plan a damn thing. David and I did all the ground work, and it was already done when you came in," I yelled.

"Yeah, you would say that. I remember us talking about this long before we even went to school for it," he replied.

"You still stuck on some shit that we talked about when we were in elementary. That was long before you decided that you loved the bottle more than you loved your money. Fuck outta here with that bullshit," I roared.

"Man, it's whatever. Like you just said, I'm already fired, so there's no need to keep talking about it. Fuck both of y'all and this job," he hissed. David tried to pull me back when I went to grab him, but I was too quick. After delivering two vicious blows to his face, he went stumbling to the floor with blood gushing from his nose. I got in two more good licks to his face before David grabbed me.

"Let that clown make it. It's not even that serious," David said while holding onto my arm.

"Get the fuck out of here before I knock your bitch ass out," I yelled through clenched teeth. Usually he would be popping off at the mouth, but he knew better than to test me right now.

We watched as Scott got up from the floor holding his bloody nose. He got into his car and sped out of the parking lot. Over ten years of friendship and this is what it boiled down to. I don't have any regrets, and I would do it all over again if I had to. I would rather have one hundred enemies than one fake friend like him. Aside from all the drama with Brooklyn, that's one less problem that I have to worry about.

CANDACE

For the past few weeks, David's house has become our hangout spot every Sunday. He and Dominic would get on the grill or Bryce would boil seafood for everyone. I usually stayed the night and went home Monday morning when he left for work. That was the plan for today until I received a very disturbing call from Nadia's mother, Cheryl, early this morning. Cheryl had moved to Virginia a few years ago, and she hasn't looked back since then. She's been begging Nadia to join her and the rest of their family, but she keeps refusing to go. I was surprised when she called me, but that soon turned into shock. According to her, Nadia was locked up, and she needed my help to get her out. Working prevented her from coming down to do it herself, and I'm the closest thing to family that Nadia has in New Orleans. She wired me the money and David, and I rushed to the St. Tammany Parish Jail in Slidell to bail her out. I've never known her to ever hang out in that area, so I had no clue as to what was going on. I don't know what has gotten into Nadia, but this is not like her at all. I never asked Cheryl what she was charged with because she's already upset about everything. I'm thankful that David has taken the day off from work to be here with me. I don't know the first thing about talking to a bail bondsman, so he did all of the talking for me.

"It's been over two hours. I wonder what's taking them so long to release her," I complained. We're sitting in the waiting area where the prisoners are released from, but Nadia still hasn't come out.

113

"It's a long process. They have to do all kinds of paperwork and stuff before they release somebody," David informed me.

"I can't believe she's in here in the first place."

"Now that was a shock to me too. Nadia has never been the type to get into anything. She must have gotten mixed up in something with somebody else."

"It's like she can't catch a break. If I were her, I would move to Virginia and be closer to my family. Maybe a fresh start is what she needs," I said. My poor friend has been going through a lot lately. She hasn't really been herself since she had her heart broken by Dominic. Because of her insecurities, no other relationship seemed to work out after that. She automatically assumed that every man was out to do her wrong.

"Here she comes now," David said as we both stood up. I looked towards the sliding glass doors and spotted Nadia walking towards us. She looked awful. Her hair was all over her head, and she seemed to have aged overnight. It also looked like she's lost some weight since I saw her at the restaurant the last time.

"Hey," she said smiling weakly. "Thanks for coming to get me."

"You're still my best friend, Nadia. You know I'm always here whenever you need me," I assured her while giving her a hug.

"I'm just so embarrassed. My mama is mad at me, and I don't even know where my car is," she cried.

"Where were you when you got arrested?" David asked her.

"At a strip mall not too far from here," she replied. "But that was three weeks ago."

My head shot up, and my eyes widened in surprise when she said that.

"You've been in here for three weeks Nadia?" I asked her.

"Yeah," she nodded.

"Oh my God Nadia! Why didn't you call me? You know I would have been here the same day to get you out," I replied.

"I don't know Candace. I was just too ashamed. I haven't been a very good friend to you lately," she admitted.

"Girl, forget about all of that. We've always had each other's backs. Even if we don't talk as much as we used to I would have been here in a heartbeat had I known what was up."

"Come on, let's go see if we can find out where your car is," David suggested.

After talking to a few people at the police station, we were no closer to finding her car than we were before. David decided to go back to where she was arrested to see if they knew anything. It only took us about ten minutes to get to the strip mall that Nadia led us to. He told us to sit in the car while he went in to speak with the manager of the place.

I wanted to ask her what she did to get locked up, but I decided against it. I figured that if she wanted to talk then she would come to me whenever she's ready.

"The manager said that the police towed your car a few days after you went to jail. Most likely it's been impounded," David said when he got back to the car.

"So what does that mean?" Nadia asked.

"The first thing we need to do is go to the auto impound lot. He said they don't have one out here, so it's probably at the general one on North Claiborne. Do you have your keys?" David asked.

"Yeah, they gave them back to me with my other belongings. But I don't have any money on me to pay for it. My phone is dead, and my debit card is at home," she said sadly.

"Don't worry about that. Let's just see if it's there first," David said.

After stopping to get Nadia something to eat, we were on our way. It took us almost an hour to get from where we were to where we needed to be. Since there was nowhere to park, David stayed in the car while Nadia and I got out and talked to someone. It didn't take long for us to be switching places. After almost going to jail for slapping the rude ass lady who was trying to help us, David made me sit in the car while he went in with Nadia. I was pissed that we stood there for almost ten minutes, and the bitch never asked if we needed any help. When she did decide to help us, her attitude was ridiculous. She was popping her gum and talking on her cell phone at the same time. Then when I went off on her, she threatened to call the police and have me arrested. We did find out that Nadia had to pay three hundred dollars to get her car back. I had given her the money before I left to go back to the car. She promised to pay me back, but I'm really not worried about it.

"Hey Ms. Cheryl," I said when I answered my phone for Nadia's mother.

"Hey, Candace. Nadia's phone is still going straight to voicemail. Were you able to get her out?" She asked.

"Yes, ma'am, me and my boyfriend are at the police impound trying to help her get her car back."

"I can't believe she could be so damn stupid. And who the hell is Shannon Franklin?" She asked.

"I know a Shannon, but I don't know her last name. Why?"

"That's who she got arrested with. I had somebody that I used to work with look it up for me," Nadia's mother had been a police dispatcher for years when she lived here. She knew just about everybody in all of the police precincts and she still kept in contact with most of them. Even now that she lived somewhere else, she's still in the same line of work.

"Well, what did she get arrested for?"

"Check fraud. Can you believe that shit? She was going around cashing counterfeit checks. If she needed money all she had to do was call me. I've always helped her out when money was tight," she fussed.

"What! Where in the hell did she get counterfeit checks from?"

"I don't know, probably from that no good ass nigga that she was messing with."

"I didn't know that she was messing with anybody. I mean she told me that she had a friend, but that was a while ago," I admitted.

"She's been messing with some loser named Kyle. I called her phone one day and heard him cursing her out like a dog in the background. Then she tried to cover for his ass and said that it was his brother cursing out his girlfriend. I'm not stupid, and I specifically heard him saying her name when he was going off," she rambled.

After she said Kyle's name, everything that she said after that was a blur. I didn't want to believe that it was the same Kyle that I use to deal with, but it would make perfect sense. I thought that Brooklyn being with Dominic is what was keeping her away. Now it was a possibility that it was more than just that. I didn't want to just jump to conclusions, so I asked a few questions just to be sure.

"Did she tell you anything else about Kyle, Ms. Cheryl?" I asked.

"No, not really, only that he lives with his younger brother and the brother's girlfriend," she replied.

"Is his brother's name Kevin?"

"Yep, I remember her saying that it was Kevin who was cursing that time and not Kyle," she confirmed.

"Wow," was my only reply. Never in my wildest dreams would I have thought that Nadia would do something so conniving to me. I've always prided myself on being a good friend, but obviously I was the only one. I could care less about

118

Kyle. He fucked anything with a pulse. I'm just hurt that my best friend fell for it.

"Well, I won't hold you any longer Candace. Tell my stupid daughter to give me a call," she said.

"Alright Ms. Cheryl," I said right before she hung up. I held my phone in my hand as I stared off into space. I'd just given up my whole day to bail this bitch out of jail. I even took three hundred dollars of my hard earned money to get her car back for her. Now I know why she said that she hadn't been a good friend to me lately. That also explains why she's been hanging with Shannon all of a sudden. She's been sleeping with the enemy. I'm beyond pissed and nothing she says can calm me down right now. As a matter of fact, I don't even want to talk. I pulled a hair tie from my purse and pulled my hair up into a sloppy ponytail. I took off my earrings and got out of the car. The longer I waited, the more infuriated I became. About twenty minutes later, I saw Nadia and David walking back towards me. She was smiling, so I guess she got some good news about her car.

"Candace thank you so much. I promise I'll pay you back every penny before the day is over. I just have to go around the corner to pick up my car," Nadia said happily.

I didn't reply, but as soon as she got close enough to me, I grabbed her hair and slung her to the ground. She didn't even hit the pavement good enough before I pounced on her and started beating her ass.

"Oh shit! Candace what's wrong with you," David said as he tried to pull me off of her.

119

"Get off of me David!" I screamed as I banged her head on the concrete sidewalk. He ignored me and picked me up off of her and wrapped his arms tightly around my waist. Nadia sprang to her feet and used that as an opportunity to get a few licks in. She hit me one good time before David let me go to defend myself. I ran at her full force, and she was back on the ground in a matter of seconds. I delivered blows to her face so fast that she didn't even have time to block them all.

"Alright mama, that's enough. What the hell is going on?" David said as he pulled me up and stood in between us.

"You dirty bitch. Why would you fuck with Kyle of all people? I've been nothing, but a good friend to you and that's how you do me?" I yelled out of breath.

"If you're so much of a good friend why would you hook your cousin up with my ex? I know that you had something to do with Dominic and Brooklyn being together," she cried while holding the back of her bloody head.

"You must really be crazy. I came to you and told you what was going on before it came from anywhere else. Brooklyn and Dominic are grown. I can't control what they do."

"Yeah right, now you know how it feels to have someone you trust stab you in the back. And don't be mad because Kyle came to me. Obviously you weren't enough for him," she screamed.

"Girl, I don't give two fucks about Kyle. I got a man. It's just the principle of it all. Trust and believe that you're not the only one he's fucking.

And where was that nigga when you were sitting in jail for three weeks dumb ass?" She stood there looking at me with a stupid look on her face when I asked that. I know firsthand how selfish Kyle can be. He doesn't care about anybody but himself and sometimes Kevin.

"Yeah, that's what I thought. He left your stupid ass in jail and is probably laying up with the next bitch. You can keep that lil money I just gave you. Three hundred dollars is a small price to pay for getting rid of a snake," I yelled as David pulled me to the car. We left her standing there looking stupid while we sped away. David looked over at me, and I could tell that he wanted to say something.

"Say what you have to say," I demanded as I stared right back at him.

"You sure you're not mad about her being with ole boy?" David asked me as we drove home.

"Hell no, I can't believe you would even think that. I'm very happy being with you. Kyle is the biggest dog I know, so nothing that he does surprises me. Honestly, it's not even about him. Nadia was my best friend, and she should have known better. I knew that something was wrong, but I'm happy I know for sure now," I replied honestly.

"Alright, I was just asking. But you're right Nadia shouldn't have crossed that line. At least you found out before it was too late. First it was Scott now Nadia is on some foul shit. That word loyalty don't mean nothing no more," he said while shaking his head.

I hate to admit it, but he was absolutely right. A lifetime of friendship was gone down the drain all behind Kyle's no good dog ass.

NADIA

I've never felt so stupid in my life. I lost my best friend over a man that doesn't give a damn about me. I'd spent three weeks in jail hoping and praying that Kyle would come and bail me out. Shannon and I were in the holding cell together for the first day, but we got separated after that. I just assumed that she was still locked up as well, but I soon found out that I was wrong. After talking to one of the male guards who kept flirting with me, I found out that Shannon had been bailed out after only two days of being in there. As stupid as it sounds, I thought it would be only a matter of time before they came back for me. After the first week I gave up hope, but I was too scared to call anybody. By week number three, I thought that I was going to lose my mind, so I ended up calling my mother. She was so upset, but she still came through for me just like she always does. I hated for her to get Candace involved, but I was ready to get the hell out of there. I'd lost so much weight because I refused most of the meals that were offered to me. A few times I'd luck up and get something decent to eat, but it wasn't that often. I'm so thankful that my rent had been paid up for a few months, or I'd probably be evicted by now. I have a few thousand dollars saved up from before, but that won't last me too long. I still have to go to court and legal fees will probably eat that up. Even though I'm a first-time offender, the dollar amount of the checks we cashed was so high. I pray that I just get probation, and I don't have to do any time in jail. I'm bound to go crazy if I do.

I spent my first night home soaking in a hot tub of water and nursing the bruises on my face and body. Candace went into full beast mode and practically killed me with her bare hands. I understand that she's mad, but she took things a little too far. Deep in my heart, I knew she didn't help Dominic and Brooklyn get together, but that was my only defense. I really don't have a reason as to why I started messing with Kyle, so I tried to turn everything around on her. She's right about everything that she said about him. He left me in jail and went on as if I never existed. I've been calling his phone nonstop since I've been home. At first, he would send me straight to voicemail. After a while, he blocked me out altogether. I called Shannon's phone, but she didn't answer either. She did send me a text telling me that she would call me later, but that call never came. I'm giving him a few days to think it's all good before I show up at their house. There's no doubt in my mind that we're over, but he owes me money that I want and need.

"I see you finally decided to call me back," I said when I answered the phone for Shannon. I know I shouldn't be, but I'm pissed with her too. Obviously, she didn't care enough to help me out of my situation either. I called her three days ago, and she's just now returning my call.

"I had to wait until Kevin wasn't around to call you back," she replied.

"So you can't talk to me in front of Kevin? When did that start?" I asked.

"I don't know. I guess he's listening to Kyle. He's been in a foul mood, and I'm not trying to do anything to piss him off."

"Oh, so Kyle doesn't want you talking to me? That bastard left me in jail even though it was his fault that I was there. Then he tries to shut me out like it never happened. He owes me thousands of dollars and I want it," I yelled.

"I doubt if you'll ever see it. It's been so crazy around here. Since we went to jail the whole check scam thing is over with. The dude that was helping him doesn't even want to deal with him anymore. He won't print up anymore checks for him either. Kyle claims that the money is running low. He's been talking about hitting up somebody's stash that they know," Shannon said.

"How the hell is money running low? We gave him all the money that we made not even a month ago," I yelled.

"That's the same thing I said. He's been gambling like crazy, and Kevin said he owed somebody some money. He was even trying to get Kevin to help him rob somebody outside the club a few days ago. Then he's been having that bitch Tiffany here every day like she lives here or something," she informed me.

"Are you serious?"

"Dead ass," she replied.

Candace had his ass right. I was locked up, and he was laid up with the next bitch. I'm not going to tell Shannon, but she'll be seeing me sooner than she thinks. I'm about to pay Kyle's ass a much needed visit.

****

It had taken me an entire week before I worked up enough courage to finally pay Kyle a visit. I spoke with Shannon earlier, and she told me that Tiffany hadn't been there for the past two days. I didn't tell her that I was coming because I'm sure she would have told Kevin. I don't know what I'm walking into, so I'm going prepared for a fight. I pulled my hair up into a high ponytail and threw on some leggings with a long spaghetti strap tank to match. I slipped on my Nikes and was out the door. The drive to Kyle's house took me about forty-five minutes, and I had a lot of time to think while I drove.

I'm so ashamed of how I betrayed Candace, and I want nothing more than to apologize. I can honestly say that she has always been a great friend to me. Her family welcomed me in and never treated me like an outsider. I tried calling her, but just like Kyle, she blocked my number too. I could have gone to Bryce's shop to talk to her, but I knew that I was asking for another beat down if I did. I'm sure that she told Co-Co and everybody else about what I'd done by now. I didn't need any more embarrassment.

As soon as I pulled up to Kyle's house, I saw his truck parked out front. I parked on the side of the building and turned my car off. Before I got out, I spotted Kevin's truck pulling up right behind Kyle's. I rushed out of my car and met up with him just as he unlocked the door.

126

"Where is Shannon at Kevin?" I asked startling him. He looked me up and down lustfully before he answered my question.

"I just dropped her off at the hair salon. What are you doing here?" He asked.

"I'm here to get my money from your brother. Y'all just said fuck me and left me in jail to rot. He's damn sure not keeping the money that I got locked up for," I snapped.

"Don't say y'all. I didn't have shit to do with that. He could have bailed you out when I went to get Shannon, so don't blame me for that. And I really don't think this is a good time for you to be here right now. You need to call him before you just show up."

"Maybe I would have called if he hadn't blocked my number. I'm already here, and I want to talk to him now," I yelled as I pushed passed him and went inside.

"Aye girl, don't be busting your ass up in here like you running shit," Kevin yelled as he came after me.

By then I was already halfway upstairs heading towards Kyle's room. I heard the radio playing and the red light illuminated from underneath his bedroom door. I twisted the knob on the unlocked door right as Kevin grabbed my arm.

"Let me go!" I yelled as I busted into the bedroom. Aside from the glow of the light, I saw red as I witnessed Kyle and Tiffany lying in bed butt ass naked. He was on top of her, and they were actually having sex. Hearing about it is one thing, but to catch them in the act is something totally different. They broke their connection and reached for the covers when I burst through the door.

"What the fuck are you doing here Nadia?" Kyle yelled at me. Tiffany was still trying to cover herself up, but it was too late for all of that. I already saw everything that I needed to see.

"I hate you!" I screamed as I ran towards Kyle. I used all the energy I had and punched him right in his mouth. I found a little more confidence when I saw that his lip had started bleeding. I kept swinging, trying to hurt him just as much as he'd hurt me over the past few weeks. Tiffany used this as an opportunity to get out of bed and get dressed. I wanted a piece of her ass too, but I was more focused on him for now. Of course, he didn't sit there and let me win for long. As soon as he was able to stand up he reached back and slapped the shit out of me. He hit me so hard that I went flying to the floor from the impact.

"Man, get this bitch out of here before I hurt her," Kyle yelled to Kevin as he started to get dressed. I rubbed my stinging face and stood to my feet once again. I wasn't done, but this time I wasn't after Kyle. I'm like a crazy woman and all common sense is gone at this point. I ran over to Tiffany and started swinging on her next. She tried to cover her face, but she never did try to swing back. I had her cowering in the corner while I gave her an ass whipping that she would never forget. Some of my anger was reserved for her cousin, but she got it all since she's the only one here. I felt my ponytail being forcefully pulled, and I was being hauled across the carpet like a rag doll. Kyle had come to her rescue and pulled me off of her.

"Get off of me! You left me in jail so you can play house with this hoe. Nigga, where is the money that I got locked up for?" I screamed.

"Bitch, I don't owe you anything. Thanks to you getting caught I lost my fucking hook up," Kyle replied angrily. He stood in front of Tiffany like he was her bodyguard or something. She was trying hard to fix herself up, but she was still a mess.

"Take me home Kyle," she cried like a scared little girl. He grabbed her hand and started leading her out of the room. I tried to get at them again, but Kevin held me back.

"Bitch you better not be here when I get back," Kyle spat before leaving out of the room.

"Fuck you!" I yelled while trying to break free from Kevin's hold. I kicked and screamed trying to get to him again, but it was of no use. He and Tiffany walked down the stairs and straight out the front door.

"Calm down girl," Kevin instructed while still holding me. He had me in a bear hug as he guided me out of Kyle's room and closed the door.

"Just let me go Kevin," I begged as the tears started falling from my eyes. He released his hold on me and allowed me to fall to the floor and cry. This just can't be my life. How could I lose not one, but two men to two cousins? This shit sounds just like a lifetime movie.

"Come on girl, get up. Don't let nobody have you acting outside of your character like this," Kevin said.

129

I allowed him to help me up from the floor and stand me up straight. He put his hand underneath my chin and lifted my head. We made eye contact, but I turned my head away in shame. I hated for him to see me act this way, but I couldn't help it. He used his thumb to wipe away my tears, and I was very surprised by his gesture. I've never seen him be this affectionate with Shannon. Before I knew what was happening, he leaned in and planted a kiss on my lips. His lips were so soft that I just had to do it again. This time when I kissed him, he stuck his tongue in my mouth. As wrong as it was I opened my mouth and willingly accepted it. We stood in the hallway kissing for a few minutes before I finally broke away from him.

"I'm sorry," I mumbled as I tried to walk away from him.

"I'm not complaining," he replied as he pulled me back.

When he kissed me this time, he started fumbling with the buckle of his belt. If I wanted to stop him, now would have been the time. He dropped his pants and boxers to the floor in a matter of seconds. I didn't protest when he pushed me down on my knees and guided his rock hard erection into my warm mouth. He gripped the back of my head as I took all of what he offered to the back of my throat. I looked up and smiled when I saw his eyes rolling to the back of his head. Since Kyle had done me wrong, sleeping with Kevin was ultimate payback. Shannon didn't do anything to deserve it. She's just a casualty of the war that Kyle started.

BRYCE

After being up under Taylor and my girls for the past few weeks, I'm happy to get away with my brothers for a while. One of my tattoo artists had just purchased his first home, and he threw a little housewarming party to celebrate. He's newly divorced, so it's more of a bachelor's pad than anything. We had to drive all the way to Pearlington, Mississippi, but it wasn't too bad. It wouldn't have been a party if Dominic and David weren't there, so we had to invite them to come with us. We stayed at the gathering until everyone else had gone home before we decided to call it a night. After helping my boy get his house back in order, we hopped in Jaden's Navigator and headed back home.

"Man, who are you texting back and forth with like that?" David asked Dominic. It's almost midnight, and he's been on his phone texting for over an hour.

"What you mean? I'm texting my girl," he replied like David should already know.

"Oh, I didn't know you had a girl. Last time I checked you were single," David laughed.

Baby is still trippin', and she's been at my house for the past week. Any other time Dominic would be going crazy by now, but he's trying to teach her a lesson. He didn't come down there all day bothering her like he usually did when she was acting stupid. He had DJ upstairs with him, and he only came down to drop him off or pick him up.

"Nigga you don't believe that yourself. She's trippin' on me right now. Talking about what I'm doing out this late. If she doesn't want me no more, she shouldn't care how late I stay out. I got something for her ass though," he replied.

"Baby needs to stop acting like that. Her ass is too spoiled," Jaden fussed.

"Y'all are the ones that got her like that. I'm suffering because of what you niggas did before I came into the picture," Dominic replied.

"You played a big part in it too. Don't act like you don't give her what she wants," David chimed in.

"That's different, I'm her man. I give her what she wants in order to get what I want."

"Stop," I yelled with my hands in the air. "I don't even want to hear no more." I know that Baby is not a virgin, but I'll be damned if I sit here and listen to the details of her sex life. Everybody started laughing, but I was dead ass serious.

"I don't know why you acting like it's a surprise. You already know they're having sex. Shit, she's on baby number two," Jaden said.

"I know that, but I still don't want to hear about the shit," I stressed.

"Jaden stop at the next gas station. I need some more cigars," Brian requested. We just entered Slidell and were about to get on the twin spans bridge to go back home. It only took about five minutes before another gas station came into view.

"Let me hop out and buy Brooklyn and DJ some snacks," Dominic said as he exited the car with Brian. The rest of us stayed put while they went in to make their purchases. It was late, but the gas station was filled to capacity with all kinds of cars. There's a pizza place next door to it and most of the crowd seemed to be over that way. Two police cruisers were in plain view with four officers standing near them.

"Man, look at this shit," Jaden said while pointing towards the pizza place.

I had to do a double-take when I saw Kyle walking out with his arm draped around Tiffany's waist. They're both smiling hard like they're the only two out here. We watched as they walked over to his truck that was parked right next to one of the police cruisers. They never got in, but they stood up against it and kissed like two kids in love.

"That dude is really foul," David observed from the back seat.

He said the exact same thing that I was thinking. Maybe he's the reason why Tiffany stopped bothering me. If that's the case, he did me a huge favor. Candace put me up on what happened with him and Nadia too. He just didn't know how to keep it real with nobody. I just hate that my cousin lost her best friend behind his sad ass.

"What are y'all looking at?" Brian asked when him and Dominic got back into the car. I pointed out the scene across the lot while they followed my gaze.

"That nigga there," Dominic said shaking his head. "Him and his brother just can't get it right."

He had it in for both Kyle and Kevin since everything went down with Brook. I never had anything against Kevin until I found out about him putting his hands on my sister. Now, he's on my shit list right along with his brother.

"Damn, I wish the police wasn't out here right now," Jaden said angrily.

"We need to wait here and follow his ass," Dominic suggested.

"That's what I'm talking about," Jaden agreed while bumping fists with him.

"Let that shit go man. Just know to keep your grass cut low so you can see the snakes. That one got passed me, but it will never happen again," I promised.

"We'll see him again," Dominic said.

"Yeah, and I like seeing people when they don't see me," Jaden said with a sneaky grin as we left them in our rearview mirror and headed home.

DOMINIC

Brooklyn's ass thinks it's a game, but I'm really done playing with her. She's been at Bryce's house for two weeks now, but she comes up here to our apartment whenever she feels like it. I hate when I get my hopes up high thinking that she's staying only for her to leave and go sleep downstairs. I made it clear that my son is not going with her, and she knows better than to ask. She even came up here and cooked when I was at work, but she would be gone by the time I came home. I want her home, but I'm not about to beg her. It's time for me to show her that she's not the only one who can act a fool.

"How many keys do you need Mr. Roberts?" The locksmith asked me. I'm having the locks changed on our apartment, so Brooklyn can't bring her ass in here unless I'm home. She was trying hard not to face me, but I'm not giving her a choice.

"Give me five," I replied as I handed him a check for what he charged me. I have to give our leasing office a key, besides the ones I had made for me, Brooklyn, David, and Bryce. After she sees that I'm not bullshitting with her, she'll be running home, big belly and all. Her new key will be ready for her whenever she decides to come back.

"I can't believe you're doing my girl like that," David said shaking his head.

"Bruh, I'm tired of playing with Brooklyn. She needs to bring her ass home and stop being so damn childish. She comes down here every day to cook and clean, but she's still sleeping at Bryce's house," I complained.

"That's good for her lil ass. You need to show her better than you can tell her," Jaden replied.

I handed David his key and prepared to go pick DJ up from my mama. Brooklyn won't be home until later since she has a class that starts at six. She always comes to our apartment to chill with DJ for a while before she goes back to Bryce's house.

After picking my son up, I fed him and gave him a bath. We sat in the living room watching cartoons waiting for Brooklyn to show up. It was a little after eight, so she should be on her way.

"I sleepy," DJ whined while rubbing his eyes and climbing onto my lap. I know he's tired since my mama said that he didn't take a nap all day. I rocked him to sleep and carried him to his bedroom. I sat back down just as I heard keys fumbling at the front door. I sat down and flipped through channels on the TV, waiting for Brooklyn to knock. I heard her insert the key into the lock, but it never did turn. She kept trying to play with it, but she was wasting her time.

"Dominic," I heard her yelling from the other side of the door. She started ringing the doorbell while yelling my name. I fell out laughing just imagining the look on her face. I took my time getting to the door. I made sure the security chain was in place before I decided to open it.

"What's up Brook?" I questioned while peeping through the small crack.

"What do you mean what's up? Why is my key not working and why are you not opening the door?" She asked all in one breathe.

"Oh, I got the locks changed, but what's up?" I asked again.

"Why did you get the locks changed and why do you keep asking me the same damn question?"

"Did you want something?" I asked ignoring all of her questions. I could tell she was getting upset, but she was trying hard to remain calm.

She sighed. "Where is my baby Dominic?"

"He's asleep. I'll bring him down to see you in the morning before I go to work," I offered. I looked behind me at nothing in particular and she really went off after that.

"What are you looking behind you for? I know you not stupid enough to have a bitch in there around my son," she yelled.

"Stop talking so loud before you wake DJ up. Nobody is in here, but me and my baby."

"Well, open the door and let me see for myself," she demanded.

"I'm not doing nothing. You said it was over so it shouldn't matter if somebody is in here or not. You live downstairs now, right?"

"Fuck you Dominic! Nigga you lucky I'm pregnant, or I'd have this fucking door hanging off the hinges," she warned angrily.

I laughed as I watched her waddle away while still cursing me out. I watched her get on the elevator before closing the door and sitting down again. I'm not into playing mind games, but she needs to know that she's not the only one who can play them.

****

138

Three whole days had passed, and Brooklyn still wasn't home. I tried hard to get under her skin, but I'm driving myself crazy instead. She used to come down and cook and clean, but since I changed the locks she can't even do that anymore. The house is a mess and DJ, and I have been eating out for the past few days. When we left the house this morning, it took everything in me not to ask my mama to come clean up for me. It wouldn't have been bad if I was by myself, but trying to do certain things when my son is around is almost impossible. The laundry basket is overflowing, and the dishes haven't been washed in a while. I'm ready to walk down to Bryce's apartment and drag Brooklyn's stubborn ass back home.

"What you got to eat over there?" I asked David on the speakerphone in my truck.

"I wouldn't even do that to you lil brother. I'm feeling Candace and all, but she can't cook for shit," he laughed. I'm happy that DJ is sleeping because he would have been repeating the curse words.

"Are you serious bruh?" I asked because I really thought he was joking.

"Hell yeah, I'm serious. She cooked something the other day, and she didn't even want to eat it. I told her don't even worry about cooking no more after that. I'm not all that pressed behind a home cooked meal anyway. I can come to your house if I ever want one," he replied.

"Good luck with that. I can't even get one of those."

"Brooklyn better bring her ass back home and stop playing," he commented.

"I'm going to get her ass tonight, but I swear this is my last time trying with her. If she doesn't come home tonight, she doesn't have to come back at all. I'll take care of my kids, and that's that," I said seriously.

"Nigga, you don't mean that shit and you know it," David laughed.

"Yes, I do. I'm tired of going back and forth with her like we're kids. Yeah, I fucked up, but so did she. How many times do I have to apologize for the same shit? Nothing even happened between me and Kennedi for her to be acting like this. I could have moved out when I found out that she was still talking to that nigga Kevin, but I didn't. I know how to talk about what's bothering me instead of always running away from it."

"I guess you're right, but I hope y'all don't break up over that stupid shit," David said somberly.

I know how he feels. I don't want us to break up either, but the choice is hers.

"Same here man. I'm going to get DJ ready for bed. I'll call you later and let you know what's up."

"Alright, lil brother. Make sure you call me too. It doesn't matter what time it is," he replied before we hung up.

I got my sleeping son from his car seat and got on the elevator. I saw Brooklyn's truck in the parking lot, so I knew she was out of class. I don't know if DJ was sleep for the night or not, but she and I had to have a talk. I fumbled with my keys trying to open the door with my son in my arms. As soon as I stepped foot inside, the scent of food hit my nose letting me know that someone had been in here. I turned on the light in the living room and was pleasantly surprised. The mess that was there when we left this morning had been cleaned up. It didn't take long for me to figure out that Brooklyn had come through. She probably convinced Bryce to let her in while I was at work, but it's cool. I laid DJ down on the sofa and ventured further into the apartment. I saw some pots on the stove on a low fire, but I didn't look to see what was in them. I got excited about the possibility of her still being here. I'm sure she wouldn't have left pots cooking on the stove if she wasn't. I looked inside the laundry room, and all of the clothes had been washed and put away as well. Our house was finally back to looking like it did before Brooklyn left. I walked into my bedroom and smelled her Jasmine Vanilla soap as soon as I opened the door. I heard the shower water running, and I knew that's where she was at. If DJ hadn't been on the sofa sleeping, I would have stripped down and joined her. I looked in the closet and smiled when I saw that all of her clothes were back where they belonged. I guess that little stunt I pulled worked, after all. I walked back out of our room and grabbed my phone to call David.

"Tell Brooklyn she better have me and my girl a plate of food like she promised," he said when he answered.

"Huh?" I asked in confusion.

"I kept my end of the deal, so she better keep hers," he replied.

"So you already knew that she was here?"

"Who do you think let her in? I'm the one that had to carry all that heavy shit back up there for her cry baby ass," he laughed.

"Cry baby? What was she crying for?"

"Talking about you had somebody else up there the other day. She said you changed the locks and wouldn't let her in."

"Man, I didn't have no damn body up here. She should know me better than that."

"I know that, but you know Brook and her hormones. She cries about everything," he replied.

"Well, you already know I appreciate you. Let me go talk to her, I'll see you tomorrow."

After hanging up with David, I picked DJ up and carried him to his room. I laid him in his bed and went to talk to Brooklyn. She walked out of the bathroom at the same time that I entered the bedroom. She had a towel wrapped around her making me lick my lips subconsciously.

"So I guess this means you're back home, huh?" I asked while taking a seat on the bed.

"Yeah," she replied while rummaging through her drawer.

"You better not leave no more Brooklyn. That's not always the answer. I'm sorry for not being upfront with you about everything. Next time we need to sit down and talk. Even though, I was mad about what went down with you and Kevin I didn't leave you. Once I calmed down, I came to

you and told you how I felt. We're better than that,"
I said looking her right in her eyes.

"I know, I won't leave again," she promised.
"But I need to ask you something and I need you, to
be honest."

"I'm always honest with you Brooklyn. I tell
you the truth even when I know it'll make you
mad."

"Okay, well did you have somebody else in
here with you the day when you wouldn't let me
in?" She asked.

"Are you serious?" I asked laughing at her.

"It's not funny Dominic. You changed the
locks and didn't let me come in when I asked. Then
you kept looking behind you like somebody else
was in here," she said sounding like she was about
to cry.

"C'mon Brook, I can't believe you even
coming at me like this. I would never do no shit like
that. I don't care what's going on with us at the
time. Everything I did including changing the locks
was only to get you to come back home. I know you
saw how the house looked when you came in here.
I've been going crazy in here trying to take care of
me and DJ by myself. I was planning to drag your
ass back here tonight if you wouldn't have come on
your own," I admitted.

"But changing the locks and stuff, did you
really have to take it that far Dominic?" She asked.

"I guess I did. I see you came back home. Oh
yeah, let me give you this before I forget," I replied.
I walked over to my drawer, pulled out a key and

handed it to her. I sat back on the bed while she put the key on her key ring.

"Where's my baby?" She asked.

"He's in his bed sleep. Come here," I said pulling her to me. I palmed her round belly while she ran her hand through the waves in my hair. It's been a minute since anything popped off between us, and I'm more than ready. I pulled the towel from around her and watched it drop to the floor. As much as I love foreplay, I'm just not in the mood for it right now. I hate to rush, but I don't know if DJ is going to wake up or not. Once he gets up everything comes to a halt. I hurriedly kicked off my shoes followed by my jeans and boxers.

"I see you're ready," Brooklyn laughed referring to my already hard erection.

"I'm always ready," I replied while pulling her closer to me. I lifted her up slightly and sat her down on my stiffness, instantly filling her up. It felt so good I had to bite down on her shoulder to keep from crying out like a bitch. I started out slowly moving her up and down, but I must have been going too slow for her. After a few minutes, she pushed me down on the bed and really went to work. I held on to her hips and enjoyed the ride. Not even three minutes had passed when she suddenly stopped.

"Oh shit, I forgot about the food. It's probably burning," she panicked. I wanted to say fuck the food, but she wouldn't have listened.

"Wait baby. Give me like five more minutes," I begged.

"Dominic no, it's going to take you longer than five minutes and you know it."

"No, it's not Brook, don't stop," I pleaded desperately.

"I just need to turn the fire off. I'll be right back, I promise," she said trying to get up. I pulled her arm to prevent her from leaving.

"Wrap your arms around my neck," I instructed as I sat up in the bed. She was still straddling me, and I wanted her to stay that way. Once her arms are securely wrapped around my neck, I stood up with her pregnant body wrapped snugly around mine.

"Dominic what are you doing?" She said in a panic.

"I'm going to turn off the fire," I replied never missing a stroke. I walked down the hall while still drilling into her.

"Boy, it ain't even that serious," Brooklyn laughed.

"Play crazy if you want to. It's been a minute. You know I'm used to getting it every day," I said as I walked to the kitchen and turned the fire off on the pots. Instead of going back to the bedroom I sat in one of the kitchen chairs while Brooklyn gave me the ride of my life.

KENNEDI

"It's a girl!" The ultrasound tech proudly exclaimed. My mother, Tiffany, and I screamed like crazy when the sex of my baby was revealed. I was so excited to be having a little diva of my own. I can't wait to start shopping for her. I'm five months pregnant, and everything is going great. This is the longest that I've ever held a baby without having any complications. Although I'm excited, the moment is bitter-sweet. I would love nothing more than to have Dominic at my side to share the good news. Instead, he's off playing house with his other baby mama and their son. I hadn't talked to him since we had lunch. He tried calling, but I always sent him to voicemail. We have two months to go before our divorce is finalized, and it's killing me.

"I'm going to be a nanny," Tiffany said shaking me from my depressing thoughts. She rubbed my small round belly and smiled at the thought.

"And you're going to be a grandma," I said directing the comment towards my mother.

"Oh no, she will not be calling me grandma. I want her to call me Honey," she replied proudly.

"Why do you want her to call you that? Where did that even come from?" I inquired.

"I've been doing my research on modern names for grandparents. I fell in love as soon as I ran across that one," she replied. It's just like my mother to do things differently. Tradition is not something that she sticks with.

"Get dressed so we can go get something to eat," Tiffany suggested.

"Y'all can go ahead without me. I have some business to take care of. You can get a ride home with Tiffany," my mother told me.

She picked me up to accompany me to my doctor's appointment, but I'm not mad that she's leaving. She's still pissed at me for signing the divorce papers and walking away with nothing. My lawyer and I tried to explain to her what the judge said, but she wasn't trying to hear it. She made a huge scene outside of the courthouse and cursed Dominic and his entire family out. It took Dominic and David to pull Mrs. Liz away because she was about to kill my mother. Once we left the courthouse, she turned her rage on me and my lawyer and cursed us out as well. She even refused to pay my lawyer the remaining balance of what we owed her for representing me. She felt like she didn't fight hard enough to get me what I wanted.

"Are you going to call Dominic and tell him what you're having?" Tiffany asked once we were in the car.

"Hell no! He hasn't been here for me, and I don't owe him a damn thing," I yelled in anger.

"He hasn't been here because you and Aunt Karen won't let him be here."

"Did I tell you that he fired Scott? I feel so bad since I'm the cause of him losing his job. Dominic even broke his nose during the confrontation."

"You don't have anything to feel bad about. Scott got himself fired. He knew what the outcome would be if Dominic ever found out."

"Yeah, but he was never supposed to find out. I let Dominic sweet talk the information right out of me. I should have known that he didn't have a change of heart about our divorce. Especially after the way he behaved in court," I said beating myself up.

"So what is Scott doing now?"

"Thanks to me getting him fired, he's collecting unemployment. He said it was a long time coming so he's not upset with me. I just feel like shit about how everything went down," I admitted.

"You need to stop being so hard on yourself Kennedi. None of that is your fault. If you ask me you're letting Dominic off way too easy," Tiffany said.

"How am I letting him off easy?"

"I understand you being hurt and everything, but you're just letting Brooklyn and Dominic go on as if you never existed. You need to make it hard on their asses. He bought his son thousands of dollars' worth of stuff, but your baby doesn't have anything yet. Don't be crazy. I would bother his ass so much he wouldn't even get a good's nights rest. Bryce is lucky that I've moved on because I would do the same thing to him and that bitch Taylor," Tiffany rambled.

"I don't need him to do anything for my baby," I said stubbornly.

"Kennedi we're family so let's keep it real. Without Dominic, that little money that you have saved up is nothing. It'll be gone in a few months. You better be happy that the lease is paid up for the rest of the year. You're letting Brooklyn spend money that's rightfully yours."

I hate to admit it, but Tiffany was right. I have a few thousand dollars saved up, but that won't last too much longer. If I have to buy everything for my baby and pay bills at the house, I'll be lucky to survive for another six months. I still have my job, but that's not enough. I have an addiction to shopping, and I want my baby to have the best of everything. My mother said she'll still pay me while I'm out on maternity leave, so that's a good thing. I thought about trying to make up with my father, but I don't want to hear the "I told you so" speech about Dominic leaving me. At least I know he'll give me financial assistance if I need it.

"So what about a baby shower?" Tiffany asked interrupting my thoughts.

"Who are we going to invite Tiffany? Our family is too small, and my mama would die before she invited Dominic's people."

"You need to stop listening to everything your mama says and start making your own decisions," Tiffany spat.

I didn't reply because she's right once again. I still remember Dominic telling my mother that she's one of the reasons why he left me. It hurt to hear it, but I believe him. She was always putting herself in our business, and I never did anything to stop her. Even now, I want Dominic to be here with me, but she's not having it. I really need her in my corner right now so pissing her off was not an option.

"What are you going to name her?" Tiffany asked.

"I've been playing around with a few names for boys and girls. Since I know for sure that it's a girl I want to name her Diamond Starr," I replied proudly.

"That is so pretty," Tiffany cooed. "What about her last name?"

"My mama is adamant about me going back to my maiden name once the divorce is final in two months. I guess it'll be Henry unless Dominic signs for her to get his last name." I don't know about other states, but in Louisiana if a father doesn't sign the birth certificate, the child is automatically given the mother's last name.

"He better sign for her to get his last name. He signed for that bitch's baby, and she wasn't even his wife," Tiffany fumed.

"That was his first, so that wasn't a surprise to me, but I think I'm going to take your advice. Diamond needs a lot of stuff, and her father needs to pay up in order for her to get it," I smiled while rubbing my small baby bump.

"That's what the hell I'm talking about. When you finish with his ass you won't even need a baby shower," Tiffany said hyping me up. I was feeling good about everything as long as I was with her. I just hope I don't lose my nerve when the time comes for me to act on it.

BROOKLYN

"DJ sit down!" I yelled at my overactive almost two-year old son. I was in the kitchen trying to cook, and he's driving me crazy. He's standing in his high chair throwing his cookies all over the kitchen. Dominic is at a meeting with David pertaining to their company. That left me home to deal with my bad ass son all by myself. I'm seven months pregnant, so the task is not easy. I've been tempted to call Bryce to come get him, but I'm trying to do better with spending time with my own baby. I promised myself that if I didn't have anything important to do then I would have him at home with me. DJ is going through his terrible two phase, and I'm praying for Dominic to walk through the door to get him out of my hair. Aside from that I'm so excited for Dominic and David. They've been offered a year's worth of work from an out of town Construction Company that has a few projects to do in the New Orleans area. They want to use some of the trucks from Dominic's company to transport their tools and supplies back and forth until the jobs are complete. They're negotiating the cost and signing the contracts to get started on that as soon as possible. Dominic said if all goes well we'll be looking for a house and moving before I have the baby. He loves our apartment, but he wants to buy a home for us to raise our kids in. I don't mind moving, but I want to wait until after the baby is born. I know that we need more room with two kids in the house, but I don't feel like this is a good time. DJ is turning two years old next month, and I'll be having a newborn baby the month after that.

Then Dominic is talking about us getting married as soon as his divorce from Kennedi is finalized. It's just too much coming up at the same time. It's not that I want a big wedding; I just don't want us to rush into anything. I always said that I wanted to be married on a beach, and that's all I needed to make me happy.

"I'm about to whip your bad ass," I yelled at DJ over my iPod music.

"Girl, you better not hit my baby," Dominic said walking into the kitchen. I didn't hear him come in, but I was so happy to see him.

"You better get your son before I hurt him. Look at the mess he made," I said as I gestured to the cookies and juice that was all over the kitchen floor.

"I got him," Dominic said taking him from his high chair. He washed DJ's face and hands before cleaning up the mess he made.

"Are you ready to eat?" I asked Dominic.

"Yeah, but damn, you didn't give me a kiss or nothing. DJ made you mad, and you're taking it out on me. We're supposed to be celebrating, and you got a frown on your face," he laughed.

"I'm sorry, but he drove me crazy today. He didn't want to take a nap or nothing," I complained as I stepped up and gave him a kiss. Of course, I had to kiss my baby too since he wants to do everything that his daddy does.

"So how did your meeting go?"

"It went better than I thought. After we pay our employees and take care of the other expenses, David and I should walk away with at least two hundred thousand for ourselves. And I'm talking about two hundred thousand each for a year's worth of work. The contract we signed is for one million. They have a lot of work coming up, and they need a lot of help transporting their materials. I don't understand how a company that big wouldn't have trucks of their own, but I'm not complaining."

"Damn, that's a lot of money for a year of work. Especially since y'all really don't have to do anything," I replied.

"Right, but that's not even including what we'll be making on our own. That's just with them. We'll probably have to hire about four more drivers within the next month. We're going to need the help."

"But you can help sometimes too right?" I asked.

"I can, but I'm not. I'm not leaving you and my kids at home alone while I'm driving trucks all night. That's the reason why I opened my own business. The point was for me to hire other people to do the work, so I don't have to," he replied.

I fixed him and my baby a plate and sat down at the table with them while they ate.

"So what are we going to do about the baby's room?" I asked changing the subject. "We have to get rid of that bedroom set and put some baby furniture in there." I still don't know what I'm having, and nobody is giving me any clues. We haven't even started shopping for our new addition as of yet.

"I really want us to start looking for a house Brooklyn. It's gon' be too cramped in here with us and two small kids. Then I have to think about when the other baby starts to visit. This apartment is not going to work."

"I have two more months to go before this baby gets here. Plus, you're trying to throw DJ another party on top of all of that. Then you want us to get married right away. That's a lot to make happen in the short time that we have," I admitted.

"It's really not though. The only thing that would hold us back is money. We have plenty of that, so I don't understand what the problem is," he shrugged.

"I don't know the first thing about looking for a house," I whined as I washed the dishes that they had just eaten out of. "Maybe I can get my mama and daddy to help us out."

"Baby, I love you to death, but you really have to grow up. Your mama and daddy are not going to be living in the house we are. We have our own family now. We need to go look for us a house together," he said pointing back and forth between the two of us.

"You're right, but where do we look Dominic?"

"I don't know. We can get a real estate agent to help us out. Just tell me where you want live, and I'll take it from there."

"I like the westbank, but where do you want to go?" I asked. Both of our parents live in the westbank, and I want our kids to be close to their grandparents.

"As long as you're happy I'll go wherever," he replied causing me to smile. The moment was short lived because his phone started ringing soon after. When I saw the frown on Dominic's face, I already knew who it was.

"That's Kennedi calling again?" I asked even though I knew. Kennedi has been on some bullshit lately. She would call Dominic all times of the day and night telling him that she needed money to start buying stuff for their baby. When Dominic asked her what she was having she told him that it was none of his business. He was done talking to her after that.

"Yeah, that's her bipolar ass," he replied sounding disgusted.

"That bitch is really nuts. She doesn't want you to be a part of the baby's life, but she wants you to finance everything. She won't even tell you what she's having," I fumed.

"I know, but I'm not about to play these games with her," he replied.

"Maybe you should just buy whatever she's asking for so she can stop calling you all throughout the day."

"That's exactly what I'm not doing. She doesn't call the shots around here. If I do that, she'll just find something else to call about. I'm not putting any money in her hands, and I'm not letting her mama pick out my baby's shit."

I nodded my head in understanding, but I didn't reply. Even though Dominic and I are together, I still try to stay out of him and Kennedi's business. Legally, she's still his wife and the soon to be mother of his child. She's always throwing my name in the mix, but I ignore her most of the time.

Dominic always puts her in her place, so I don't have to.

"Don't let her stress you out. Go take your shower so we can watch a movie," I suggested. Once he and DJ were gone, I put the food away and cleaned up the kitchen.

****

"That's just why your ass gets pregnant every year," Co-Co said loudly calling attention to Dominic and me as we exited the bathroom. It's Sunday, and all of us were chilling at David's house while he barbecued. Aside from me and Dominic, Co-Co and his boo, along with Candace, Tiana, Taylor, and Bryce were all in attendance as well. Co-Co was always noticing things that other people don't really pay attention to. I got up to go to the bathroom a little while ago, and Dominic had to follow me in there. After being gone for almost thirty minutes, it didn't take long for anybody to figure out what we were doing. Nobody really cared except for my big mouth cousin.

"You are too nosey and I do not get pregnant every year," I snapped at him.

"Oh yeah, I meant to say every other year," he said making everybody laugh. "What is it with y'all and the bathroom?"

I flipped him my middle finger just as David came in with a pan of whatever he and Bryce were grilling.

"Y'all can come eat," David yelled right before he went back outside. Co-Co and Candace jumped up, but Dominic was much faster than the both of them.

156

"I hope y'all don't think y'all are eating before my girl gets hers," he yelled. DJ is with Dominic's parent, so we didn't have to worry about feeding him.

"Look at you. Brooklyn took you in the bathroom for a few minutes, and now you acting like a little trained puppy. I know they better have enough food in here for my boo to eat," Co-Co fussed. Co-Co has recently been spending a lot of time with a man named Dwight. He's very nice, and we all took to him immediately. He's unattached to a man or a woman, and that just makes us like him more. Co-Co usually falls for men that are unavailable so this is a good thing for him as well. This is Dwight's second time really hanging out with us and Co-Co always keeps him laughing. When David and Bryce came back inside we all sat around in the living room eating and talking.

"I'm still hungry," I complained while rubbing my huge belly.

"Damn Brooklyn, you just had a big ass plate of food," Tiana yelled.

"Don't worry about her. As long as she's feeding my baby she can eat as much as she wants," Dominic said as he got up to get me some more food.

"That's right hater," I said sticking my tongue out at Tiana. Dominic came back and handed me another plate of food just as his phone started ringing for the third time in the last ten minutes. He kept sending Kennedi to voicemail, but she was still calling him back to back.

"That's that crazy girl again?" Taylor asked.

"Yep," Dominic replied as he declined her call. Not even a minute later the phone started ringing again.

"Let me answer it. She's getting on my damn nerves," I yelled as I held my hand out for Dominic to hand me his phone.

"Put her on speakerphone," Co-Co demanded.

"Hello," I answered putting the call on speaker like I was asked to.

"I need to speak with Dominic," Kennedi said sounding upset. Dominic shook his head saying no while Co-Co stood next to me waiting for something to pop off.

"He's busy right now. Is there something that you want me to tell him for you," I said as nicely as I could.

"Lil girl put my husband on the phone and know your place. Whatever I have to say to him does not concern you," she hollered. Co-Co snatched the phone out of my hands and started going off on her.

"Bitch, you must have eaten your Wheaties for breakfast, huh? Maybe you need to be reminded about that beat down that was delivered to you a few months ago," he yelled.

"Fuck you and everybody that's in there listening. I called to speak to my husband so put him on the phone," she screamed putting emphasis on the word husband.

"Kennedi what the hell do you want?" Dominic finally spoke up.

"I should have known that you were sitting there listening while your bitch answered the phone for you," she said angrily.

"I got your bitch," I yelled.

"This is my last time telling you about disrespecting my girl and this is my last time asking you what the fuck you want," Dominic yelled.

"You already know what I want. I need to furnish and decorate our baby's room, and you need to pay for it. That's the least you can do. It's not like you can't afford it."

"I don't even know what you're having Kennedi. How can I start buying anything?" He asked with a frown.

"Why does that even matter? What does the sex of the baby have to do with you providing for it?"

"You got me fucked up. I keep telling you that I'm not playing these games with you. Since you don't want me to be a part of anything then do all that shit by yourself," Dominic said.

"And since you wanted a blood test for my cousin's baby we need one for yours too hoe," Co-Co yelled before he hung up.

"Co-Co sit down and stop being so damn messy. You have company, and you're minding everybody else's business," Candace told her brother.

"He already knows how I am, don't you boo? I was about to fight his whole family the first time I met them," he said seriously.

"I know you're joking right?" Taylor asked with raised brows.

"Oh, no I'm not. You better tell them Dwight," Co-Co yelled excitedly.

"Yeah, his first meeting with my family didn't go too well," Dwight shrugged.

"That's a damn shame. Can't even bring your ghetto ass nowhere without you wanting to fight somebody," Bryce commented.

"They tried to come for me cousin, but I shut the whole family picnic down. I had them bitches putting the fire out on the grills and everything," he laughed while Bryce just shook his head.

"It's always some drama with you," Taylor said.

"You got some ice cream in here David?" I asked moving on to another subject.

"Girl, you greedy as fuck," David laughed.

"Nigga ain't nobody ask you all that. Do you have some ice cream or not?" Dominic said taking up for me.

"That baby really got you eating a lot," Taylor said.

"I know, I never ate this much with DJ so it can't be another boy," I said fishing for clues. I really wanted to know what I was having, but I wanted somebody to tell me without me having to ask.

"Stop trying to be slick. Nobody is telling you nothing," Tiana said catching on to the little game that I was playing.

"I don't want anybody to tell me nothing. I'm just saying that it can't be another boy because this pregnancy is so different," I replied with a shrug.

"See, y'all can keep playing this game with this dizzy hoe if y'all want to, but I'm tired of it. Bitch you're having a girl. Your man already picked out a name for her and everything," Co-Co blurted out.

"Co-Co you make me sick. You talk too damn much. Just learn to shut the fuck up sometimes," Candace yelled angrily.

"I keep telling y'all to stop telling me shit, but nobody seems to be listening.I don't give a damn if you're mad. That's y'all fault," he replied like he didn't care.

"Yes! I'm having a girl," I yelled excitedly as I danced in my seat. "But we need to talk about what name you came up with."

"I want her name to be Dominique after me and her brother," Dominic replied while rubbing my belly.

"Dominique? That's too common. What about Diamond?" I suggested.

"That's common too. I like Dominique better."

"Okay, but you can't decide on that without including me. We need to get this together before she gets here."

"Let's vote on it at your baby shower," Taylor suggested.

"What baby shower?" I asked looking around at everybody. I made them promise not to give me another baby shower, but it looks like they weren't listening.

"I swear you bitches got diarrhea of the mouth today. Y'all can't keep a secret for nothing," Candace fussed.

"We know you said you didn't want another one, but it's going to be something small. It's really just your family and Dominic's family. When Mrs. Liz found out that you were having a girl, her and your mama started planning the same day. You can't use any of DJ's things because it's all boy stuff," Tiana spoke up.

"I guess," I said nonchalantly. It's not that I don't appreciate the gesture. I just don't want them making a fuss over me like they did the first time. Nobody is obligated to buy me a gift, and I don't want them to feel like they are.

"That's why I told you that we needed to move before she gets here," Dominic said trying to further prove his point about purchasing a house. I nodded my head, agreeing with what he said.

"You want me to answer that David?" Tiana asked referring to the ringing of David's doorbell.

"Yeah, you can get it," he replied.

"Can I help you?" Tiana asked the person once she cracked the door open. I didn't hear what they said, but the look on her face spoke volumes. She looked kind of nervous, so Candace got up to see who it was. Things went from zero to one hundred quickly after that.

"Um David, you need to come handle this shit right here," Candace yelled with a frown on her face. All of us jumped up and peeped out of the window when she said that. David started going off as soon as he saw who his uninvited guest was.

"Man, I told you that whatever we had is over. I have a girl now," David said as he wrapped his arm around Candace's waist. Dominic and I glanced at each other with a knowing look. This is the same woman that showed up wearing a trench coat and heels in the middle of the summer a while ago. That was also the same day that Dominic found out I was a virgin. All of that was long before David and Candace got together though.

"You never told me that you had a girl," the woman replied with her arms folded across her chest.

"That's a damn lie!" David shouted. "I can show you the text message where you were begging me to come over here. I told you no because I have a girl."

"Okay, so now you know. It don't matter if he told you before he's telling you now," Candace said.

"I don't believe I was talking to you," she said as she raised her hand to stop Candace from talking. Candace didn't get a chance to respond before Co-Co flew out the door to confront the girl for her.

"Bitch you must have gone to Wiz and got you some courage. I promise you that this is not want you want," Co-Co yelled.

"And you are?" She asked while staring Co-Co down.

"I'm the bitch that's about to drag you back to that raggedy ass car that you just pulled up in," he replied taking a step towards her. Dwight had grabbed him by his arm before he got too close.

"You need to bounce and make this your last time coming here," David said.

"No problem. Nigga, you ain't all that anyway," she replied seemingly embarrassed.

"Girl, you don't even have edges and trying to talk about somebody ain't all that. You petty hoes kill me," Co-Co said as she walked away.

"Let me go get my stuff and take my ass home," Candace said angrily as she pulled away from David's hold.

"I know you're not mad at me behind that shit," he said following her into the house.

"This is the second time that a bitch showed up to your house when I was here. There won't be a third time because I'm staying at my own house from now on."

"Just like a nigga showed up to your house when I was there, but I didn't trip. We both have a past, and we knew that before we decided to get into a relationship. I told her what was up just like I did with the one before her. Don't even start with all that," David said.

"I'm not saying anything else. I'm about to get my shit and go home," Candace said walking to the back of the house. David waved her off and resumed his position on the sofa.

"Man you better go talk to your girl before she leaves your ass," Dominic told his brother.

"She ain't going nowhere," David said dismissively. "She just likes to play mad for the make-up sex. I keep telling her she doesn't have to do all that to get me to beat it up. All she has to do is ask."

We all laughed, but I knew that he was serious. His relationship with Candace is like nothing that I've ever seen before. They both try to play hard to cover up how they really feel about each other. I got up and walked to the back of the house to make sure that my cousin was alright. I expected to see her packing her clothes, but she was stretched out on the bed watching TV instead.

"I thought you were leaving," I asked while stretching out right next to her.

"Girl please, he knows I'm not going nowhere," she said waving me off. "Trust me it'll pay off tonight when everybody is gone."

David had her right. She did all of that just to get some make-up sex.

"He said that's what you were doing, but I didn't believe him. Y'all are crazy," I said laughing.

"I don't know why you're laughing. You and Dominic are just as crazy. The only difference is that you really do leave his ass," she laughed.

I thought about our relationship and wondered if we looked as stupid to other people as David and Candace look to me right now.

NADIA

"Stop crying friend. You know he's coming back," I've been trying my best to comfort Shannon over the phone since she called me crying ten minutes ago. She's upset because Kevin hasn't been home for two days straight. I have her on speakerphone while I stood in the mirror flat ironing my hair.

"That's not the point Nadia. He's stepping out and coming in all hours of the night like he's single. I let that shit slide when he did it with Brooklyn, but I'm not doing it again. This time I'm showing my ass and whatever bitch he's messing with," she cried.

"You think he's messing with her again?"

"No. Tiffany told me that Brooklyn lives with her baby daddy. She's pregnant by him again and everything," she answered.

"And you believe that bitch?"

"Yeah, I believe her. She doesn't have a reason to lie to me about something so stupid. She said that he left her cousin to be with Brooklyn. I saw them on a bunch of pictures and stuff on Facebook. After seeing her man, I don't blame her for not wanting Kevin. I don't see how you let his fine ass get away," she said referring to Dominic.

"Girl please, he ain't all that like you making it seem," I said getting pissed off.

"That's a lie. That nigga looks good, and he's paid. Brooklyn hit the jackpot," she said rubbing it in.

"Good for her," I snapped.

"You sound kind of salty. I know you're not jealous," she laughed.

"Jealous? Girl if you only knew," I said laughing right along with her.

"What don't I know? Tell me what's up then."

"It's nothing girl don't worry about it. I'm about to get out of here. Call me if you want to talk later."

"Okay, I will," she said sadly before hanging up.

"So that's what you have to put up with every day, huh?" I asked Kevin, who was stretched out in my king sized bed. He is so cute. If you ask me he's way too cute to be with somebody like Shannon. We've been kicking it almost every day since I fought Kyle and Tiffany at their house. After I had given him oral sex that day, he ended up following me back to my apartment. That was the first, and I assumed the last time that we had sex. It must be something about me that Kevin likes because he came back the very next day. Unlike Kyle, Kevin even spends some nights here with me. I should feel bad for betraying Shannon, but I don't. She seems to have formed a friendship with Tiffany, so she's getting everything that she deserves.

"I told you that she's crazy. I need to take my ass home before she loses her damn mind," Kevin replied.

"I thought we were going out for a little while," I said with an attitude.

"We might have to do that another time," he said making me mad.

"You've been here getting sucked and fucked for two days straight. Don't try to act like you have a conscious now. Staying out for a few more hours won't hurt her," I snapped.

"You better watch who the fuck you're talking to like that. I'm not even supposed to be around this way to begin with. The purpose of me staying inside is so I won't be seen. Me and my brother have too many enemies for me to be running the streets with your ass," he yelled.

"We're not running the streets. Nobody even goes to the bar that I want us to go to. It's always empty. Let's just have a few drinks and get something to eat. I'll drive, and I'll bring you back to your truck as soon as we're done." I would always let Kevin park his truck in my apartment complex's enclosed garage while I parked in one of the guests' spots. He's always so paranoid when he comes to see me. I know it had something to do with all the dirt that he and Kyle did before they moved to Slidell.

"I'm giving you two more hours of my time, and then I'm out," he said agreeing to my demands. He had a frown on his face, but I didn't care.

"Stop looking so mean all the time. You know I'll make it worth your while before you go home," I promised.

We rode the fifteen minutes to the bar in silence. Bottom's Up Bar and Grill is a small establishment that's located on a dead end street of a residential neighborhood. If a person doesn't know exactly where it is, it's almost impossible to find. Candace and I stumbled upon it one night when we got lost, and we started going there whenever we wanted to get away. Aside from a few older men in the back shooting pool, we would be the only patrons in the bar at times. I love them because they don't water down their drinks, and the food is good.

"You're right about nobody being in here," Kevin observed when we walked inside. Besides us, the bartender was the only other person here. She looked bored out of her mind sitting behind the bar. I heard the voices of a few people in the back shooting pool, but the lounge area was empty. Kevin and I placed our orders, sat down at one of the tables and waited.

"Loosen up. Nobody that you know is coming here. This is not that kind of place," I said to Kevin. He kept looking around nervously like he was expecting something to happen.

"I see that. I never even heard of this place before. I might make this my new hang out spot," he replied.

"As long as you don't bring your brother or your bitch here with you," I hissed.

A few minutes later, the bartender, who was also the waitress, sat our food and drinks in front of us. We sat there eating and talking like he didn't have a girlfriend to get home to. He said that he was giving me two more hours, but he's not in a hurry to leave. It doesn't matter to me if he stays another night at my house. I'm really starting to feel him so Shannon might be getting a run for her money.

BRYCE

"I'm ready to go," Dominic announced for the second time tonight. I swear I hate going places with him sometimes. He acts like he can't stay away from Brooklyn too long. He's called or texted her every five minutes since we've been here. We're at a hole in the wall bar shooting pool and having drinks. Aside from us two, David and Jaden were here as well.

"Man, Brooklyn ain't going anywhere," I yelled at him. "You not gon' get in trouble if you stay out late."

"I think Brooklyn be beating on my lil brother," David said with a straight face. "I don't want to get the police involved, but I will if I have to."

We all looked at Dominic and fell out laughing. As tall as he is, I couldn't imagine Brooklyn trying to fight him. He has to damn near kneel down just to kiss her.

"You niggas better stop playing with me. We don't do violence in our household," Dominic said.

"Let's go before his ass starts crying in here," David said still messing with his brother.

"I need to use the bathroom first. Y'all got me laughing so hard I'm about to pee on myself," Jaden said as he walked toward the back.

That's always the case whenever David was around. He keeps everybody laughing no matter what mood you're in. He's the type that's funny without even trying to be funny.

"What's going on with the house hunting?" I asked Dominic while we waited.

"We found a few that we like. Brooklyn fell in love with the one in English Turn. I really hope we get that one. The real estate agent put in the offer a few days ago. She said it could take up to four to six weeks before we hear something, but sometimes it may come sooner," he answered.

"English Turn? You're trying to spend some real money, huh?" English Turn is a gated golf and country club community. It's nothing for a house to run for three to four hundred thousand or more.

"It's a foreclosed property, so the price isn't bad. It was only built like eight months ago. It's like six bedrooms with a pool."

"Y'all don't even need that much space. Baby is buggin' for real," I said.

"That's what she wants and that's what she's getting. I just hope they accept my offer. The agent is confident that they will," Dominic replied.

"Ain't that the same place that Kennedi wanted to move to?" David asked.

"Yep," Dominic replied calmly.

"You better not tell Baby that shit. She might change her mind if she finds that out," I joked with him.

"I hope y'all do get it. I'm posting that shit on a billboard just to make sure Kennedi's ass see it," David swore.

"Let's roll," Jaden said coming from the bathroom.

We all made our way out to the front of the almost empty bar. Candace showed us this place a few months ago, and we've been coming here ever since. There's never a crowd, and the food and drinks are decent. Besides us, there was no one else in the bar except for a couple who was hugging and kissing at a table across the room. Dominic walked ahead of us as we talked and headed for the front door. He slowed his stride, but I didn't pay attention as to why. All of sudden he broke out and started running to the other side of the room. When he got close to a table where the couple sat, he punched the man in his face, knocking him out of his chair. We rushed over to try and stop him until we realized who it was that he started beating.

NADIA

"Dominic stop!" I screamed to the top of my lungs. After eating and having a few drinks, Kevin and I were enjoying each other's company. We were so busy hugging and kissing that we didn't even see anyone coming towards us until it was too late. Dominic came out of nowhere and started throwing jabs at Kevin. David, Bryce, and Jaden were with him, but nobody tried to intervene.

"Get up nigga! You like to fight women, fight me back," Dominic yelled as he continued his attack.

I've seen Kevin fight Shannon more times than I can count, but he was letting Dominic wipe the floor with him. He was swinging back, but his licks must have been too soft. Dominic was shaking them off like they came from his son. I don't understand why he even had a problem with Kevin aside from the fact that he had a brief relationship with Brooklyn. They're back together, so that shouldn't matter anymore. He kept saying that Kevin likes to beat on women, but I'm wondering how he knows about that. More importantly why does he even care if Kevin beats on his girlfriend? Something isn't adding up.

"Somebody stop him," I continued to yell. I tried pulling Bryce's arm for him to do something, but he snatched away from me.

"Don't touch me. That nigga deserves that ass whooping for putting his hands on my sister," he replied angrily.

"He didn't put his hands on your sister," I yelled in Kevin's defense.

"Shut up Nadia. You a straight up hoe. You're standing here defending this nigga when you were just fucking his brother a few weeks ago. You don't know what he did so stop speaking on it," Jaden barked.

I looked up and saw the bartender standing by the bar looking petrified. She's been glued to the same spot she's been in since we got here earlier.

"Don't just stand there looking stupid, call the police," I screamed at her. Her dumb ass just looked at me like I was crazy, but she still didn't budge.

"Damn Nadia, I use to consider you family at one time. I would have never thought you would turn out like this," David said looking at me in disgust.

"I'm not about to just stand around and let your brother kill him," I replied in my own defense.

"Come on lil brother, chill out. Let that nigga make it," David said as he pulled Dominic off of Kevin.

I rushed over to Kevin and helped him off of the floor. He was barely able to stand after the beat down that he just received. I had to practically stand him up and sit him back down in the chair. He had a huge knot on his forehead, and his right eye was almost swollen shut. I grabbed a hand full of napkins and tried to stop the blood that dripped from his lip, but he snatched them from me.

"I guess that's why you beat on women. You can't fight for shit," Jaden laughed and shook his head at Kevin.

174

Dominic stared at Kevin with pure hate in his eyes. If David wasn't holding him back, I'm sure he would have finished him off.

"Let's go," Bryce suggested. He walked out first followed by Jaden, who wore a sneaky grin on his face. He's crazy as hell, and I never did trust his ass.

"You good man?" David had asked Dominic before they walked out. Dominic nodded his head, and they slowly made their way to the door.

They were almost gone when Jaden stopped and walked back towards us. We didn't even get a chance to react before he grabbed a bottle from the table and smashed it across Kevin's head. Kevin fell back to the floor while I jumped up and screamed.

"I never did like your pretty boy looking ass," he spat with a frown on his face.

"Let's go Jaden!" Bryce yelled to his baby brother.

"I got a bunch of pretty bitches ready to put in work for me whenever you ready for it Nadia," he threatened before walking out with the rest of his crew.

I knew that was a warning for me not to get the police involved. Jaden doesn't make threats he makes promises and I knew not to take them lightly.

"Are you okay?" I asked while trying to help Kevin up from the floor.

"Get the fuck off of me!" He snarled angrily.

"I'm only trying to help you. You look like you need to go to the hospital."

"I should have never let you talk me into coming here. All this shit is your fault. You probably set the shit up."

"How is any of this my fault? I didn't know that they were going to be here. I wouldn't have come here if I did."

"Just take me to my truck and stop talking to me," he quipped.

I watched as he pulled himself up from the floor and staggered to the exit, barely making it to the door. I couldn't believe he would even think that I had something to do with Dominic beating him up. As much shit as he talks, I thought for sure he at least knew how to fight. He hit so soft I wonder how Shannon even got those black eyes that he gave her.

"At least let me put something on your face before you leave," I offered.

"Whatever," he replied brushing me off.

We traveled the rest of the way to my apartment in complete silence. I kept stealing peeks at Kevin, but he just stared straight ahead. Dominic had really done a number to his face. Thanks to Jaden, he had a nice size gash in the back of his head as well. I wanted to ask him when and why did he put his hands on Brooklyn, but this was not a good time. That was a huge mistake he'd made, and I'm sure he knows that now.

"Are you coming in?" I asked Kevin once we pulled up to my apartment complex. "Please, just for a minute."

I didn't have anything to do with what happened, but I do feel bad about it. I'm also concerned about him driving home in the condition that he's in. He barely made it to the car, and he's all banged up. After thinking about it for a while, he got out of the car and started towards my apartment. I hopped out, followed behind him and opened the front door. I rushed to the bathroom and got my first aid kit and some peroxide. After grabbing some cotton balls, I went back to the living room and sat next to him on the sofa. He played on his phone while I tried my best to bandage up his wounds.

"Ouch," he winced in pain when I got to the sore area at the back of his head.

"Sorry," I mumbled. After working on him for about ten more minutes, I finally finished. After cleaning all the blood away, he looked just a little bit better, but not much. I've seen Dominic in action more times than I can count. He's like a young Muhammad Ali when it comes to fighting. Even if Kevin could fight, he probably wouldn't have won.

"Get me a mirror," Kevin requested.

I put away my first aid kit and handed him the small mirror that I kept in my bathroom. I watched as he frowned at the damage that Dominic had done to his face. I would hate for this incident to be the thing to possibly tear us apart.

"Kevin, I'm so sorry about what happened. I swear I didn't know they were going to be in there. I've been there a million times, and I've never seen Dominic or any of Brooklyn's family there," I swore. Instead of answering me he kept his head down playing on his phone. I heard my own phone ringing, so I got up to answer it.

"Your girlfriend is calling me again," I said blowing out a breath of frustration.

"She keeps texting me. Answer your phone," he insisted.

"Hey Shannon," I answered trying not to sound aggravated even though I was.

"Hey Nadia, are you busy?" She asked sounding upset. I looked at Kevin shaking his head telling me to say no.

"No, what's up?"

"I just need to get out of this house for a while. I feel like I'm going crazy. Kevin is gon' make me kill him and his side bitch," she cried.

Hearing her say that made my heart beat just a little bit faster. She doesn't know that I'm the side bitch, and I plan to keep it that way.

"What happened?" I asked just to see what she knew.

"I've been calling him all day and he hasn't answered. Then he had the nerve to text and asked me what I want. I know he's somewhere laid up with a hoe, but he better pray that I never find out," she fumed.

"Girl, don't worry about that. He's probably somewhere getting his mind right. You should be happy as much as y'all fight. I wish I could come get you, but my car is in the shop. It's been acting up on me lately," I lied.

"Damn. As much as I don't want to I'm about to take this bitch Tiffany up on her offer," she replied pissing me off.

"What offer?" I asked.

"She asked if I wanted to go have a drink with her and I said no. I'm about to call her and tell her that I changed my mind. I'll talk to you later."

Shannon forming a friendship with Tiffany was making what I'm doing with Kevin that much easier. She's not loyal to me so why should I be loyal to her.

"What do you even see in her?" I asked Kevin once I hung up the phone. That's been something that I've wanted to ask him since the first day I laid eyes on her.

"You wouldn't understand. She might not have the best shape or the prettiest face, but she's loyal. She'll do whatever she has to do to make me happy, and I only have to ask once. I never have to worry about her leaving or cheating on me because I'm all that she knows. If it came down to my life and hers she would gladly leave this world for me," he said seriously without a doubt in his mind.

"How do you think she would feel if she knew that you were here with me right now? What do you think she would say if she knew that you had been here for the past two days? You don't think she would leave you then?" I asked curiously.

"Not at all. After she beats your ass, she'll be giving me a blowjob and bringing me breakfast in bed. I've seen it happen a million times before," he replied arrogantly.

"What makes you think she would beat my ass? And what makes you think I would let her?"

"Don't underestimate her. Y'all are from two different worlds," he answered.

"Fuck Shannon! If she was all that you wouldn't be here with me. That bitch wants to be Tiffany's friend so let her be. I felt bad about being with you at first, but I don't anymore," I ranted.

"So you said that you're sorry about what happened to me today, huh?" Kevin asked changing the subject.

"Yes Kevin, I really am," I confirmed.

"Well, show me then," he replied with a sexy smirk.

He didn't have to ask me twice. I crawled over to him on the sofa and sat on his lap. After sharing a long passionate kiss, I dropped down to my knees and did what I always do before we have sex. Kevin loves oral sex, but he's not like Kyle. He never returns the gesture. After a few minutes of me trying to swallow him whole, I got up from the floor and straddled him.

"Are you seriously going to play with your phone right now? I asked in aggravation. "That game can wait."

Once he put his phone down, he grabbed my hips and started drilling into me like he was drilling for oil. At the moment, Shannon was a distant memory for me. If things went right with me and Kevin, she would be a distant memory for him too.

BROOKLYN

After putting DJ to bed, I sat in the living room talking on the phone with Tiana about her boyfriend. Her and Taylor walked up on him at the movies with another girl. After Tiana had beaten the girl up, she threw a brick through the windshield of his car and left. Her feelings are hurt, and I'm trying my best to make her feel better. We've been on the phone for over two hours, and he's been knocking at her door the entire time, begging her to let him in. I've also been texting back and forth with Dominic. He's out shooting pool with David and two of my brothers.

"So what are you going to do?" I asked my friend.

Tiana and her boyfriend Travis have been together since she was a freshman in high school. They were each other's first everything. I really couldn't see them being with anyone else besides each other.

"Nothing, it's over," she replied nonchalantly.

"Now you know I have to call you out when you're wrong. You did the same thing to him twice before, and he didn't break up with you."

"So, he only knew about the one time, but that's not the point. He lied to me, and I'm done with him," she fumed.

I was just about to tell her how selfish she was when I heard Dominic fumbling with his keys at the front door. I ended my call with Tiana and got up to greet him with a huge smile on my face. That was quickly replaced with a look of shock when I saw him.

"What happened to your hand?" I yelled frantically when Dominic walked through the door. He had a white towel wrapped around his hand, but I could tell that it was bleeding.

"I'm good, but I finally ran into that nigga Kevin," he replied calmly.

"What happened? I hope you didn't get yourself into any trouble," I said as I followed him down the hall to our bedroom.

"I told you I'm straight, but your friend is all fucked up."

"That is not my friend and I'm not worried about him. As long as you're alright that's all that matters," I went to the bathroom and got some peroxide and Neosporin. I gasped when I removed the towel and saw how bruised and swollen Dominic's hand was. He had a few cuts and scratches that caused the blood that I saw on the towel.

"Don't trip it looks worse than it is," he said when he saw my reaction.

"Are you sure you didn't kill the boy? If your hand looks like this, I would hate to see his face."

"His punk ass will live, but Jaden bashed him over the head with a beer bottle," he said laughing.

"Why am I not surprised?" I replied sarcastically. Jaden is as crazy as they come. Any time there's drama he was never too far away.

After cleaning and bandaging Dominic's wounds, I cleaned up my mess while he prepared to take a shower.

"Oh yeah baby, I forgot to tell you the best part about tonight," Dominic said right before he went into the bathroom.

"Better than the fight?" I asked with a smile.

"Yep, much better than the fight. When I walked down on ole boy, he didn't see me because he was all hugged up with a woman."

"It was probably his girlfriend Shannon," I replied with a shrug.

"No, it wasn't his girlfriend. He was in there with Nadia," he revealed.

"Are you serious?" I asked while sitting up in the bed to see his facial expression.

"I'm dead ass serious. She jumped out of bed with one brother and climbed right in with the other one. I never even knew her to be so shady," he said before disappearing into the bathroom.

Candace had already filled us in about Nadia's relationship with Kyle, but this was my first time hearing about her and Kevin. Bryce had also told us about seeing Kyle with Tiffany not too long ago, but this is just too much to take in. Kyle seems to change women like he changes underwear, and nobody is off limits to him. Even though he and Bryce are no longer friends, Tiffany should have never been on his radar. And Nadia is just proving herself to be an untrustworthy hoe that's capable of doing anything.

I waited until I heard the shower turn on to grab my phone and called Candace. I'm sure David probably already filled her in, but I wanted to talk to her about it as well. I'm so happy that she found out about Nadia before it was too late.

****

Three weeks later, we were celebrating DJ's second birthday. I had to damn near beg Dominic to do something small for him. He wanted something big like his first one, but I just wasn't in the mood. We agreed to give him a party at the bounce house instead. All of the food was included, and we only had to buy a cake and party favors for his guests. Mrs. Liz and my mama went a few hours earlier and decorated the place for us. I'm eight months pregnant, so I was happy to let them do it. Aside from that, we're also preparing to move into our new home. A few days ago Dominic finally got the call that he's been waiting for. The bank accepted his offer for the house. He already signed all of the necessary paperwork and picked up the keys. I'm so excited that we got the house that I really want. I won't be able to really decorate until after I have my baby, but I'm looking forward to doing it. I fell in love with the huge red and stainless steel kitchen the first time I laid eyes on it. Not to mention the six bedrooms and three and a half bathrooms that came along with it. The lighted pool and deck in the rear sealed the deal. I can't wait to have my first poolside gathering.

Dominic is happier about the price. The property was owned by the bank due to foreclosure, and it was almost fifty percent cheaper than the original price. It's newly built, and the previous owners only lived in it for three months before they went to prison for drug trafficking.

So much is going on right now, and I'm beginning to feel overwhelmed. I had my baby shower last weekend, and our apartment is a mess. They told me that it was going to be something small, but it was almost as big as the one I had with DJ. I have so much stuff for my baby that Dominic and my brothers had to take most of it to the new house. We weren't officially moving for another week because Dominic had someone to come in and paint DJ and our daughters' rooms. We went there almost every day to drop something off or just look around.

"These damn children are wearing me out," Taylor complained as she sat down next to me. Her, Tiana, and Nyla were playing more than the kids.

"Don't blame it on these children. You've been running around here like a big ass kid," I said laughing. I got in the spacewalk for all of five minutes before Dominic had a fit. He's in the back playing with DJ on the inflatable slide, but he's keeping a close eye on me to make sure I don't do it again.

"You're just mad because Dominic made your fat ass sit down. Poor Dominique is probably all shook up in there," she said while rubbing my belly.

"I hate that damn name," I frowned. I listened to Tiana and Taylor and let the guests at my baby shower vote on the two names that Dominic and I chose. They didn't know which one was our favorite, but everybody picked the name that he liked. Knowing him, he probably cheated and told them which one he wanted.

"Girl, that's cute. Did y'all ever find out what Kennedi is having?" Taylor asked.

"She still won't tell him. She still calls all day begging for money though. We saw her daddy the other day, and he said she wouldn't tell him either. He didn't even know that her and Dominic were about to be divorced."

"She didn't tell the man?"

"Nope, he said that she's still mad at him about that wedding stuff."

"That heifer is really crazy. She's gon' be a headache for y'all once she have that baby."

"Her daddy said that her mama is in her ear. He's giving up on trying to get through to her. I feel bad for him because that's his first grandchild. I'm not worried about her being a problem for us. I won't be pregnant forever," I replied.

"Somebody needs to whip her mama's ugly ass. Kennedi is gon' be a lonely old maid just like her," Taylor said before she walked away.

As soon as she left, Dominic made his way over to where I sat. I looked at him and rolled my eyes, letting him know that I'm still pissed about him ruining my fun.

"You can roll your eyes all you want to. You know you ain't have no business in that damn spacewalk," he fussed.

"I can't wait to have this baby," I complained. "You gon' be looking for me with a flashlight in the daytime."

"Yeah alright, play crazy if you want to. I might have to put another one in you just to make sure you chill out," he laughed while pulling me onto his lap.

"You must be crazy. I already gave you a son, and I'm giving you a daughter next month. Not to mention whatever Kennedi is having. You should be good on kids for a while," I replied.

"Yeah, you right when you say whatever she's having. I guess I'll find out when the baby gets here."

"She might tell you if you buy what she's asking for. You have to at least buy something before the baby gets here."

"I already told you that she's not calling the shots. You know I don't have a problem providing for my kids, but I'm not about to play these games with her. Her stupid ass must be listening to somebody else. She wouldn't have done anything like this on her own. I can't wait until this divorce is final next month."

"She'll come around when she sees that you're not playing with her. You already know that she's going to use that baby as a weapon. I just hope she doesn't try to keep it away from you. I really want all of the kids to know each other," I replied. Dominic nodded his head in agreement.

I was about to get up and check on DJ when I heard Co-Co and Taylor yelling at somebody. Everybody turned their attention to the front door to see what all the commotion was about.

"Girl, I know you didn't come to my nephew's party with your bullshit," Taylor yelled angrily.

"She must be trying to go into premature labor coming around here. You already know how this family gives it up," Co-Co said.

Mrs. Liz blocked the door, preventing anyone from going outside. Dominic and I jumped up trying to see who was trying to ruin our son's party. I got heated when I peeked outside and saw Kennedi standing there frowning.

"Sit down baby, let me go see what she wants," Dominic said.

"I'm good right where I am. I'm not trying to do nothing to her scary ass," I replied.

"Brook, please don't wild out up in here," Dominic begged.

"I told you I'm good. She just better not say anything to me."

"David come here," Dominic yelled to his brother. David walked over with DJ in his arms. "Don't let her ass come out there."

"I don't need no damn babysitter. I told you that I'm not coming out there," I yelled with my hand on my hips. He's really doing too much right now acting like I'm his child or something.

"Come on and sit down slugger," David said laughing. He grabbed my hand and led me over to the seating area right as Dominic went outside. My mama went to the door and grabbed Taylor and Co-Co. I'm happy that she did before things got worse than they already were.

KENNEDI

Showing up to DJ's party wasn't the best idea, but I wasn't thinking clearly at the time. Dominic has been avoiding me for weeks and I'm sick of it. The final straw was when Tiffany showed me some pictures on Instagram that David posted a few days ago. My heart stopped when I saw Brooklyn and Dominic's smiling faces standing next to the sign that said "SOLD" in front of their brand new house. She was holding up the keys while he had his hands secured around her very pregnant belly. Then, if that wasn't bad enough, he got that bitch a house in the exact same location that I wanted us to live in. He denied me everything that I've ever wanted only to turn around and give it all to his side bitch. My daughter and I are going to be living in a two bedroom condo while Brooklyn and his other kids live it up in a six bedroom home with a pool.

I ignored the remarks being made by Taylor and Brooklyn's cousin and turned my attention to Mrs. Liz instead.

"Can you call Dominic for me, please?" I asked her. Before she could leave to go get him, I saw him making his way over to where I stood. I could tell that he's upset, but I really didn't care.

"I'm trying to be civil and handle this like an adult, but you're really trying to make me go there with you," Dominic said as he walked up on me.

"I don't give a damn about none of what you're saying right now. You out here buying cars and houses and shit, but I can't even get a bag of diapers for our baby. This is your son's second party, but I haven't seen a dime for this baby yet," I yelled.

"Don't worry about what I do for my son. I don't have a problem supporting this baby, but I'm buying what I want to buy. You don't run shit over this way, and you should know that by now."

"I don't want your bitch picking out nothing for my baby. Just give me the money, and I can do it myself. I'll get my mama to help me," I replied.

"I'm not putting one dollar in your hand. And since you and your mama always want to run the show y'all can do that shit on y'all own," he said as he started to walk away.

I lost it after that. I walked up behind him and slapped him on the back of his head.

"I hate you!" I screamed trying to hit him again.

He spun around with fire in his eyes, and that scared the hell out of me. Mrs. Liz rushed over to us just in time. Dominic looked as if he was about to knock me on my ass. I saw Brooklyn trying to break away from David to come outside, but his hold on her was too strong. I didn't need her wild ass coming out here too.

"You better keep your fucking hands to yourself," Dominic fumed.

"Go back inside Dominic. Let me talk to Kennedi for a minute," his mother requested.

"Yeah, go back to your hood monkey," I yelled at his departing back.

"That hood monkey got what you want though, huh," he smirked right before disappearing into the building.

As much as I still love my husband, I'm starting to hate him even more. I would never have thought that we would be in the place that we're in right now.

"Now Kennedi, you know that I try to mind my business and let you and Dominic handle things on your own, but you have crossed the line this time. This is my grandson's party, and you shouldn't have come here with all this mess," Mrs. Liz said.

"I know that, and I apologize, but he left me no other choice. I'm tired of him ignoring my calls and texts. Brooklyn is not the only one that's having his baby. I have three more months before my baby gets here, and Dominic hasn't done anything to help me. I don't have anything for when my baby arrives," I said as I fought back the volcano of tears that threatened to erupt.

"Kennedi you know my son and you know how he feels about kids. Dominic is going to take care of his baby and my husband, and I are going to help just like we do with DJ. It's hard for us to even start shopping when you're refusing to tell us the sex of the baby."

"It's a girl okay? I don't know why that's even important, but I'm having a girl," I snapped.

"You can lose the attitude honey. I'm only trying to help you."

"I'm sorry Mrs. Liz. I'm just stressed out, and that can't be good for her," I replied while rubbing my small baby bump.

"No, it's not good for her, so you need to relax. There's no need to stress over something that you can't change. I'll talk to Dominic. Maybe you and I can go shopping for her next weekend if you're free," she suggested.

"Thank you so much, Mrs. Liz," I said giving her a tight hug. "I'll let you know if I'm free or not."

"Okay, you know my number if you need anything," she replied right before walking away.

I felt a little better after talking to her. I would have rather it be Dominic saying those things instead of her, but at least it's a start. As soon as I got in my car my phone rang, displaying my father's number. He'd been calling me non-stop for the past few weeks, and I'm over it.

"Yes," I yelled once I connected the call.

"Hey sweetheart, how are you"? He asked sounding happy. It sickened me that he and everybody else could be so happy while I am feeling like I'm living in hell on earth.

"I'm fine," I answered with ice dripping from my voice.

"I was calling to see if we could meet up for lunch or dinner one day this week."

"No, we can't. I have too much on my plate right now."

"Kennedi we really need to sit down and talk. It's time for us to put the past behind us and move forward. You're about to give me my first grandchild, and I want to be in his or her life. I truly apologize for whatever I did to make you angry," he said.

"Don't try to downplay what you did. You told Dominic things that he should have never known about," I yelled.

"I'm not downplaying anything. I'm trying to apologize if you'll just let me."

"No, I won't let you. Because of you, my husband almost called off our wedding."

"Why does that even matter now? Y'all are about to be divorced in a few weeks anyway," he bellowed.

I sat there staring at my phone in stunned silence, wondering how he knew about my impending divorce. The last thing I wanted him to do was gloat about how right he was.

"Who told you that?" I asked angrily.

"It doesn't matter who told me Kennedi. I just want you to know that I'm here for you. Whatever you and the baby need I'll be happy to provide. Please don't shut me out. I want to help you as much as I can," he replied almost begging.

"I'm fine and I don't need your help. My mama will help me just like she's been doing since you abandoned me to go play house with your new wife and kids," I snapped.

"I don't know what Karen has been telling you, but I never abandoned you. I've always wanted to be a part of your life, but she wouldn't let me. Everything had to be done on her terms or not at all. My money was always good enough, but I never was. I damn near had to wait until you were an adult to have a relationship with you thanks to your mother," he ranted.

"Well, it's a little too late for all of that now don't you think?"

"You're absolutely right and I'm done trying. I'm tired of kissing your ass and begging you to let me be a part of your life. I feel bad that your mother has turned you into a younger version of herself. God knows I never wanted that for you."

"Are you done?" I asked impatiently.

"More than you know," he said before hanging up. It really didn't matter to me how he feels at the moment. I tried to let him into my world, and he almost had it crashing down around me. I'm good on him and anybody else who has a problem with what I do.

****

Three weeks later, Tiffany and I were coming from my doctor's office before going into work. Today marks the seventh month of my pregnancy, and everything is perfect. Since I'm considered a high-risk patient, I have to start seeing the doctor twice every week until my princess is born. Mrs. Liz called me to go shopping with her a few times, but I always turned her down. Although I appreciate the gesture, it's not her job. She's doing everything that her son should have been doing. I hadn't seen or heard from him since DJ's party. I did find out through Tiffany and her social media stalking that he and Brooklyn had moved into their new house. They posted pictures of how each room was decorated, and it's absolutely beautiful. It's also how I found out that she too is having a girl. I don't know her exact date, but she should be due to have her baby any day now. I just can't win for losing with her. It wasn't enough that she gave Dominic his first and only son now she's giving him his first daughter as well.

"You want to get something to eat before we go to the office?" Tiffany asked me.

"Yeah, and I need to go check my P.O. Box. I know it's piled high with junk mail," I replied. I looked down and smiled at the text message that I'd just received from Scott. I'm so happy that he didn't blame me for causing him to lose his job. I helped him put together a resume for a few jobs that he expressed interest in. He'd just informed me that he was offered a job as a driver for Budweiser. It doesn't pay as much as he made when he worked for Dominic, but it's enough to get him back on his feet. He's been collecting unemployment, and that's barely enough to pay his rent.

"What are you smiling so hard for?" Tiffany asked when she pulled up to the post office.

"None of your business nosey," I replied while getting out of her car and responding to Scott's message. I opened my P.O. Box and instantly started throwing away most of the junk that was stuffed in there. While shifting through everything, a bright green card caught my attention. It informed me that I needed to go into the office and sign for a package. Being seven months pregnant made me lazier than I've ever been, but curiosity got the best of me. Since I'm not having an actual baby shower, a few of my mother's friends had started sending me gifts for my daughter. I got excited about the thought of getting something else and hurried to see just what it was. I told Dominic and Mrs. Liz that I didn't have anything, but that's none of their business anyway. If I have to lie to get my baby girl everything that she needs then so be it.

"Can I help you?" The clerk asked me. I handed her the card and watched her walk to the back to get my package. She was only gone for a few minutes before she came back with a big brown envelope and handed it to me.

"Is this all?" I asked with an obvious attitude.

"Yes, that's all we have for you," she replied matching my tone. I snatched the envelope from her hand and walked away.

"Let's go get something to eat," I told Tiffany went I got back in the car.

"Okay, I want some chicken," she replied. As soon as she pulled off, I tore open the envelope and pulled out the contents. My heart skipped a beat when I read "Dissolution of Marriage" in big bold letters at the top of the page. Tears immediately started to fill my eyes.

"Kennedi did you hear me?" Tiffany asked.

I had completely zoned out as I read over the paperwork that confirmed the end of my marriage. Tiffany pulled her car to the side of the road when my hands started shaking, and my breathing became irregular. She jumped out of the car and rushed over to me.

"Kennedi are you alright?" She asked in a panic filled voice. I handed her the papers to read as silent tears crept from my eyes.

"I can't believe it's really over," I mumbled sadly.

"Oh Kennedi, I'm so sorry about all of this," my cousin said while embracing me. I welcomed her hug and held on to her as tightly as I could.

"I should have been celebrating my one year anniversary around this time, but I'm not even married anymore," I cried harder.

Tiffany held me and rubbed my back while I cried until I didn't have any more tears left. I thought back to all the drama that I took Nadia through to get Dominic and I ended up losing him the exact same way.

"We don't have to go to work if you don't want to. I'm sure your mama will understand," Tiffany said.

"No, I need to do something to get my mind off of all of this. I'll go crazy if I sit inside and think about it all day."

"You don't have to go home either. You know you can stay with me for as long as you want to," she suggested.

"Thanks, Tiffany. I'll get some clothes and come over after work. You can still go get your food, but I'm not hungry anymore."

"My goddaughter is probably starving so I'm getting you something too," she said as she pulled up to the drive-thru at Popeye's. My stomach was growling so I didn't protest when she shoved a box full of chicken and biscuits in my hands. We sat in the parking lot of the restaurant and ate before heading back to work.

"You feel better?" Tiffany asked when we were almost to our office. "You know you don't have to do this if you don't feel up to it."

"I know, but I'm..." I started talking, but my words got lodged in my throat when we pulled up to our office building. There were about five marked and three unmarked police cars in front of the building, blocking us from getting into the parking lot. Tiffany stopped her car, and both of us jumped out in a hurry. We ran over, trying to see what happened until a police officer stopped us from going too far.

"What's going on? We work here," Tiffany yelled while pulling away from the officer.

"Oh God Tiffany! My mama's truck is here. Did something happen to my mother?" I yelled out to anyone who was listening.

"Calm down ladies. I'll get somebody out here to talk to you," the masculine looking female officer said to us. She walked away right as she summoned another officer over to make sure we didn't try to go in.

"What if somebody tried to rob us? They probably did something to my mama," I cried out in fear.

"Stop thinking like that Kennedi. They don't have any yellow tape out here, so nobody is dead," Tiffany rationalized.

"I don't care about any of that Tiffany. Something must have happened. Look at all of these police cars out here. I just need to know if my mother is okay." Just as I finished talking the police lady who restrained us before came back out of the building with another man. He wore a suit and tie, but I didn't miss the badge that rested on his side.

"Which one of you ladies work here?" He asked while looking at me and Tiffany.

"Both of us do. My mother owns this place. Is she alright?" I spoke up.

"She's fine, but the place is closed indefinitely," he replied.

"What! Why?" Tiffany yelled.

"Just stay right here. We might need to ask both of you a few questions before you leave," he said before walking away.

"Something's not right. I can feel it. I just need to see her to make sure she's alright," I said to Tiffany through teary eyes.

Right when the words left my mouth, I watched as two police officers escorted my mother out of the building. A sense of relief washed over me until I noticed that her hands were cuffed behind her back. Despite the circumstances, she still held her head high like she didn't have a care in the world. I rushed through the crowd of police officers and headed straight to her. I didn't care that I was told to stay back.

"Kennedi come back here," Tiffany yelled as she raced after me. Her yelling caused a group of officers to turn around and stop me just as I made it to my mother.

"Calm down before you hurt yourself and your baby ma'am," one of the officers who held me back instructed. I tried to break free to see what was going on.

"It's okay Kennedi. This is all a misunderstanding that will be over very soon," my mother said as she was placed in the back of an unmarked car. Seeing her in that position took all of the fight out of me. I broke down and cried like a baby.

"I feel sick," I said right before I relieved my stomach of the lunch that I'd just eaten. Tiffany was right at my side while I threw up all over the grass where we stood. The same plain clothes officer that came out and talked to us before came back and handed me a bottle of water and some paper towels. Tiffany poured some water on the napkins and gave me the rest to drink.

"Here you go, have a seat," another officer said, sitting a folding chair down in the grass for me.

"Can somebody please tell me what's going on?" I begged while taking a seat.

"This is still an ongoing investigation, but your mother has been arrested for embezzlement and fraud. We were alerted by the bank a few months ago about the possible misappropriation of funds on several accounts that belong to her. After investigating a little further, we noticed that it was much deeper than we originally thought. This whole loan and finance company seems like nothing more than a cover-up. As of right now she's in federal custody, and there is no bond," he said all in one breath.

I felt lightheaded after he had finished talking. Not only were my cousin and I out of a job, but my mother was now a federal inmate. Without my mother's financial help and no job, I'll be broke in a matter of months.

"I need to talk to her. Will she be able to call me?" I asked.

"Yes, she'll be given the opportunity to make a few calls. Here's my card. Call me if I can be of any further assistance. I'm sure your mother will let you know about her court dates or anything else of importance," the detective said before handing Tiffany and I a card and walking away.

"Come on Kennedi, let's go get you some clothes so you can stay with me for a while," Tiffany said while helping me stand to my feet. I followed behind her like a zombie. Aside from Tiffany and my soon to be new addition, my mother was all that I had. Dominic left me, and I had basically pushed my father away.

"I don't know what I'm going to do Tiffany. I can't afford to pay bills and take care of this baby without a job. I'll have to use my all of my savings, and then I'll be broke," I cried to my cousin.

"The first thing you need to do is talk to Dominic about helping you. If he still refuses, take his ass to court, and they'll make him pay. You know your father will help you if you need him to," she replied.

I never told her about the last conversation I had with my father a few weeks ago. He told me that he was done trying with me, and he meant it. He hasn't tried to call me again since then. Knowing him, he'll probably be happy when he finds out that my mother has been locked up. I'm not about to give him anything else to throw in my face. I'm still wondering how he found out about me and Dominic divorcing. My pride will never allow me to call him and beg for help. I would never make him think that I needed him even though I really did.

DOMINIC

"Come on baby, just one more time around and we can leave," I begged Brooklyn. We're at the park doing a few laps around the walking trail. Co-Co is doing a few laps with us while Candace played on the slide with DJ. Since Brook is nine months pregnant, I try to make her walk for at least an hour every day. Most days we barely get in thirty minutes and today is most likely going to be one of those days. She's due to have our baby girl any day now, and I'm too excited. I'm also excited about our new house. Brooklyn was supposed to wait until after she had the baby to decorate, but she started on it anyway. With the help of my family and hers, everything was just about done. Brooklyn has good taste, and her decorating skills are something serious. The only thing missing is some patio and pool furniture for outside, but she still hasn't come across anything that she likes.

"Dominic I'm tired. We already did three laps. I'm ready to sit down," Brooklyn complained.

"Y'all can go sit down, but I'm going around a few more times. I didn't get this hour glass figure by being lazy," Co-Co said as he kept walking. We couldn't leave right now anyway since we rode to the park with him. Co-Co had just purchased a silver G-Wagon, so he volunteered to drive.

"Come on lazy ass," I grabbed Brooklyn's hand and led her over to one of the park benches. We sat down and talked while watching DJ play.

"Have you heard from Kennedi again?" Brooklyn asked.

"No, she's been in contact with my mama though. I think I'm just going to give my mama some money and let her go with her to shop for the baby. I feel bad for her, but I still don't want to be around her ass."

"I feel bad for her too," Brooklyn replied sadly.

According to my mama, Kennedi's mother had been arrested, and things aren't looking too good for her. She finally stopped being a bitch long enough to tell my mama that we're having a girl. As much as I can't stand Kennedi's ass I have to put my feelings to the side and be there for my daughter. Kennedi's mama is basically all that she knows. Her not being here for the birth of her first child is going to be hard on her.

"It's crazy how I went from having no kids a few years ago to having three back to back," I observed.

"It doesn't matter how many you have as long as you take care of them," Brooklyn replied.

She's right, but that's a given with me. Brook and all of my kids are going to be well taken care of. I make enough money to make sure of that.

"So what's up with this marriage thing?" I asked changing the subject. "I'm divorced now, so you don't have any more excuses."

"I wasn't trying to make excuses, but you've only been divorced for a week. We couldn't do anything until that was final."

"Well, it's final so what's up?" I asked again. I didn't care that it sounded like I was begging. When I want something, I won't rest until I get it.

"As soon as I drop this load I'm all yours. When I heal up that is," she said smiling.

"Baby, I'm serious. Don't tell me what you think I want to hear just to shut me up."

"I'm not, but I need at least four to six weeks to get back to myself," she responded.

"You got that. Don't worry about anything. I'll take care of everything."

"No Dominic, I don't trust your taste. You got me naming my damn baby Dominique. I do not trust you with planning my wedding."

"You know I don't know anything about all of that. I'll hire somebody to do it for me. I know your likes and dislikes. And nothing is wrong with my baby's name. She'll be named after me and her brother."

I laughed when I saw Candace walking our way with DJ. He was doing his best to get away from her, but she had a death grip around his legs. He hated to be held, and he's trying hard to get down.

"Take this bad ass lil boy," Candace said handing him over to me. As soon as I got him he jumped down and started running around.

"Y'all ready?" Co-Co asked as he came over to us.

"Yes, I am so tired. Get your son Dominic," Brooklyn said standing to her feet. I picked up my son and followed everybody to Co-Co's truck.

"And make sure y'all don't have any dirt on y'all shoes. I don't want my rugs to get dirty," Co-Co fussed.

"Man, just take us home. You have too many damn rules when somebody rides with your ass. I didn't say all that when me and my girl had to pick your pissy ass up from the club when you couldn't drive," I replied. I knew that it was about to be an issue when he stopped and snapped his head around to face me.

"Don't even go there with me Dominic. If you don't like my rules, then take your fat ass girlfriend and your demon seed son and walk home. You can beat your feet right along with them since you think its funny Candace," he spat.

"Say that shit when you show up to our house looking for something to eat," Brooklyn said.

"You got a point, so you can get in Brooklyn. The rest of y'all better shut up before y'all be walking home," he replied.

"Bitch act like he never had a decent car before," Candace mumbled making me laugh.

"Say that shit loud enough for me to hear it Candace," Co-Co replied. We all ignored him and hopped in the truck. Brook sat up front while Candace and I sat in the back with DJ's car seat in between us.

"I hope y'all don't mind, but I need to pick up something from Dwight," Co-Co said.

"I mind, my back and my side are starting to hurt again," Brooklyn complained. She's been complaining about the same thing for the past two days. I noticed that she tried to turn sideways in her seat, but her stomach wouldn't allow her to.

"You good baby?" I asked when I noticed the uncomfortable look on her face.

"That bitch better be good. Don't be trying to go into labor in my brand new truck," Co-Co yelled dramatically.

"You think you need to go to the hospital Brook," Candace asked.

"I don't know, I might. My back is really killing me all of a sudden," she replied with a pained expression.

"I knew I shouldn't have let your overdue ass ride in my shit. I'm returning this shit if your water breaks in here. Brook I swear if you mess up my truck I'm kicking your ass when you have that baby. Let me call Dwight and tell him to meet me at the hospital," Co-Co fussed.

We all ignored him as he drove in the direction of the hospital. I called my mama and Mrs. Pam to meet us there as well. Candace called David, and he's swinging by the house to grab Brooklyn and my daughters' things. Even though I'm nervous, I can't help myself from laughing at Co-Co's crazy ass. He's on the phone telling Dwight how wrong Brooklyn was for deciding to have our baby in his new truck like she had a choice.

"Somebody help us, please. Come get this bitch out of my truck," Co-Co screamed and blew his horn when he pulled up to the hospital's emergency ramp. This nigga is always doing way too much.

"You are so stupid. Nobody is going to come out here. Let me go get her a wheelchair," Candace replied. I jumped out and helped Brooklyn out of the truck just as Candace returned.

"Bring DJ in with you Candace," I instructed before wheeling Brooklyn in. I already knew the routine, so I bypassed triage and headed straight upstairs to labor and delivery. As soon as the elevator door opened, we were greeted by Brooklyn's family and mine. I'm surprised to see my father here because he usually stayed at home with my brother and sister. Since Nyla and Ivan are at my aunt's house for the week, I guess he decided to come along.

"She's already checked in. Just ask the nurse what room they're putting her in," Mrs. Pam instructed.

"Where is my grandson?" My daddy asked.

"Right here," Candace replied when she stepped off of the elevator with DJ in her arms. Co-Co walked in with her while Dwight trailed close behind. I left all of them standing in the hall while I went and talked to the nurse. She informed me that Brooklyn's doctor is on duty, and he would be coming to check on her soon. With her help, I escorted Brooklyn to her room and helped her change into a hospital gown.

"Are you in any pain Brooklyn?" The nurse asked her.

"Just my back," Brooklyn replied.

"That's just labor pains. They come in your back and side sometimes too. I paged your doctor, and he should be here shortly," she said before walking away.

A few minutes later Mrs. Pam and my mama walked in with Brooklyn and the baby's bags. That let me know that David had arrived too. Just like when DJ was born, the waiting area was full of our family. The only difference this time is that

Brooklyn and I are officially together. We don't need anybody to stay at our house with her because I'll be there every step of the way. If Kennedi allows me to, I'll be in the delivery room with her when our daughter arrives as well.

"Good afternoon everybody," Dr. Martin said when he walked into the room. "How are you feeling Brooklyn?"

"I feel alright, but my back is killing me," she replied.

"Alright, let me check you and see if baby girl is ready to meet her parents yet," he smiled. He did his normal hygiene routine before examining her. We were all shocked to learn that Brooklyn was already five centimeters. I guess all the walking I made her do paid off. She's not in as much pain as she was with DJ, but she got an epidural anyway. Once all of that was done, we just sat around waiting for something to happen.

****

Three hours later, we welcomed eight pound, eight ounces Dominique O'Mya Roberts into the world. Just like DJ, she's an exact replica of me. She has a head full of curly black hair, and I fell in love all over again. After Brooklyn and the baby had been cleaned up and situated in their room, everybody was allowed to come back and visit. The room was big, but it's still not big enough for all of us. My aunt had just arrived with my little brother and sister, and they're going crazy over their new niece. DJ just keeps staring at her and holding her hand like she's not real.

"As cute as she is I would've whipped her little ass if she would have popped out in my truck," Co-Co said.

He's being overly dramatic as usual. I feel bad for Dwight. There is no way in hell that he can handle his crazy ass. I looked at David, who kept nodding his head for me to step out into the hallway. I followed him out of the room and down the hall to the vending machines.

"What's up?" I asked him.

"What, you changed your mind or something?" He asked as he shoved the small light blue Tiffany box into my hand.

"No, I didn't change my mind, but I'm nervous man. I don't want do it in front of everybody. I'm waiting until we're by ourselves," I replied as my hands shook. Brooklyn and I had just talked about marriage a few hours ago, but now it's about to be real.

"Nigga what the hell are you shaking for? I don't know what you're scared of. You almost drove me crazy about helping you find a damn ring. Y'all got two babies and a house together. This is the only thing left for y'all to do. As much as you spent on that ring her ass better say yes," David said.

"But what if she says no?" I asked him.

"Then propose to me. I'll marry your fine ass if you put that big rock on my finger," he laughed.

"Your punk ass better stop playing with me," I yelled while laughing with him. "But you can have the ring I gave Kennedi though."

"I don't want that cheap shit. You must have forgotten that I was with you when you bought both rings. You did right by giving it to Nyla."

Kennedi must have thought she was doing something when she mailed her wedding rings to my mama's house. That shit didn't even put a dent in my pocket, so I really didn't care. When my sister asked me if she could have it, I handed it over to her with no problem.

"But seriously lil brother, you already know what she's going to say," David assured me.

He's right, but that still didn't calm me down. I knew without a doubt that Brooklyn would marry me because we always talk about it. I just don't want to rush her into something that she's not ready for.

"I know you're right, but I don't want her to feel like I'm rushing her. And then I just got divorced, and I'm trying to do this shit all over again."

"That's just your nerves talking right now. You and Brook got together in a crazy way, but it's real. Y'all got something that you never had with Kennedi and anybody else. I really think y'all were made for each other, and I know you feel the same way," David replied.

My brother is in his very first relationship, but he's always given me some good advice. After talking to him for a while longer, he made me feel better about my decision. He made a lot of good points just like he always does. I saw things clearer after our conversation, and I made a decision. As soon as Brooklyn and I are alone, I'm going to ask her to be my wife.

BRYCE

"Co-Co you need to stop all this damn performing before you wake Brooklyn's kids up," Candace said to her drama king of a brother. He's always doing too much, and he's getting on everybody's damn nerves. David, my brothers, and I only came over to help Dominic put together him and Brooklyn's patio and pool furniture, but I'm ready to take my ass right back home.

"I don't give a damn. My man is cheating on me and y'all don't even care about how I feel," he cried.

Well, he's not just crying he's actually rolling around on Brooklyn's floor like a damn fool. Brooklyn had my niece two weeks ago, but Co-Co doesn't care. He's bringing all this drama to her house behind some foolishness. Jaden stopped helping us a long time ago and started recording his stupid ass with his phone. I told him to put his ass on World Star for everyone to see how crazy he is.

"Shit happens Co-Co. You deal with other people all the time, but you're mad because he's doing the same thing," Candace said.

"And not to mention how you embarrassed the man today," Taylor chimed in.

Taylor told me how my cousin showed his ass on Dwight and some woman that he was with outside of the mall. She was scared that they were going to be arrested because the police had to be called.

"So I see him with a woman and I'm not supposed to say anything?" Co-Co asked pointing to himself.

"But did you have to try to fight them out in public like that? Then your dumb ass jumped on the hood of the man's car while he was driving. You always go overboard with everything that you do," Candace said.

"You bitches don't care about me. You and Taylor got a man and Brooklyn is about to have a husband. I just feel like I can't breathe," he said gasping for air like he was having an asthma attack. Nobody even tried to help that clown because it wasn't that serious.

On another note, I'm happy for Baby and Dominic. He popped the question the night that she had their daughter, and they're making it official very soon. Her ring looks like it cost about the same as the house they live in, but it's not my place to ask about the price. Brooklyn is kind of nervous about the idea of marriage, but I tried to assure her that they're doing the right thing. I spent over two hours on the phone with her the night she came home with Dominique. They're already living together so there wouldn't be much of a difference. Looking at what she and Dominic have makes me want to take it to the next level with Taylor. They met at a crazy time, but it's not hard to see how much they love each other. Taylor and I had our issues in the past when I was with Tiffany, but we've been on the right track ever since we got back together.

"Nigga, shut up!" Jaden yelled out angrily. "You didn't even know dude that long for you to be acting like that."

"Leave him alone Jaden. His feelings are hurt," Brook said while rubbing our cousin's back.

"Brooklyn you were always my favorite cousin," Co-Co told my sister while enjoying the sympathy that she was giving him.

"Don't pacify that clown, Baby. He looks like a damn fool crying over Dwight's ole receding hairline ass," Jaden fussed. Just that fast Co-Co forgot all about being depressed. He jumped up and started going off after Jaden's last comment.

"Oh no, you didn't Jaden. That last bitch we saw you with was built like an ice cream sandwich so don't even go there with me," he yelled.

"Co-Co you fake as hell. You were just crying a minute ago, now you ready to fight," David laughed.

"I'll finish crying in a minute. I just had to check this clown right quick for talking about my man," he replied.

We all fell out laughing after that. As mad as Co-Co made me sometimes I wouldn't trade him for nothing in the world. He kept us laughing with his flip mouth and non-stop drama. Jaden was always giving him a hard time, but he's crazy about him too.

"She might have been built bad, but her head game was so good she deserved her own reality show," Jaden replied.

"Stop talking to me Jaden, I'm too depressed to be arguing with you," Co-Co said as he forced out some more crocodile tears. And just like that he was back on the floor cutting up again.

"Why don't you just call the dude and talk to him," David suggested.

"No, the hell I'm not. I probably would have felt better if I caught him with another man, but that was a slap in my face to catch him with a woman. I just want to know when his fraud ass decided to start playing for the other team," Co-Co replied.

"He's playing for the right team. Maybe you should try it, and you and ole boy can do a threesome," Jaden said laughing.

"Brook you got some Benadryl or something? My allergies are starting to act up," Co-Co said.

"Boy, shut up. You don't even suffer from allergies," Candace yelled.

"I keep telling y'all that I'm allergic to vagina. I'm already breaking out in hives just by talking about it," he replied as he started scratching his imaginary itch.

I laughed so hard that I fell out of my chair and onto the floor. You never know what to expect when all of us get together, but it's always fun. After about an hour, we finally finished our task. It turned out better than I thought. It looked even better when we put everything where it belonged. Baby and Dominic's house was laid like something on MTV cribs. She picked out all of the furniture and our mother helped her decorate everything. I'm almost scared to touch anything it's so pretty. Once we were done, we sat around eating the pizza that Dominic ordered while Baby fed my niece. My daughters played with DJ while he sat in his high chair making a mess of his food. Brooklyn might be their mother, but both of her kids look exactly like Dominic.

After a few minutes had passed, Candace got up from the table and went outside. She'd been gone for about ten minutes when she came back in followed by Dwight. That's all it took for Co-Co to start up with his grand performance again.

"What is he doing here?" He asked pointing to Dwight.

"Me and Brook called him to come over here. You need to stop acting stupid and talk to the man," Candace said.

"We don't have anything to talk about. I gave you the best four months of my life. I even gave you my virginity, and this is how you do me. If you wanted a woman, you could have at least picked somebody that actually looks like one. That ugly bitch you were with needs to be put to sleep."

I started choking on my beer when he made the comment about his virginity. Dwight doesn't seem like he's lame, but if he believes that shit then he's a damn fool. Co-Co has been around the block more times than the garbage man.

"That was my cousin Co-Co. If you would have just listened instead of blowing up, you would have known that," Dwight replied.

"That bitch wasn't your cousin. You're just embarrassed because she looks like Wesley Snipes with a bad wig."

"See, that's your problem. You went from zero to one hundred without even knowing what was going on. Your ass is crazy for real."

"And you knew that when you met me. Don't start complaining about it now."

"I'm telling you that's my cousin and you're wrong for talking about her like that. She remembers you from our family picnic and everything. She's the one that you threatened to cut when you were going off on everybody."

"Honey, I threatened to cut a lot of people that day. You have to be more specific than that. And besides, I would have remembered seeing a face like hers. That's something that a bitch will never forget as ugly as she was," Co-Co said.

Dwight is a cool dude, but I really felt like my cousin was way too fast for him. I don't know much about the gay lifestyle, but Co-Co could run circles around him.

"I'll be right back," Dwight said as he walked out the front door. About a minute later, he came back in with another woman.

"This is my cousin Drika y'all," Dwight said introducing her to everybody. One look at her and I had to admit that Co-Co was right. There was absolutely nothing cute about her. She kind of reminded me of the comedian Jamie Foxx when he played Wanda on In Living Color. She had a dark chocolate complexion with bright red lipstick covering her huge lips. The blonde wig she was wearing only made her look worse.

"Hey everybody," she said waving at us. "And how are you Co-Co?"

I prayed that this clown didn't act a fool on this girl in Baby's house. But to my surprise and relief, he's on his best behavior.

"Hey, Drika girl. You look so cute. I was just telling Dwight how pretty you are," Co-Co lied with a straight face. He walked over and gave her a hug like they were the best of friends. Dwight looked at him and shook his head. Drika was blushing at the false compliment, and I had to keep myself from laughing once again.

"Thanks and I love your hair," she said as she attempted to touch my cousin's short platinum colored hair. We always joked and told him that he looks like Sisqo from Dru Hill, but he always said that he looked better. He really does remind me of the singer except he's not as short, and he can't sing for shit. A few other people said it too so it must be true.

"Oh no honey, please don't touch the do," he said seriously.

Co-Co doesn't play about his hair, so he moved away before her hand connected with his head. Brooklyn offered them some food, and they made themselves right at home. They ended up staying over there for a while as well. We played cards and chilled up until a little after midnight. This day just like any day with my family proved to be one that I would never forget thanks to Co-Co.

BROOKLYN

Six weeks and four days after I gave birth to Dominique, Dominic and I got married on the beach in Key West, Florida. When he came to me with the idea, I was skeptical at first. He wanted to do everything by himself and that made me nervous. As soon as I stepped on the beach and saw the layout I was in awe. I don't know who he got to help him, but everything was perfect. The view was breathtaking. Dominic and I stood in a heart that was made of roses and recited our vows in front of all of our family and friends. The colors were coral, and cream, and everyone was dressed to match the decorations. There were about one hundred chairs decorated and lined up in the sand behind us. I cried the entire time when my dad walked me down the makeshift aisle to meet Dominic underneath the gazebo. Never in a million years would I have thought that we would be here today. When he married Kennedi I just knew that it was over between us for good, but fate has a way of making the impossible happen.

Once the ceremony was over, we retired to the wraparound deck where the reception was being held. I didn't want to leave my babies to go on a honeymoon, so Dominic rented the entire villa on the beach for us to stay in for a week. It was big enough for all of us to have our own rooms with lots of space left. They had lots of activities for us to enjoy, and we had babysitters for whenever we wanted to do something. As much as my mama didn't want us to be together, even she was happy and smiling. All of our parents were staying there as well as our siblings. Since they planned to stay for the entire week, Bryce had somebody else running his shop until they returned.

I was also happy to see Dominic smiling and happy again. He had a huge smile on his face for the entire wedding. Kennedi had been stressing him out for the past few weeks. He gave Mrs. Liz his credit card to take her shopping for their daughter, but that didn't go too well. That crazy heifer wanted a custom made crib in the shape of a carriage that cost almost four thousand dollars. When he told her that he wasn't paying for it, she threw a tantrum and said that she didn't want anything if she couldn't have what she wanted. She said her baby wasn't wearing or sleeping in anything cheap. After two days of shopping, the only thing they ended up getting for the baby was some pampers, wipes, and a few onesies for her to sleep in. Mrs. Liz was ready to kill her. She said Kennedi bitched and complained the entire time they shopped. She gave Dominic his credit card back and gave up. I told Dominic that we would go out and buy everything that the baby needed when we got back home. If she refused it, then that would be on her.

"Damn Brook, it's almost three o'clock and y'all are just now waking up," Co-Co complained when Dominic and I met them on the beach the following day. "I hope your fertile ass is on some birth control."

"Um, we did get married yesterday just in case you forgot. And we had to make sure our kids were straight before we left," I replied. I ignored his comment about birth control because I'm probably overdosing I'm on so much medicine. I love my babies, but I'm not ready to have anymore anytime soon. Even though Dominic and I are married now, I want to finish school and focus on my career before even thinking about having more kids. Dominic's sex drive is through the roof so I have to protect myself or we'll have a house full of babies.

When I was younger my mother and I never really talked about birth control. She always told me to tell her if I ever felt like I was ready to have sex and we would take it from there. Of course, that never happened. I would have never felt comfortable enough to tell her something like that. It was those times that I often wished for a sister. All my brothers ever told me was don't do it. They drilled that in my head for so long until I almost didn't do it. They had me so scared of everything that I was almost anti-social at one time. If anybody even expressed interest in me, they scared them off before it went anywhere.

"Well, let's get this show on the road. Dwight is only here for two more days, and I want us to have some fun before he leaves," Co-Co said shaking me from my thoughts. Dwight works as a cameraman for one of the local news stations. His hours are crazy, and he barely gets time off. He had to practically beg one of his colleagues to fill in for him just to be with us for a few days.

"I'm ready," Taylor said walking away.

"You might as well bring your hot as right back here," Bryce said as he grabbed her hand. "You're staying with me since you wanted to wear that small ass bathing suit."

Taylor and Tiana were so tiny that they could get away with wearing anything. I have to be careful because my ass is too big for certain clothes. Having two babies back to back only made it bigger. We all have on two piece bathing suits, but I'm wearing the boy shorts instead of the underwear bottoms. Dominic still doesn't like it, but he let it go because I'm with him. Candace is wearing a wrap over her bathing suit, and that kept David's mouth closed too.

"Let's get on the jet skis," David yelled excitedly.

"I'm not getting on them things," I replied nervously. I looked out at all the people who were on them, and they're going too fast for me. A few people fell off, but the skis kept right on rolling.

"C'mon baby, you can get on with me," Dominic said as he pulled me along. We all followed David's lead as he walked us over to the rental booth. We have five more days of vacationing left. I just hope we're all still in one piece to be able to enjoy it.

KENNEDI

I've been holed up in my house all day crying my heart out. I've cried so much until I didn't think there were anymore more tears left. That was until I looked at Dominic and Brooklyn's wedding pictures again. I can't believe he really married that bitch. He refused to buy what I wanted for our daughter, but he gave her a lavish wedding on the beach. They're still in Key West living it up without a care in the world. I guess Tiffany got tired of me asking her what was going on with them because she gave me her password for me to look whenever I wanted to. I'm already in a foul mood and seeing that only made it worse. I was finally back at home relaxing after being gone all day yesterday. I'd drove for almost four hours to visit my mother in the federal facility where she's being held in another part of Louisiana. I'm due to give birth in less than three weeks, so my doctor advised me not to go. Tiffany was supposed to drive me, but she canceled at the last minute. I didn't have anyone else to take me, so I drove myself there. I just had to see my mother before having my baby. I don't know when I'll be able to see her again.

She tried to keep a smile on her face, but I saw the worry in her eyes. Things aren't looking too good for her, and she'll probably have to do federal time. We couldn't even hire a lawyer because all of her accounts had been frozen. She keeps telling me that everything will be alright, but I know that's a lie. The Feds don't come for you unless they have solid proof. She's guilty of everything they accused her of, but she'll never admit it. Now I understood why she was always so afraid to get the police involved in anything.

I cried almost the entire ride back home. Just seeing her in those prison clothes was enough to drive me crazy. Then, if that wasn't bad enough, I had to come home and get hit with the pictures of Dominic marrying his side bitch.

"Yes," I snapped into the receiver of my phone when I saw Tiffany calling. I was so pissed with her for so many reasons. Ever since she moved in with Kyle, she's been putting me on the back burner. Not only did she cancel on me yesterday, but she was supposed to be here to get me earlier this morning. She promised that we were going to spend the day together just so I could get out of the house, but she never showed up.

"I'm outside, come open the door.I have food so you better hurry up," she said laughing.

I wasn't in a laughing mood, but the thought of food had me rushing down the stairs. I unlocked the door and swung it open, ready to tell her off for standing me up. My words were lodged in my throat as anger took over my body when I saw Kyle standing there with her.

"What is he doing here?" I asked with a frown on my face.

"I'm here with my woman, that's why I'm here," he replied with an attitude.

"Are you going to let us in or not?" Tiffany asked me. I stepped to the side and allowed them to come in. Kyle walked in and immediately started looking around while Tiffany took the food to the kitchen.

"You can have a seat," I said when he started touching some of the paintings on my wall. His ghetto ass was acting like he'd never saw art before. He gives me the creeps, and I don't know why my cousin brought him here. He ignored my invitation for him to sit and continued looking around at everything. I rushed into the kitchen with Tiffany to give her a piece of my mind.

"You can go sit down. I'll bring your plate to you," she said when I walked in.

"Why the hell did you bring that loser here? He's in there looking like he's checking out my house so he can come back and rob me," I snapped.

"You can't be serious right now," she said frowning at me.

"I'm very serious. I don't trust his broke ass and I damn sure don't want him in my house," I whispered angrily.

"Bitch, I'm far from broke and I don't want to be in your house either. I only came because my girl begged me to come," Kyle said from behind me. I jumped when I heard his voice because I didn't know that he was standing there.

"Kyle chill, we'll leave in a little while," Tiffany said trying to defuse the situation.

"Nah, I'm ready to leave right now. I see why Dominic divorced her stuck up ass and married Brooklyn," I'm sure Tiffany is the one who told him, but he didn't have to throw it in my face.

"Fuck you!" I snapped angrily.

"From what I heard you can't even do that right," he laughed.

"Kyle stop," Tiffany begged.

"Tiffany, if you're not out of here in five minutes I'm leaving without you," he said as he walked out and slammed my front door.

"Did you really need to say all of that Kennedi?"

"I don't know what the hell you see in him. You should have left him alone after he let that bitch Nadia beat your ass," I yelled.

"He didn't let her do anything. He can't control what his ex does. You just need to stop looking down on everybody. That's why you're single right now," she replied hurting my feelings further.

"I'd rather be single than be a broke nigga's punching bag," I replied.

She couldn't respond to that because she knew that I had her right. I lost count of how many times she showed up to my house with a busted lip or bruises on her face. She always makes excuses as to why Kyle hits her, but it's all bullshit to me. In my opinion, he's a coward who can't keep his hands to himself.

"I only came here to give you some money for my God-daughter. You can have the food. I'm not even hungry anymore," she said as she handed me a wad of money. I looked at all the hundreds that she'd just stuffed into my hand, and my jaw hit the floor.

"Where did you get all of this money from Tiffany?"

"Don't worry about where it came from. I know you need it to get some things for the baby. I'll call you tomorrow," she said as she walked out.

I locked my door and sat down on the sofa, staring at the two thousand dollars that Tiffany had just given me. She and I needed to have a talk very soon. Both of us are unemployed, so I want to know where she got this kind of money from. Looking at Kyle, I'm sure it came illegally. I just pray that whatever he's doing doesn't affect my cousin in any way.

BRYCE

After being in Key West for a whole week for Baby and Dominic's wedding, we were all on our way back home. Dominic rented three vans for us and his immediate family to get to and from the airport. The rest of our family left the day after the wedding, so it was only a few of us left. Damion, one of my tattoo artists, has been running things for me in my absence. He called me every day to let me know that everything was running smoothly. The barber and beauty shop was closed for the week since all of us were gone. Damion blocked off the front of the shop and had all of the clients who wanted tattoos to come in through the side entrance. He was the first artist to work for me when I opened my shop years ago, and I trust him to the fullest.

When we got back to the airport in New Orleans, it was a little after nine that night, but we were all worn out. I was ready to grab Taylor and my girls and go home. We all boarded the airport shuttle buses that were there to take us to our cars. I didn't want to park my car at the airport lot for an entire week, but I'm happy that Taylor convinced me to do it. That way I didn't have to wait for anybody else to take us home. Both of my daughters were sleeping so I had to pick them up and put them in the car. As soon as I finished putting in the last of our suitcases my phone rang displaying Damion's number.

"I'm just now getting in town D. Let me call you back tomorrow after I get me some rest," I said when I answered the phone.

"Aye Bryce, I need you to get to the shop like right now," he yelled above all the noise in the background.

"Why, what's wrong?"

"Man, the whole damn shop is on fire," he said knocking all of the wind out of me.

"What!" I yelled causing everybody to stop and stare at me. "Damn, I'm on my way!"

"What's wrong baby?" Taylor asked me.

"Damion said that the whole shop is on fire," I said repeating what I was just told.

"Oh Lord no! My tropical fish were in that shop," Co-Co said right before he collapsed to the ground. His ass is just too extra, and I don't have time for it right now.

"Co-Co get your ass up. Fuck those ugly ass fish," Candace snapped. "Bryce's shop is on fire and you're worried about fish."

"I paid a lot of money for my fish, but it's not just about that. What about all of our supplies and stuff? And let's not forget that we're out of a job. I just can't take this right now," he said as he stood to his feet.

"Everybody just calm down," my pops yelled. "Y'all put the kids in my truck and go see what's going on. Call me if you need me Bryce."

Dominic put him and Baby's kids in the car while I laid my daughters on the third-row seat of my daddy's truck. All of us had our own cars except for Candace and Co-Co. They rode with David as we all left the lot and headed to my shop. I started smelling smoke as soon we were around the corner from my building. When we got on the street, it was impossible to drive in front. We parked on the corner and walked the rest of the way. I couldn't believe what I saw when I walked up. My entire building was engulfed in flames. The firemen were working hard to put it out, but it wasn't an easy job. I walked through the crowd until I found Damion.

"Did they say what happened?" I asked when I spotted him near a group of people.

"No, but you can talk to the fire chief. I told him that you were on your way," he responded.

I went over to the man that he pointed out. He led me away from the crowd and asked me some questions. They wouldn't know what happened until they did an investigation, but I had a feeling that it was done intentionally. After talking to him and getting his card, I went back to join my family. A crowd of people was standing around looking, and I heard Co-Co's mouth before I even got to them.

"We lost everything. Y'all might as well take me to the hospital right now. I feel an asthma attack coming on," he cried.

He was acting a pure fool just like always. Candace looked like she's ready to knock fire from his ass, and I didn't blame her. I shook my head in embarrassment at the way he was behaving in front of all these strangers. He was on the ground screaming and crying about his fish and being out of a job. He cut up so bad that one of the firemen came over and tried to give him some oxygen. A representative from Red Cross came over to speak with us, and even she ended up consoling him. She also offered to assist us with getting our supplies back whenever we're ready to open up another shop. My tattoo artists and I always take our supplies home with us every day, so we're good on that. Unfortunately, Taylor and everybody else will have to purchase everything all over again. The fire seemed to have started in the front of the shop, and they lost all of their supplies.

"Nigga, you don't even have asthma. Get your stupid ass up off of that ground before I knock you out," Jaden threatened Co-Co.

"I wish you would put your hands on me. Don't get it twisted Jaden. You already know how I get down," he yelled. His eyes were dry, and he was back up on his feet in no time after that. That's just how fast he switched things up.

"Look at your fake ass. You don't even have any tears," Jaden fussed. He and Co-Co went back and forth until Candace made them shut up.

I ignored everybody and watched as the firemen battled the blaze that was once my shop.

****

Three days later, Taylor and I met with the fire chief to discuss what happened. He informed us that it was indeed arson, and the building was set on fire with an accelerant. They even had surveillance videos from two nearby offices, but none of that helped. All we were able to see was three figures dressed in black hoodies throwing something through the front and side windows. The camera quality wasn't the best so I couldn't even make out who it was. After getting nowhere with the fire chief, we went to meet with the insurance agent. I filled out the necessary paperwork and gave him the

231

report that the fire chief had given to me. My shop and everything in it was fully insured. I also received some good news earlier this morning. James, whose shop Taylor once worked in, offered to let us use his old shop free of charge. He'd recently moved to a bigger place, and the old one was vacant. It's not as big as my shop was, but it would get the job done until I got my spot up and running again. I offered to pay him whatever he wanted, but he refused anything that I offered. I know it's because he feels indebted to me. I paid for a lawyer for him a few years ago when he got himself into a bit of trouble. He's been trying to find a way to repay me ever since. He didn't even charge Taylor booth rental when she worked in his shop.

Once all of the business was handled, we got the keys from James and prepared to go clean up his old spot. David, my brothers, and my cousins came over and gave us a hand. When we finished, it looked like a brand new shop. They still had all of the chairs in the waiting area as well as the stylist chairs. Since I have a business card, I decided to foot the bill to get some new dryers and supplies for everybody. I would get it back once the insurance money came in. I don't know who set my shop on fire, but they did me a huge favor. The insurance money is going to be three times what my shop was worth. There's an empty lot next to my shop that I've always wanted to purchase. Thanks to the unknown hater, I now have the money to get it. I plan to rebuild from the ground up and this time it'll be bigger and better than it was before.

NADIA

"Mama, I told you that I'm going to think about it. I can't just up and move anyway. I'm still going to court," I yelled into my speakerphone.

I've been on the phone arguing with her for the last thirty minutes. She's been stressing me out about moving to Virginia, but I'm just not ready. I've been to visit more times than I can count, but I don't know about moving there. Virginia is okay, but it's just something about New Orleans that I can't explain. Even the food here is worlds apart from anywhere else. I can't walk into a corner store and get boiled seafood in Virginia like I can do here. They might sell it, but I can guarantee that it won't be the same.

"I don't know who the hell you think you're yelling at. It's not like you go to court every day. You can fly back when you have a court date."

"I already told you that I can't take care of your house and mine. This is my last time sending your ass money. Either you come live here or get a damn job. I'm sick of this shit," she fussed right before she hung up on me.

I hate having to call her for money. I've already used up most of my savings on bills. I ended up having to get a public defender to help me fight my charges because I can't afford a real attorney. He's fresh out of law school, so he's trying to prove himself to his colleagues. He's been working hard to ensure that I only walk away with probation. I've already had two court dates, but they keep pushing it back.

Kevin said that he was going to help me, but he's been acting kind of distant lately. I've barely seen him since the altercation with Dominic. He came over a few times, but once he got what he wanted he was out the door. A few times he ran off right after I gave him oral sex. He said he knew that I didn't have anything to do with it, but his actions were showing otherwise. Even now, I've been calling and texting him for over an hour, and he still hasn't responded or answered his phone. I'm pissed, but there isn't much I can do about it.

Even Shannon has been acting shady lately. She's so far up Tiffany's ass that she barely answers when I call her. She always tells me that she'll call me back, but she never does.

It's times like these that I really miss my friendship with Candace. She always made time for me no matter what. Just thinking about her made me want to see what she has been up to. I sat down on my sofa and pulled up my Facebook page. Candace had unfriended me when we had the fight, but David didn't. He's never on here, but I'm still able to keep up because Candace tags him in all of her posts. That's how I was able to see Brooklyn and Dominic's daughter. After scrolling through my timeline, I typed in David's name. I almost died from shock when I saw Brooklyn and Dominic's picture with the caption, "Mr. & Mrs. Roberts," right above it. I scrolled through about twenty more pictures of them on the beach with their family and friends or with their kids. I was in shock by the fact that they're actually married.

In the beginning, I thought that maybe it was just the sex between them. Even after she had his son I didn't think, it was that serious. Obviously, I was dead wrong, and the pictures in front of me proved it.

When I looked on further and saw their house, I was livid. It's beautiful inside and out. I couldn't take it, and I didn't want to see anymore after that. I logged off and resisted the urge to toss my phone across the room. How that dumb naïve bitch managed to get Dominic to do all of that for her is beyond my comprehension. I felt myself getting depressed, and I didn't know how to stop it. I picked up my phone to call Kevin, but it started ringing right when I did.

"Well damn, it took you long enough to call me back. I guess your new friend don't want to be bothered with you no more," I snapped when I answered the phone for Shannon.

"Let me find out you're jealous," she laughed. "What are you doing?"

"Nothing, I'm bored out of my mind," I replied honestly.

"Come get me and let's go somewhere," she suggested.

"Where's Kevin?"

"He's probably with one of his bitches. I haven't seen him all day," she replied.

I got heated hearing that. I guess that's why his dog ass didn't answer the phone when I called. He's not my man so I shouldn't be mad, but I am.

"Where do you want to go?" I asked her.

"Somewhere quiet so we can talk and drink," she replied. That's music to my ears because I'm definitely in need of a drink.

"Okay, let me put on some clothes and I'm on my way."

"Wait, I didn't even tell you where I am," she yelled.

"You're at home right?"

"Yeah, but we don't live in the same place anymore."

"Damn, y'all moved again?"

"Yep, but I'll meet you somewhere. I don't want any drama with Kyle. You can pick me up in front of the Walmart on Bullard."

"I'll be there in a few minutes," I said before hanging up. Since I'd just taken my shower, I found a pair of leggings with a matching shirt to put on. After putting on my tennis shoes, I touched up my straight hair with the flat iron and made my way out the door. The Walmart where Shannon wanted to meet was about fifteen minutes away from my house. She claimed they moved, but I think that's a lie. Tiffany is probably there, and she doesn't want to cause a scene. She doesn't have to worry about that though. I'm no longer interested in Kyle. It's her man that I want.

As soon as I pulled up to the store I saw Shannon standing out front on her phone. I turned my head and laughed when I saw the leggings that she wore. Shannon has the worst shape that I've ever seen in my life. I can't believe she even feels comfortable enough to wear tights. Then she had on a short shirt calling attention to her flat backside.

I'm still trying to figure out what the hell Kevin saw in her.

"Hey girl," I said when she hopped into my car.

"Hey," she said dryly like she didn't feel like being bothered.

"What's wrong with you?"

"Nothing, I just have a lot on my mind," she answered. She sounded happier when I talked to her a few minutes ago. She probably got into it with Kevin. That always puts her in a bad mood.

"So where are we going?" I asked her.

"Get on the interstate, I'll direct you," she answered.

"Okay, let me get some gas first." I drove a few blocks down and pulled up to the gas station. When I got out to pump, I saw Shannon texting on her phone. A few seconds later I heard her on the phone arguing with somebody who I'm sure was Kevin. I can't make out what she was saying, but she was mad about something.

"Are you alright girl?" I asked when I got back in the car.

"Yeah, I'm fine."

"Don't let Kevin's dog ass stress you out."

She looked at me like I was crazy, but she didn't reply. The rest of the ride was quiet with the exception of her giving me directions on where to go. When we got to the drawbridge downtown, I had a feeling that I knew right where she was taking me. We're headed to the same bar that Kevin and I went to not long ago. It's the same place where we saw Dominic and Brooklyn's brothers. There isn't any other place around here that we could be going to. I'm curious as to how she knows about the place, so I try to pick her brain.

"Where are you trying to go? It looks deserted around here," I said.

"It's a bar that Kevin took me to. It's quiet, and not many people go there," she replied.

I wanted to scream when she said that. I showed that bastard my little getaway spot and he had the nerve to bring Shannon's trifling ass there. I'm surprised that he even went back after the beat down that Dominic gave him. I couldn't wait to see his ass just to tell him off. Shannon was talking, but I was so mad that I tuned her out. I'm too busy focusing on how I want to handle her man whenever I see him.

"Nadia," Shannon called out shaking me from my thoughts. We were in front of the building, but I'm in another world.

"I'm sorry friend. What were you saying?"

"Friend?" She questioned with raised brows.

"Yes, I've always called you friend. So that's a problem now?" I asked.

"It wasn't before, but it is now. Especially since you're sleeping with your so called friend's man," she snapped.

"What the hell are you talking about?" I asked nervously. I tried to be extra careful when dealing with Kevin, so I wondered how she knew. It really doesn't matter because I'll never confess to anything no matter what she says.

"I'm talking about you sitting on the phone with me while I cried to you about my man. You knew where he was the whole time because he was in your bed. Please don't play yourself and lie to me. I already know everything that happened including you bringing him here. You set him up for Dominic and Brooklyn's brothers to get at him," she said.

"I don't know what Kevin has been telling you, but that's a lie. I didn't have anything to do with him getting beat up, and I've never slept with him," I lied.

"So whose voice is this? And whose lips are these wrapped around my man's dick?" She asked angrily.

Silent tears crept down my cheeks when she pulled out Kevin's phone and played a video. I remembered that day clearly. It was the same day that Dominic beat Kevin up. I thought he was on his phone playing a game, but he was recording me the whole time. He recorded when I talked on the phone with her and when I talked about her to him. If that wasn't embarrassing enough, he even recorded me giving him oral sex. I felt like a damn fool, and I'm sure I looked like one too. The way I've been behaving for the past year is not like me at all. I let a man take me off of my square, and my life has gone downhill ever since. Now I know why Shannon called me out of the blue all of the sudden. The only thing I could do at that point was apologize.

"Shannon, I'm so sorry. I swear I never meant for any of this to happen. I got into a fight with Kyle and Tiffany, and Kevin were there. He kissed me first, but I shouldn't have let it go as far as it did. It's over, and it'll never happen again," I cried.

"If that's true then why are you still calling and texting him? Why are you begging him to come see you? At one time, I considered you my only friend. I told you everything about my past and my family. You knew all about me being hurt in the past, but you turned around and did the same thing. No apology you give me will ever be good enough for how you betrayed me. I should have known that you couldn't be trusted when you started sleeping with Kyle behind your best friend's back. But unlike her, I'm not letting you have what's mine," she said as she punched me in my face.

It wasn't just a regular punch. She had something in her hand because it felt like a bone or something in my face cracked. She tried to hit me again, but I slapped her hand away, and a silver padlock fell out of it. That's when I realized that Kyle and Kevin were right. This bitch is really crazy. When she reached down to pick it up, I started swinging on her like I was just as crazy as she was. She shook the licks off and still managed to pick up her lock and hit me again. My nose snapped, and blood started pouring from it like a hose. That still didn't stop her because she kept swinging. I turned my head and got most of the licks to the back of my head. I was so scared, but I refused to give up. I tried to open my car door to get out, but she grabbed me back by my hair. This time when I swung I hit her in her right eye. The lock fell from her hand again, but she didn't try to pick it up this time. This crazy bitch pulled a blade from her bra and started swinging it at me. I raised my arm to block her from cutting my face and ended up getting my arm sliced open.

"Ahhh," I screamed as the pain shot throughout my entire body. It's like my entire life flashed before my eyes. I know if I don't do something fast I probably won't make it out of this alive. Kyle, Kevin or any other man was worth me losing my life. Shannon had a crazed look in her eyes that I had never seen before. I wasn't about to let her cut me again, so I shifted my entire body to the side and lifted my leg up to kick her. Thankfully the kick was hard enough to shake her and allow me to open my door. The interior of my car was full of blood, but that was the least of my worries right then. I needed to make it out of this situation alive and get some help before I lost too much blood. There are only two other cars in the parking lot, and I prayed that someone was in the bar that could help me. I felt the swelling in my left eye, and I could barely see out of it. As soon as I got out of the car I saw Shannon rushing to get out as well. I tried looking on the ground for something that I could use to defend myself. She wasn't fighting fair, and neither would I. I couldn't even make it to the door of the bar before she ran up on me again.

"Don't get scared now bitch. You weren't scared when you had my man's dick halfway down your throat," Shannon yelled.

When she grabbed my hair again, it was like something in me clicked. I forgot about all the pain that I was in, and I started swinging on her like my life depended on it. I didn't care about the deep cut to my arm or the swelling in my eye. She needed to know that she bleeds just like the next bitch. It didn't take long before I got the best of her and had her on the ground. I soon found out that without her weapons to help her she really couldn't fight. I grabbed a handful of her braids and started banging her head into the concrete the same way that Candace had done me a few months ago. My arm was killing me, but I refused to let up on her. I wanted to knock her out and use that as an opportunity to run. Unfortunately, that never happened.

A few minutes into the fight, my hair was pulled from the back as I was forcefully slammed to the ground. The impact was so hard that I actually saw stars. My entire body was on fire, and I couldn't move even if I wanted to.

"Get up Shannon," I heard a male voice say.

I looked on in horror as Kevin helped his girlfriend up from the ground. That bastard was in on it the whole time. He must have been sitting close by watching her attack me. He never even made an attempt to intervene until Shannon started losing the fight. As soon as she was up on her feet she rushed over and started her attack again. She punched me in my face and pulled my hair while Kevin just stood there and watched. I closed my eyes and said a silent prayer begging God to either let me pass out or die. The pain was just that unbearable.

"That's enough Shannon somebody's coming," Kevin whispered. I saw headlights headed in our direction, and I was grateful to whoever it was for possibly saving my life.

"Being set up don't feel too good, huh?"
Shannon had said before they ran off.

I couldn't move or respond to anything that she
said. I heard the screeching of tires a few minutes
before two women discovered my beaten and
bloodied body on the sidewalk near my car.

****

I woke up in the hospital to find my mother's
tearstained face at my bedside. Her eyes were red
and swollen, and I knew that she had been crying.
She was on the phone, so she didn't even know that
I was up.

"Ma," I called out weakly to get her attention.
She immediately ended her call and rushed over to
me.

"Thank God you're up. How are you feeling
baby?" She asked as she grabbed my hand.

"My whole body is hurting, and my mouth is
dry," I complained.

"You had to get thirty stitches in your arm,
Nadia. Not to mention the black eye, broken nose,
and bruises all over your body. The police came to
talk to you, but the medicine they have you on has
kept you sleeping so much. What happened baby?"
She asked in a concerned tone.

I thought back to everything that led up to me
being here and tears immediately came to my eyes.
I couldn't believe what Shannon had done to me.
It's even harder for me to believe that Kevin was
right there with her. He was right when he said that
she would never leave him. She's his fool, and he
knows it. But for him to even think that I set him up
has me madder than anything else. My mama sat

there staring at me waiting for me to answer her question.

Before I could say anything, the door opened, and a nurse walked in with the machine to check my vitals. I had a bandage on my arm, so she had to help me sit up. My mother excused herself to the hallway to let her do what she needed to do. Another lady walked in soon after to change the bedding on my hospital bed and clean my room. She looked familiar to me, and I tried hard to place her face. I waited until the nurse was done before I started talking to her.

"You look familiar, but I can't think of where I've seen you before," I said looking up at her. My lip was swollen, so I hope she understood what I was trying to say.

"I don't know. I live uptown with my boyfriend. Maybe you've seen me around that way before," she answered.

"My friend does hair uptown at So Xclusive, but I don't really know too many other people around that way."

"Yeah, that's Bryce's shop. He's cool with my boyfriend, Vamp. Co-Co does my hair," she said smiling.

That's where I know her from. She was in the shop a few times when I was there. That's not what piqued my interest though. The name Vamp rang a bell loud and clear. According to Candace and numerous other people, Vamp has been looking high and low for Kevin and Kyle. They supposedly robbed him and a few other people, and he wants them in the worse way.

"Where is your boyfriend at now?" I asked. She looked at me sideways, and I had to quickly explain myself. "Oh, it's nothing like that. I have some info that he might be interested in."

"What kind of info?" She asked with her hand on her hip. I could tell that she was ready to check me, but she didn't have a reason to.

"I really don't want to tell his business like that," I replied.

"Baby, there's nothing you can say that I'm not aware of. I know everything about his business," she clarified.

"Well, I heard that he's been looking for Kyle and Kevin."

"Yeah, they robbed him and his brother," she responded. I guess she really does know everything.

"Well, I know where they live," I replied.

I still wasn't buying that story that Shannon gave me about them moving. That was probably her way of throwing me off because she knew that she was going to attack me. Even if they did move, they aren't that hard to find. I don't want the police to get involved. Jail is too good for them. If everything goes like I hope it does, Shannon will get hers too.

"Okay, but what's in it for you? Why would you give them up to somebody that you barely know?" She asked skeptically.

"Aside from Kyle crossing me and stealing my money, Kevin is the reason why I'm in here. He and his girlfriend jumped me," I said trying to fight back tears.

She looked at me with pity in her eyes, but I could tell that she was still unsure. After a few minutes, she pulled out her phone and dialed a number. She talked to the person on the phone in code, but I knew that it had to be Vamp. She talked for a little while longer before handing me her phone.

"He already knows who you're talking about so don't say names," she instructed. I took the phone from her and did something that I never thought I'd do. I snitched on Kevin and Kyle, telling Vamp everything that I knew. He thanked me for the info, but it was my pleasure. I couldn't wait until they were met with the same fate that Kevin and Shannon tried to deliver to me.

CANDACE

"Girl my nerves are bad as hell," I complained to Brooklyn as Co-Co and I rode around with her and her kids. Dominic is going crazy about her changing her last name on all of her documents, so we went with her to handle her business. She was able to use their temporary marriage license to get everything done. We'd just left from meeting Dominic at the bank. He added Brooklyn's name to the bank account and the house that they'd just purchased. He wasn't divorced when they first got it, so he waited until it was finalized. We're now on our way to Mrs. Liz's house for lunch, and I'm a nervous wreck.

"I don't know what you're scared of. You've been around Mrs. Liz a million times," Brooklyn said.

"I know, but that was before I was in a relationship with her son," I replied. Mrs. Liz was so happy when she found out that David and I were in a relationship. She said she thought that she would be dead and gone before he ever settled down. She invited us to lunch and begged us to bring my brother along. She loves Co-Co's outspoken attitude. She also loves the fact that he keeps her laughing.

"Can your mother-in-law even cook Brooklyn? I don't want to throw good food away, but I will if it's nasty," Co-Co said.

"Yes, she cooks very well. And don't you go in there acting a fool Co-Co," Brooklyn warned.

"Oh no ma'am, you can take me back home if there's going to be rules. I have to be myself no matter where I am. You need to be telling that to baby Chucky back here with his bad ass," Co-Co replied.

"Don't talk about my baby. He is not bad, he's just active."

"Girl, you can miss me with that active shit. Dennis the menace looks like a saint compared to him," Co-Co said making me laugh.

As soon as we pulled up in the driveway, David and Dominic's brother and sister ran out of the house to grab the kids. I looked down at my ringing phone and declined another call from an unknown number. I've been receiving them for two days, but I never answer. I would have thought that the caller would have given up, but they never did.

"Hey y'all," Nyla said as she grabbed Dominque's car seat. Ivan took DJ, and we all went into the house together. Brooklyn was very familiar with Dominic's family, so she went off to the kitchen while I nervously took a seat on the sofa. Co-Co's ignorant ass grabbed the remote and started flipping through channels on the TV.

"Boy, put these people stuff down. How you come in somebody's house and just start touching shit?" I asked him.

"Girl please, I'm not about to sit in here and look stupid. This is your mother-in-law's house. You need to make yourself comfortable too. You see Brooklyn walking through this bitch like she owns it," he said.

"Brooklyn is Dominic's wife so she can do that."

"Where is this shyness coming from all of a sudden? You've never been scared of anything before in your life so don't start now. Just be you and fuck whoever doesn't like it," my brother said.

I smiled and nodded my head in agreement. Co-Co is very blunt, but he always knows what to say to make me feel better. I don't have a problem with being myself, but all of this is new to me. I've never been in a real relationship, so I've never had to meet a man's parents. Mrs. Liz is cool, so I know that we'll get along just fine.

"Why are y'all sitting in here looking all uncomfortable? I'm not a stranger, so please don't act like it," Mrs. Liz said when she walked into the living room.

"Candace is scared that's why," Brooklyn said with a mouthful of food. I wanted to curse her out, but I held my tongue.

"I know she better not be scared. I've seen you in action a million times, and I know you're not shy," Mrs. Liz said looking at me.

"I'm good, but this is a first for me. I've never been in the company of a man's parents before," I admitted.

"This is a first for me too. David has never had a girlfriend before. I've never allowed him to bring any of his hoes to my house even though he probably wouldn't have anyway. He really wants us to get to know each other, and I'm all for that. I can tell that you're just what he needs. You don't take any shit from him just like me. Maybe y'all can give me some more grandbabies. Don't let

Brooklyn and Dominic beat y'all. They're already up on y'all by two," she said laughing.

"I don't know about all of that. We're not ready for babies yet," I replied.

"They might not be ready, but they have a lot of fun trying. I hear them all the time," Co-Co said.

"Alright, don't be putting everybody in my business," I said feeling slightly embarrassed.

"Whatever," he said brushing me off. "I don't mean to be rude Mrs. Liz, but is the food done? That's really the only reason why I came."

"Co-Co," I yelled looking at my brother like he was crazy. His ass is just too embarrassing.

"What?" He asked feigning ignorance.

"Leave him alone. I love his honesty. And yes Co-Co, the food is done. You can help yourself," Mrs. Liz said with a smile. She didn't have to tell him twice. He damn near ran to the kitchen with Brooklyn hot on his trail.

"Come on and get you something to eat Candace. And you are welcomed to come here anytime you want to. Don't feel like you have to be with Brooklyn to come and visit," Mrs. Liz said as she stood up from the sofa.

"Ok, thanks," I said as I followed behind her. Before I got to the kitchen, my phone rang again displaying Ms. Cheryl's number. I started not to answer, but curiosity got the best of me. I hope she doesn't ask me about Nadia because I can't tell her anything. I not only unfriended her on Facebook, I unfriended her from my life.

"Hey Ms. Cheryl," I said when I answered the phone.

"Hey Candace, Nadia said she's been trying to call you, but you didn't answer. She said it was maybe because she's calling from the hospital's phone, and you don't recognize the number."

"Yeah, I keep seeing an unfamiliar number calling my phone. Who's in the hospital?" I asked.

"She is, somebody attacked her, but she doesn't know who. She's got a broken nose and a black eye, not to mention the cut that required thirty stitches. She asked me to call you. She wants to see you," she said.

Nadia and I are no longer friends, but my heart goes out to her. I can almost guarantee that all of this has something to do with Kyle or Kevin's trifling asses. It's bad enough that she dealt with Kyle, but she turned around and started dealing with his brother too. I'm sure Ms. Cheryl doesn't know about us falling out, and I'm not going to tell her. I'll leave that up to her daughter.

"I'm at my mother-in-law's house right now, but tell her that I'll come later. Text me the information," I said right before disconnecting the call. I'm not sure why my presence is being requested, but I'm going just to see what she has to say. I joined Ms. Liz and everybody else in the kitchen for a very eventful lunch thanks to my brother.

****

Later on that night I stepped off of the elevator and headed down the hall to Nadia's hospital room. I saw her mother standing in the hall talking on her cell phone. When she saw me coming, she ended her call and held her arms open for me.

"How is she?" I asked as I gave her a hug.

"I know she'll feel better since you're here. I don't know what happened with y'all, but I know it's probably something that she did. And for you to not know that she was even in here lets me know that it's something serious. I'm so tired of trying to figure out what's going on with her. My sisters came down with me to pack up her stuff. I told her that she was going back to Virginia with me even if I have to drag her ass back," Ms. Cheryl said.

I nodded my head in understanding, but I didn't reply. I left her standing in the hall and made my way into Nadia's room. As soon as the door opened our eyes met. I wanted to cry when I saw the shape that she was in. Her face was so swollen that she was barely recognizable. One of her arms was wrapped up and put into a sling, and the other was black and blue with bruises. Her nose looked crooked, and her lips were swollen to twice their normal size.

"What happened to you Nadia?" I asked as I walked closer to her bed. As angry as I was with her before I couldn't resist the urge to hug her. She looked like she's been to the pits of hell and back. She used her one free arm to hug me back as she burst into tears. I pulled away and grabbed some Kleenex from the table and handed them to her.

"I'm so happy that you came to see me Candace. I just wanted to see you one more time before I left to go to Virginia. I can't stay here anymore. I did so much wrong to so many people. It's best if I just leave and start fresh somewhere else. I just had to apologize to you for everything that I've done. You've always been a good friend to me, and you didn't deserve what I did to you. I was jealous, but I know in my heart that you didn't have anything to do with Dominic getting with Brooklyn," she cried.

"I forgive you Nadia, but you really need to get yourself together. Dominic moved on a long time ago, but you never did. I know that you can't help who you love, but you can't make somebody love you back," I said.

"You're right and I know that now. I also know that Dominic is really happy with Brooklyn. I saw it in his eyes the very first time I saw them together. I'm not surprised that he divorced Kennedi to be with her. That's where his heart is."

"Who did this to you Nadia? Your mama said that you didn't know, but I know that's a lie." She looked away because she knew I was right. She's gotten herself into something that she doesn't want her mother to know about.

"I don't want to get the police involved. I just want to put all of this behind me and get out of New Orleans."

"Telling me is not getting the police involved. I won't tell anybody whatever you tell me. I know that Kevin and Kyle had something to do with it. I just need you to confirm my suspicions."

"I'm so stupid Candace," she cried. "I started messing with Kevin and Shannon found out. He thought that I set it up for Dominic to fight him, but I swear I didn't. He sat there and watched while she beat me with a padlock and sliced my arm open."

"What do you mean he watched?" I asked.

"He had to be watching because when I got the best of her he came and pulled me off. He slammed me to the ground so hard that my entire body went numb," she replied.

Listening to her made me happy that things between him and Brooklyn never went any further than two sexual encounters. Her brothers would have killed him if he ever did some shit like that to her.

"His punk ass is wrong for that shit. David should have let Dominic finish him off at the bar."

"I have something else to tell you. It's been weighing on my mind for months, and I have to clear my conscience," she said.

"What?" I asked as I pulled a chair up next to her bed.

"I overheard Kevin telling Kyle that he's the one who caused the accident with Taylor and Brooklyn a while ago. I swear I wanted to tell you, but I didn't want you to know that I was dealing with Kyle. He was saying that he thought it was Bryce at first. He felt bad because the kids were in the car, but he wanted to get back at Brooklyn for breaking things off with him. I even saw the damage to his truck to prove it."

I sat there in stunned silence. We racked our brains for weeks trying to figure out who could have done something like that. Kyle and Kevin crossed our minds, but we couldn't be too sure. Bryce even thought that it could have been Tiffany, but none of us had any proof.

"Wow, so what else have you been keeping from me?" I asked my ex best friend.

"That's all that I know. I promise I would tell you if there was anything else. That's the least I could do considering all the drama that I've caused you," she replied.

"Well, I appreciate all that you've told me and I'm sorry about what happened to you. But honestly, you shouldn't let Kevin and Shannon get away with what they did. I know you don't want to get the police involved, but I think you should. They could have killed you out there, and nobody would have ever known," I told her.

"I guess I never thought about it that way. Maybe I'll fill out a police report when they come back to talk to me in the morning."

"Yeah, I think you really should. Moving to Virginia is the best decision that you've made in a long time. Good luck with everything," I said as I stood to my feet and prepared to exit.

"Candace wait," she said stopping me when I got to the door.

"I know we'll probably never be best friends again, but do you think that I can call you sometimes?" She asked sounding hopeful.

"You can call, but I won't promise that I'll answer," I replied before walking out of her door and out of her life. Nadia and I had been best friends since forever. If something so small as my cousin being with her ex could make her turn on me, then I really don't need her in my life. I said my goodbyes to her mother and took the elevator back down to my car. At least my visit wasn't a total waste of time. She answered a question that we've been trying to get answered for months. I pulled my phone out and called to tell David everything that she had just told me.

KENNEDI

I sat on my living room sofa and enjoyed the strawberry cheesecake that I'd just purchased from the deli near my house. I was fresh out of the shower and enjoying a movie that I just tuned in to on Lifetime. I'm a little over a week away from having my baby, and I can't wait. My doctor told me that it could be any day now, and I'm ready. I decided to go with the Minnie Mouse theme for my baby's room. That's one of the only themes that has everything to go with it. That bitch Brooklyn called herself trying to shop for my daughter, but I wasn't having it. After she had sent Mrs. Liz here with all the bullshit that she'd purchased, I had Tiffany to help me drop it all off at Dominic's office. It's crazy because I went out and purchased some of the same things that I sent back. I just didn't want anything from Brooklyn. She may be Dominic's wife, but I'll be damned if she picks and chooses what our daughter will wear. That happened over a week ago, and I haven't heard anything from them since then. I've tried calling Dominic a few times, but he never answers the phone. I ended up using the money that Tiffany gave me to get what I wanted my baby to have. Tiffany and her dad also got a lot of stuff for her, so I'm satisfied for now. I can't wait until I give birth to my daughter. If Dominic thinks I'm a pain in his ass now, it's going to be ten times worse once I have his daughter. Brooklyn better get ready because I promise to make their lives a living hell. I got up to get me a bottle of water when my doorbell rung. I'm not expecting anyone so I looked out the window to see who it is. I saw Tiffany's car parked next to mine, so I opened the door for her. As soon as I saw her I could tell that something was wrong. She brushed past me without speaking and went straight to the kitchen.

"Well, hello to you too," I said sarcastically.

"I'm really not in the mood for your sarcasm Kennedi," she said with an attitude.

"And why are you wearing sunglasses in the house? The sun is not even shining outside."

I grabbed a bottle of water from the fridge and started to walk away until I heard her crying.

"What's wrong Tiffany? Did that bastard do something to you? I asked while rubbing her back. She didn't reply, but I got my answer when she took off her glasses. Her right eye was black and swollen to the point that it was almost closed.

"Oh my God Tiffany! Why do you keep letting him do this to you? You need to leave his crazy ass alone," I yelled.

"I did leave him, but where am I supposed to go? I gave up my apartment and moved in with him when our office closed," she cried.

"You can't be serious right now. My door has always been opened to you. I live here alone, so you don't have any excuses," I fussed.

"I know that, but you're about to have a new baby. I don't want to impose on you. I just need my eye to heal up, and I'll probably go back to my dad's house for a while," she replied.

"You are not imposing and you know it. I'm in here alone most of the time. I could use the company," I said honestly. Aside from my mother and Tiffany, I really didn't talk to anyone. Scott and I never really talk anymore either. He'll text me from time to time to see how I'm doing, but that's about all. When Dominic and I were together I tried to form a relationship with his sister, but that never worked. She seems to love Brooklyn, but I don't think she cared for me very much. At least I won't feel so lonely if Tiffany comes to live with me.

"So what happened to make him hit you this time?" I asked.

"Kevin and Shannon went to jail two nights ago, and Kyle said that's it's my fault," she replied with her head hanging low. "He was alright until he went to their arraignment hearing this morning and found out about all that they're being charged with."

"How in the hell is any of that your fault?" I yelled.

"It's a long story Kennedi. I really don't feel like talking about it right now," she said trying to get away from the subject.

"Well, that's too bad. You need to tell me everything that's going on. I don't trust Kyle's ass, and I told you that from the start. You've changed so much since you got with him."

"I'm so scared Kennedi. He's been doing all kinds of crazy shit, and he's gotten me involved in some of it. He keeps telling me that if I tell anybody I won't live to see the next day, and I believe him," she cried.

"Stop crying and talk to me. You know that I won't say anything. I don't even talk to anybody besides you."

"Well, for starters, Kevin and Kyle have been going around robbing people. I swear I didn't know what was going on at first. He would always tell me to drive, but I never saw what they did when they got out of the car. I always parked a few streets over until they came back," she confessed.

"Tiffany no, I can't believe that you got yourself hooked up in his mess. When you found out about it, you should have left him alone and moved out," I yelled.

"It wasn't that easy Kennedi. I don't have a job or any savings. I needed the money then, and I still need it now. He's been taking care of me since I've been out of work. How do you think I was able to give you money and help buy things for the baby? I've been looking for another job, but I still haven't had any luck yet," she replied.

"That still doesn't explain the black eye that you're wearing," I retorted.

"Two days ago Kyle asked me to drive while he and Kevin did their thing, but the plans changed at the last minute. Shannon ended up going with Kevin while Kyle hit a lick somewhere else. They hit up two areas in the ninth ward, but they didn't get much from that. Kevin suggested going to the French Quarters, but I was against the idea from the beginning. After Kyle called and chewed me out I finally agreed to go. I told them where I would be when they got done, but after an hour they still hadn't come back. It usually doesn't take that long, so I drove around trying to see if I saw them. That's when I spotted the police cars blocking off the street. When I got out of my car and got a closer look, I saw Kevin and Shannon in the back of one of the cars. Kyle got pissed and said that I left them, but there was nothing that I could do. I'm lucky that I didn't get arrested right along with them," she said as a steady stream of tears cascaded down her face.

Now it's all making sense to me. Tiffany has been having more money now than she had when we were working. I just hate that she got hooked up with Kyle and his mess in order to get it. I hate to see my cousin and only friend in the world go through what she's going through. Ever since Bryce did her wrong, her life had gone downhill.

"I don't care what you say you are not going back to him. You can stay here for as long as you like. Don't worry about the bills because Dominic is going to take care of that. As soon as I have my baby I'm taking his ass straight to court," I promised.

"I have something else to tell you," Tiffany said as she looked down and fidgeted with her hands.

"What is it?" I asked giving her my undivided attention.

"Kevin, Kyle, and I are the ones that burned down Bryce's shop. I know that I was wrong for participating, but he deserved it. He broke my heart, and I haven't been the same since then. Honestly, I don't even feel bad about it," she admitted.

"And you shouldn't," I said agreeing with her. "You gave him everything and he left you with nothing. If it weren't for you, his ass probably wouldn't even have that shop. Fuck Bryce!"

"So you don't think I was wrong for helping them?" She asked me.

"No, I don't and stop beating yourself up over it. He doesn't care about you so why should you care about him," I replied.

"It was actually Kyle's idea, but I couldn't let them do it without me. I only wish that Bryce and Taylor were in there to burn right along with everything else," she said angrily.

"And that bitch Brooklyn too," I chimed in. I've never hated a person so much to wish death on them, but Brooklyn is the exception.

We laid around and talked until after four in the morning. Both of us fell asleep on the sofa since we were too lazy to go upstairs. The next afternoon I got up before Tiffany only because my bladder wouldn't let me sleep any longer. I looked down at Tiffany's ringing phone and hit decline when I saw Kyle trying to call her again. He's been calling her nonstop since last night trying to apologize for hitting her. If I hadn't been there to stop her, she would have answered and been on her way back to him by now. I hate that Tiffany showed him where I lived. I don't want his rundown looking ass coming to my house looking for her. I would have the police here before he could even ring my doorbell.

After doing my normal hygiene routine, I grabbed the phone book to order me and Tiffany something to eat. I'd been craving pizza for a while, and that's exactly what I'm about to order. I was about to wake Tiffany up to ask her what she wanted when a sharp pain hit me in my side. It was so painful that I dropped the phone book and held on to the counter.

"Tiffany!" I yelled out in fear and pain. I didn't want to scare her, but I was scared my damn self. She stirred a little before turning on her side to go back to sleep. I called her name again, but this time louder than before.

"What's wrong?" She asked as she jumped up from the sofa.

"I'm in so much pain. I think I need to go to the hospital," I replied through clenched teeth.

"Ok, you want me to call Dominic?"

"No, just help me get dressed so we can go."

"You're not going to tell him what's going on?" She asked me.

"I don't know Tiffany. I'm in too much pain to think about that right now. Maybe I'll call Mrs. Liz once I get there."

She stopped asking questions long enough to run upstairs and grab me some clothes. After getting dressed, we walked to her car and made our way to the hospital. Tiffany was driving like a mad woman, and she scared me more than the impending birth of my daughter. I held on tight and said a prayer that me and baby girl made it to the hospital in one piece.

DOMINIC

Since Brooklyn has been inside with the kids for two weeks straight, I decided to take her out for a little while. She never complains, but I know it has to be hard dealing with a two-month-old and a two-year-old all day. David and I have been kind of busy too since we signed on to help the construction company. We're not complaining either because the money is flowing in. He wanted to take Candace somewhere too so we decided to do a double date. My mother-in-law agreed to watch the kids for a while to give us some time alone. We went to a movie and headed to dinner soon after.

"What's going on with Kennedi?" David asked. "She should be having the baby soon."

"She should, but I haven't talked to her. She doesn't need to call me until it's time for the baby to come. She's still on that bullshit, and I don't have time for it," I replied. Kennedi has really been doing too much lately, and I'm sick of it. She told my mama what theme she wanted for the baby, and I didn't have a problem getting whatever she needed. My wife had gone out of her way to shop and buy everything that she thought my daughter would need. When she was done, she'd spent well over three thousand dollars buying everything in the Minnie Mouse theme that Kennedi wanted. My mama and daddy packed up their cars and took everything to her house that very same night. I didn't expect her to call and thank me, but I damn sure didn't expect to see everything piled up in front of my office when I got to work the next morning. She sent me a text saying that she knew that I didn't pick out our daughter's stuff, and she didn't want anything from Brooklyn. Since Brooklyn is my wife, that was just like her saying that she didn't want anything from me either.

"I can't believe her stupid ass sent back all the stuff that y'all bought. Especially after we spent our whole day picking everything out," Candace said. She and Co-Co spent their entire day shopping with Brooklyn, and they were pissed as well.

"I don't know what to say. I guess I'll figure out what to buy once the baby gets here," I replied.

"You won't be figuring out shit," Brooklyn snapped. "She had everything that she needed delivered right to her front door. She's the one that wanted to be stupid and send it back. Since that bitch wants to be petty, I'm about to show her how it's done. I returned everything and put that money right back into our account."

"Oh well, the woman of the house has spoken, I guess that's a wrap," I said as I continued to eat my food. I can't even be mad at Brooklyn for how she feels. Kennedi is being a bitch just because she could.

"I know that's right cousin," Candace said smiling at Brook. It still amazes me sometimes when I see how much she's matured over the years. She's so good with our kids, and our house is always spotless. I can't recall one time that I didn't come home to a hot meal. She did all of that while still maintaining her grades in school. She took online classes during the summer, but she's going back on campus in a few weeks. I'm so proud of her, and I make sure I tell her every chance I get. I couldn't ask for a better wife than the one I have. When we first met, I didn't think it would go as far as us being married. My only regret is that I didn't do it sooner.

"Did Nadia leave yet?" David asked Candace.

"I don't know. I haven't talked to her since I left the hospital," she replied.

"She must have thought that she was about to die or something. That heifer was making deathbed confessions like she was on her way out of here," David laughed.

I was pissed when Candace told us about everything that Nadia had said. I was especially pissed when I heard that Kevin was the cause of Taylor and Brooklyn's accident. Bryce and Jaden wanted to go find him, but it was too late for all of that. Kevin and his girlfriend made the front page of the paper when they got arrested a few days ago. They were arrested for a string of robberies in the French Quarters and in the uptown area. According to the newspapers, they aren't getting out anytime soon. The police were even trying to see if they're responsible for more than the ones that they've been charged with. Kyle must be hiding out somewhere because he's nowhere to be found. Jaden and I even went back to the area where we saw him and Tiffany at a while ago, but that was a dead end.

"Going to Virginia was the best thing for her to do. She's too stupid to live by herself. She needs to be with her mama," Candace said.

"Brook, I'm so happy that you married this nigga. He picks the craziest bitches in the world to hook up with. Ain't no telling who he would've brought home next," David said laughing at me.

I'll be the first to admit that I didn't have the best track record with women, but that's all over with now. My marriage to Brooklyn is most definitely until death. I can't see myself being without her. I miss her even when I'm at work, and that's only for a few hours. Our chemistry is like magic, and it's been that way from day one.

"You want something else baby?" I asked Brooklyn. She only had a shrimp salad with lemon water, but that didn't look like enough to fill her up. She put herself on a strict diet after she had Dominque, but I don't want her to lose too much weight. She's right between an eight and a ten and that's perfect for me. She wants to lose ten more pounds, but I'm not having it. She's perfect to me, even after having two babies back to back.

"No, I'm good. You can get the check whenever you're ready," she replied. I called for our waitress to come over right as my phone started ringing. Brooklyn answered it and passed it to me telling me that it was my mother.

"What's up ma?" I asked when I got on the phone.

"I'm on my way to the hospital. Kennedi's cousin called and said that they've been up there since earlier today. She didn't want her to call anybody, but she snuck and called me anyway. That lil bitch is gon' make me slap her stupid ass one of these days. I don't have time to be playing these games with her. Her cousin said that she's about

267

eight centimeters now. She'll probably have the damn baby before I can get there," she rambled on.

"Alright ma, I'll be there as soon as I can," I replied. "I'm riding with David, so I need to go get my truck."

"Just tell David to drop you off. I don't want to be up here with them by myself."

"Okay, I'm coming," I said before hanging up.

"What's wrong?" Brook asked once I disconnected the call.

"Kennedi is in labor. Her stupid ass is already eight centimeters, and she told Tiffany not to call anybody," I replied angrily. When the waitress came over I paid our tab as we all got up from the table. I grabbed my wife's hand and headed for the exit.

"We can drop you off, and I'll bring your truck to you whenever you want it," Brooklyn suggested.

"What do you mean y'all can drop me off? They can drop us off because you're coming right with me," I replied.

"Shit, I'm coming too. Y'all know I'm nosey," David said when we got to his car.

"Let me call my mama and let her know what's going on. I need to be going to get my own kids instead of going to the hospital while Kennedi has hers," Brooklyn fussed.

"Just tell her that we'll come and get them as soon as we can. I really need you there with me," I said as I gripped her hand tighter.

I listened as Brooklyn told her mother what was going on. She told us that the kids could stay all night if we needed to stay at the hospital for a while.

I appreciated the gesture, but that wouldn't be necessary. There's no way in hell that I was staying at that hospital all night with Kennedi's ass. Brooklyn wouldn't let me even if I wanted to. We stopped at a red light just as my mama called me again.

I blew out a breath of frustration before I answered. "Yeah, ma."

"I just got here, but she already had the baby. The nurse said that they'll bring her back to the room once she gets weighed and cleaned up."

"So are you in the room with Kennedi right now?" I asked.

"No, that bitch had the nerve to ask me what was I doing here. Once I see my grandbaby, I'm taking my ass right back home. Her cousin and her uncle are here too."

"We're not that far away. I'll see you in a minute," I said before hanging up.

"What happened?" David asked.

"She already had the baby. She pissed mama off and you know she's ready to leave the hospital. She's waiting for them to bring the baby back to the room before she leaves though," I answered.

"What did she name her?" Candace asked.

"I don't know. I didn't even ask," I replied.

"You alright boo?" Brook asked while looking over at me.

She could probably see the aggravation written all over my face. I'm really not in the mood to deal with Kennedi and her bitching. That's one of the main reasons why I wanted my wife with me. She could always calm me down whenever things get too rough. Since Tiffany is up there, I'll probably have to calm her down too.

"I'm good, but I want you to be on your best behavior when we get to the hospital," I said smiling at her.

"What? I'm always on my best behavior," she replied.

"Tiffany is up there," I said looking at her for her reaction.

"I'm not worrying about her. I have two kids that depend on me. I don't have time to be out here fighting with nobody. I'm here to support you everybody else is irrelevant," she replied waving me off.

That wasn't the reply that I expected, but I fell in love with her new attitude. We pulled up to the hospital and took the elevator up to the maternity ward. I saw my mama standing in the hall talking on her phone, but she got off when she saw us walking up. Tiffany and her father sat in two chairs outside of Kennedi's door, but nobody said anything. My mama hugged Brooklyn and Candace and told me that I could go into the room to see the baby. I wanted my wife to come with me, but I know that wasn't a good idea. I opened the door slowly and walked into the room. Kennedi looked at me with a frown on her face as soon as our eyes connected. She was holding the baby, but she had her wrapped up in a blanket with a little pink hat on her head.

"How do you feel?" I asked only because I really didn't know what else to say. We didn't divorce under good terms, and we're far from being cordial with each other.

"I just had a baby. How do you think I feel?" She snapped with her usual nasty attitude.

I ignored her and walked over to get a good look at the baby. She tried to protest, but I took the baby out of her arms anyway. I looked down at her and put my index finger in her tiny little hand. She gripped my finger tightly just like all babies do at that age. I couldn't deny the fact that she's a beautiful baby, even though, her mother was a royal bitch. Holding her reminded me of the first time that I held Dominique, and I started to feel kind of emotional. Kennedi is watching me intently, but she never utters a word as she wipes away the few tears that fell from her eyes.

"You can't be a bitch all of your life Kennedi. The least you can do is call the man and let him know that he has a daughter. He has a right to know, and he needs to be in her life," I said while looking over at her. She didn't reply, but she broke down crying when I finished talking. She can never in this lifetime or the next try to convince me that this is my baby. She's every bit of Scott from her sandy brown hair to her almost white complexion and light hazel eyes. God must have heard my prayers even when I didn't think He was listening, and I'm so grateful.

KENNEDI

"Dominic I swear that it only happened one time," I lied. I'd actually slept with Scott a total of three times, but we only used protection twice. I never would have thought that the one time we didn't use protection I would get pregnant. I slept with Dominic the same day and two days after that. I just automatically assumed that he was the father. I was so embarrassed when the nurse came back into my room with my baby and Mrs. Liz saw her. She looked at me like I was crazy and laughed right in my face. She didn't even attempt to hold my daughter before she walked out of my room.

"One time is all it takes Kennedi. There's no need to apologize to me. You just made me one of the happiest men in the world," he said seriously.

"I never meant to hurt you Dominic," I cried feeling like a damn fool.

"What part don't you understand? I'm not hurt I'm relieved. Both of my kids are with my wife, and that's all I've ever wanted," he said.

I cringed when he referred to Brooklyn as his wife, even though, that's who she was.

"You don't have to say it like that. She's an innocent baby, don't act like she's a disease," I snapped.

"This has nothing to do with your baby. This is about me finally being rid of you for good. That's what I'm happy about. As far as your daughter, you need to call Scott and make him man up and handle his business," he said seriously.

I didn't want any advice from him, and I was about to go off on his ass until Mrs. Liz walked into the room. I don't have a problem with her, but it's who came in with her that I had the problem with.

"Who told you to bring her into my room?" I yelled angrily when I saw Brooklyn walk in. I don't know why, but looking at her always made me feel so ugly. She had her long hair curled and flowing down her back while the dress she wore showed off her almost perfect shape.

"She's here for her husband, but you better watch your tone with me. I'm done being nice to your stuck up ass," Mrs. Liz replied.

"Bring me my baby," I demanded as Dominic stood up with my daughter. He walked over to let Brooklyn get a good look at her. She looked at my baby long and hard before she laughed and shook her head.

"What's funny hoe?" I snapped as I felt my pressure start to rise.

"I'm a hoe, but both of my kids are with my husband. I didn't have to wait until I had them to know it. I knew it from the start. Give her back her baby and let's go Dominic. That's one birth certificate that you won't be signing," she replied before she walked out of my room.

Dominic handed me my daughter and followed behind his wife like a little trained dog. Mrs. Liz looked at me and frowned before she walked out on me as well. Tiffany came rushing back into the room and sat on the side of my bed.

"Are you alright Kennedi?" She asked right before I broke down and cried. She held on to me and let my liquid pain fall onto her shoulders.

273

Aside from her and my new bundle of joy, I feel like I'm all alone. Sad thing is I don't have anyone to blame, but myself.

****

I stayed in the hospital for four days before Starr, and I were released three weeks ago. I had a fever that wouldn't go away, and I stayed in a little longer than usual. I finally called Scott and told him about his daughter. He came to the hospital with his mother and aunt who demanded a paternity test. They paid to have it done at the hospital, and the results came back two days later. He was upset when I told him that I wanted to name her Diamond because he thought that it was too close to Dominic. We agreed to name her Starr instead. Since the paternity test proved that he was the father, he signed her birth certificate and gave her his last name. He's been talking about us being together, but I'm kind of unsure about that. Scott is very handsome, but he can't afford to give me the life that I'm accustomed to living. He has a job, but he's barely making it on the little money that he's being paid. His family seems nice, but I can tell that he's not very close with them. They've been going crazy buying Starr all kinds of clothes and everything else that they can think of. Tiffany laughed when I referred to them as trailer park trash, but that's what they seem like to me. Family or not, Starr would not be associating with them too much if I can help it. His mother was always asking when she can come and get her, but I didn't want to hurt her feelings.

"Please tell me that you're not going to meet up with Kyle again," I said as Tiffany walked into the kitchen. I stood at the counter making Starr's bottles when she walked in fully dressed.

Tiffany stayed at the hospital with me the entire time that I was there, but she was always on the phone with Kyle. Her black eye had finally healed, and I would hate for him to give her another one. He's been wining and dining her trying to get her back, and I could tell that it's working. She had her hair and nails freshly done yesterday, and I could see that her outfit was new. He's buying his way back in, and she seems to be for sale.

"Yes, I'm going to meet up with Kyle again," she repeated sarcastically. "What is your problem with him anyway?"

"My problem is that he uses you like you're a human punching bag. Then he comes around and sweet talks his way back into your life like nothing happened, and you let him," I replied.

"We're not getting back together Kennedi. I'm not even moving back in with him. We need money, and he's going to help me get it. We're both unemployed and damn near broke. Your plan to get child support from Dominic backfired since he's not Starr's father. Scott is broke as hell so he can't help you with too much. I'm doing this for the both of us, not just for me," she rambled.

"I still don't like it Tiffany. As much as I don't want to, I'll call my father for help if it means that you don't have to do anything illegal. He's less than a man to even have you doing that shit."

"Just trust me Kennedi. Two more days and we'll have enough money to last us for at least four months."

"Yeah okay," I said brushing her off.

"And you need to stop being so mean to Scott. I know he's not paid like Dominic, but he really does love you. That's more than you can say for your ex-husband. He's been here every day since you and Starr came home, and you won't even let the man stay the night over with his daughter.

"Don't try to take the focus off of you. We're continuing this conversation whenever you come back," I replied.

"Okay, I'm out of here. I'll be back later on tonight to get fussed at," she said as she kissed me on my cheek.

"Yeah right, just like the last time," I yelled after her.

She told me a few days ago that she would be back later and didn't come back for two whole days. I don't know what kind of hold Kyle has on her, and I don't want to find out. I finished making Starr's bottles and put them in the refrigerator just as someone started ringing my doorbell.

I peeped out of the window and saw Scott standing there in his work uniform. For the past few days, he's been coming to see the baby right after he got off. He would always ask to stay the night, but I never let him.

"Hey," I said when I opened the door for him.

"Hey. Is she up?" He asked referring to Starr.

"Nope, she never is when you come over so stop asking," I replied nastily.

"Why do you always have an attitude? I just asked a simple question," he said shaking his head.

I didn't mean to snap like I did, but this is not how I pictured my life. It's not Scott's fault, but he's the only one here for me to take it out on.

"Look, I'm sorry for going off, but I'm just aggravated."

"You're not aggravated you're miserable. You've spent your whole life getting your way, and you can't handle the fact that things have changed. I'm trying to help you with Starr, and you won't even let me do that. I'm cool if you don't want to be with me, but at least let me be here for my daughter," he ranted.

I stood there in shock. Scott has never spoken to me like that before. He's always been so passive, and I took advantage of that. I guess he must have a backbone, after all.

"I appreciate you wanting to help, but she's too young for you to take her to your house. And honestly, you need to clean that place up before I ever allow my daughter to even visit." I had been to Scott's house a few times and it's no place for a baby.

"Well, what's wrong with me staying over here once or twice a week? I can sleep on the sofa or the floor if that'll make you feel better. I'm not trying to get close to you, I'm trying to get close to my daughter," he said.

"Maybe you can stay over tomorrow night Scott," I offered.

"What's wrong with me staying tonight? I can run home and pack a bag right now," he said sounding hopeful.

My mind was telling me to say no, but my sleep deprived body screamed yes.

"I guess it's okay," I replied sounding unsure. He jumped up and left as soon as the words left my mouth. I just hope I don't regret it.

Scott is cool, but I don't want him to get the wrong impression about us. Me sleeping with him was a mistake that I didn't want to happen again. He caught me at my most vulnerable time, and he took advantage of it. He would always tell me something about Brooklyn and Dominic and then turn around and tell me how much he's been feeling me. The first time we slept together was when Tiffany and I ran into him outside of Starbucks. That was the same day that he told me about Dominic buying Brooklyn a car. He invited me to lunch, and we went back to his place after that. The whole time that we were there he kept telling me how much Dominic loved Brooklyn. He made me feel like a fool for being faithful to a man that he said was not faithful to me.

It was about two in the morning when I woke up to hear Starr screaming at the top of her little lungs over the baby monitor. Scott had her before I went to sleep, but he must have been sleeping now too. I got up and headed down the hall to her nursery. She must be hungry because she was trying to stuff her whole fist into her mouth. I picked her up and walked downstairs to warm her bottle. I saw Scott knocked out on my sofa with two empty beer cans and an empty bottle of some other kind of liquor on the floor. He must have bought it from home because I never kept liquor in the house since Dominic left.

After dealing with Starr for half of the night, I don't blame him for wanting a drink. I sat down in the recliner next to where he slept and fed Starr her bottle. I turned on the TV to keep me company since I would be up for a while. I turned on the news just as the rebroadcast came on. I listened intently as the reporter talked about a shooting that left a man and woman dead. They were found in a car in the parking lot of a casino a few hours ago. The reporter went on to say that two masked men dressed in all black were caught on camera opening fire on the couple, but they still had no leads or witnesses. They switched the camera to the earlier crime scene, and I almost dropped my baby when I saw Tiffany's car surrounded by yellow crime scene tape. I knew it was her silver Lexus because she has a bumper sticker with Bryce's shop info on the back. I had called her twice before I went to sleep, but she never answered.

"Oh God no, please don't let that be her," I mumbled as I tried to call her phone again. When it went straight to voicemail, I really started to panic. I was about to dial her father's number when someone knocked on my door.

"Scott get up," I yelled as I shook his arm. It was after two in the morning, and I knew that a knock at the door was not good.

"What's up?" He asked sitting up on the sofa.

"Somebody's knocking, I know that something is wrong, I can feel it," I said as I began to cry.

"Calm down Kennedi. Give me the baby and go see who it is," he replied calmly.

I handed Starr to her father right as my phone began to ring. My heart dropped to the pit of my stomach when I saw my uncle Thomas calling.

"Hello," I answered in a shaky voice.

"Kennedi I know it late, but I'm at your door," he replied.

I didn't respond before I hung up and rushed to let him in. He didn't even need to tell me what happened. His bloodshot eyes and tear stained face was my confirmation. I dropped down to the floor and let out a blood-curdling scream that I didn't even recognize. I begged her to leave Kyle alone, but she didn't listen. Just like I knew it would, messing with him had cost my cousin her life. And sadly, all the dirt he'd done had cost Kyle his life as well.

BROOKLYN

Since I'm headed back to school next week, Dominic decided to take the day off to chill with me and our kids. We hit up the mall and just about every shoe store that we passed. After getting my books and school supplies, we decided to take DJ to Chuck E. Cheese to let him play for a while before we went home. Dominic held the baby while I ran around with him until he got tired. Since finding out that Kennedi's baby wasn't his we hadn't heard from her anymore. We don't have any issues at the moment, but that's one less problem that we have to worry about. I can't even lie and say that I wasn't shocked by the revelation. I would have never thought that she would have cheated on Dominic with Scott of all people. Especially since she went crazy when she found out that Dominic was cheating on her with me.

I swear it's hard finding somebody that you can really trust these days. Even Kevin turned out to be a snake. When Candace told us about him being the one to cause me and Taylor's accident I was livid. I understood him being pissed with me, but Taylor and our kids didn't have anything to do with it. Dominic wanted to get at him again, but he went to jail before he had a chance to find him. He and Shannon are facing more than twenty years in jail for going around robbing people. I don't feel sorry for his ass one bit. He deserves everything that happens to him.

"I just need to swing by the office to sign some contracts before we go home. I won't be more than two minutes," Dominic said as we drove towards his office. We were on our way home when David called him to come by. DJ and Dominique were both in their car seats sleeping. As soon as we got into the car they were out cold. I plan to go home and cook dinner before they get up and demand all of my attention. As soon as we pulled up to the office I got heated when I saw Kennedi standing out front. She looked a hot ass mess. Both her hair and her clothes were unkempt. I don't know what's going on, but David and two other employees were out front trying to calm her down. She's screaming at the top of her lungs, but I can't hear what she's saying.

"Baby stay in the car and let me see what's going on," Dominic said.

"Okay," I replied as he opened his door and got out. As soon as Kennedi saw my husband she rushed over to him and started screaming. I rolled my window down and listened to what she had to say.

"That bitch that you married and her brothers are going to jail for killing my cousin," she yelled.

"Girl, what the hell are you talking about?" Dominic responded.

"You know exactly what I'm talking about. Tiffany and Kyle got killed last night, and I know they did it. Bryce probably found out that they burned his shop down and had them killed," she cried.

Hearing her say that got my attention. Dominic and I heard on the radio about a couple being killed, but they hadn't been identified yet. We never did find out who burned Bryce's shop down, but she's telling it all right now. I turned the car back on so that my babies could get some air before I opened my door and stepped out.

"Corey can you go sit in the truck with my kids please," I said to one of Dominic's drivers. I went and stood at my husband's side and waited for her to continue talking.

"I've called the police, and they're on their way here. You and your ratchet ass brothers are going to jail," she yelled as she got up in my face. I'm giving her a pass only because I know that she's hurting. As long as she doesn't put her hands on me she'll be fine.

"You better get out of my wife's face with that bullshit Kennedi. Now I'm sorry about what happened to your cousin, but my wife and my brother-in-laws didn't have shit to do with that," Dominic said while holding my hand.

"Don't stand here and try to defend this hood rat bitch," she yelled as she stepped up and pushed his head. That was all it took for me to get in her ass. I let Dominic's hand go and ran up on her. It didn't take more than two or three licks before the fight was over. I wanted to lay her ass out, but Dominic picked me up and carried me to the truck.

"That's why I told you to stay in the truck," he fussed as he placed me in the passenger's seat.

"Fuck what you talking about. I wish I would let that bitch push you and don't do nothing about it," I replied out of breath.

We sat around for a few more minutes until the police arrived. I thought she was bluffing, but that crazy bitch really did call them. When she finished telling them her story, even the police were looking at her like she was crazy. After it was all over with they told her to call the detective that's handling Tiffany's case if she has any leads. They gave her the detective's phone number and left not long after they came. She hopped in her car and sped away right after they did.

As soon as Dominic and I got home we called Bryce to fill him in on the drama. He wasn't surprised at all when he learned of who was behind the destruction of his shop. He really didn't care because he's in the process of getting the shop rebuilt from the ground up. He also has an idea about who had possibly taken their lives. Dominic told me about the visit from some man named Vamp when he was at my brother's shop a while ago. It didn't take a genius to figure out that he'd finally caught up with his intended target. I guess Tiffany was just at the wrong place at the wrong time. Even though she was a pain in the ass, I really felt bad for Kennedi. She pushed her father away, and her mother is locked up. She thought that she would be able to trap Dominic into paying child support, but even that backfired on her. She really taught me a valuable lesson though. I've learned to appreciate what I have because you never knew when it would be taken away from you.

KENNEDI

Laying my cousin and best friend to rest was the hardest thing that I've ever had to do. It was even harder when I had to go with her father to positively identify her body. It hurt me to know that somebody had riddled not only her car, but her entire body with bullets and left her to die like an animal. Thank God none of the shots were to her face or head, and we were able to have an open casket. She's my angel now, so I made sure that she wore all white with just a hint of pink. We don't have a huge family, but the few we have came out and supported my uncle during this difficult time. My mother isn't considered immediate family so they wouldn't let her out to come to the services. She was so heartbroken when my uncle and I told her the bad news. She's always looked at Tiffany as a daughter instead of her niece. Even though I give Scott and his family a hard time, they've been here for me every step of the way. I thought back to the last conversation that I had with Tiffany. Maybe she was right when she said that I should give Scott a chance to love me. I based my feelings off of what he could do for me financially, but I never really gave him a shot. Even now, we're at Tiffany's repast at my Uncle Thomas's house, and he's been dealing with Starr all by himself. He hasn't asked me to do anything, and I didn't offer. I was in my own world sitting in the corner grieving in peace.

I looked up and saw Scott walk in, but he's no longer holding our daughter. I was about to ask him where she was until I saw my father walk in not long after him with Starr in his arms. He beamed with pride whenever he looked at his first and only granddaughter. I hadn't spoken to him since before I had her, but I'm happy that he came to pay his respects. I saw him at the funeral, but I was too upset to talk to him. I sat up straight and fixed my hair because I knew that he was going to come over and talk to me. I needed to apologize to him for my behavior lately. It's not that I want to, but I'm really going to need his help soon. I'm almost broke, and he's the only person that can help me out of the mess that I'm in. If I play my cards right, I won't even have to look for a job for a few months. I watched as he held my daughter and talked to my uncle Thomas and his wife. He handed my uncle a sympathy card that I'm sure had some cash in it. When he handed my daughter back to Scott, I thought he would make his way over to me, but he never did. He walked out of the house and went straight to his car.

"Daddy," I yelled as I ran to catch up with him. He turned around to face me like I'm the last person that he wants to see.

"Yes Kennedi," he said nonchalantly.

"I just wanted to ask how you're doing. I haven't talked to you in a while," I said nervously while fidgeting with my fingers.

"You haven't talked to me because you didn't want to. You've made that clear plenty of times, and I finally got the message. I'm sorry to hear about Tiffany though. I know how close the two of you were."

"Thanks, but I also want to apologize to you for the way I've been acting lately. I had no right to be mad you, and I'm sorry. Can we just start over and work on our relationship?" I begged.

His eyes softened and for a minute I thought I had him right where I wanted him. That was until he opened his mouth to speak.

"Bravo," he said as he clapped his hands. "That was a great performance, but I'm not buying it. You're not sorry about anything. You need me right now, so you'll say anything to get your way. When I look at you, all I see is a younger version of your mother. A young money hungry woman who will stoop to any level for the sake of a dollar. My love for you will never change, but this bank is officially closed," he said as he got into his car and slammed the door.

He pulled off and left me standing there looking and feeling like a fool. I've official pushed away everybody who means anything to me. My mother has me so corrupted that I can't even have a normal relationship with anyone. The more I think about it, the more I feel like Tiffany has it easy right now. Death seems so much easier than dealing with my life right now.

Epilogue
(2 years later)

NADIA

Living in Virginia is not as bad as I assumed it would be. I've found a good job working with my mother as a dispatcher. I've also made lots of new friends. Surprisingly, I've been dating a nice guy named Darryl for the past year, and we're still going strong. I didn't want to start our relationship off with lies, so I told him all about my past in New Orleans. He also felt comfortable enough to share some of his background with me. My life is good, but that doesn't stop me from missing the one that I had back home. I really miss my friendship with Candace most of all. She never answers her phone when I call, but I understand how she feels. I did her wrong, and she doesn't want to have anything else to do with me.

I keep up with everything back home by looking at the local website. I almost died when I looked at the obituaries and saw Tiffany's picture come up. She and Kyle were killed together, and no one was ever arrested for their murders. I can't help, but feel like I'm partially to blame for that. I was the one who told Vamp everything about Kyle. I gave him his home address and told him what casino he went to all the time. I even told him what time he goes and where he parks his car. I never imagined that he would be there with Tiffany because he usually went alone. I never saw any burial information on him probably because he really didn't have any family to make arrangements.

Kevin and Shannon are still locked up, and they aren't coming home anytime soon. I took Candace's advice and told the police about what they did to me. Those charges ended up being added to the ones that they already had. After going to court for almost a year, I got three years of probation and a ton of community service for my charges. I also had to pay restitution to the courts for the counterfeit checks that I cashed. I'll probably be paying that for the rest of my life. All in all, life isn't so bad. I feel like I've been given a second chance at living, and I plan to get it right this time around.

KENNEDI

I walked into my living room and resisted the urge to walk right back out. That's how much of a mess it is. I'm so happy that my dad has Starr because I'm not in the mood to deal with a two-year-old on top of cleaning up this mess. He's been good with helping me out with her, but that's about it. He doesn't give me any money, and he buys whatever my daughter needs himself. I took a leap of faith and decided to try a relationship with Scott. That was clearly the worst mistake that I've ever made in my life. He started out being the perfect mate. He was attentive and treated me like a queen.

That all changed when he gave up his apartment and moved in with me. Things were okay at first until I noticed that he was always drinking. He couldn't go one day without a drink, and he hated to be called out on it. It got so bad that he eventually lost his job. He went to work drunk and ended up having an accident in the company truck. He was fired after he failed the sobriety test, and he wasn't eligible for unemployment. I started working as a teller in a bank about a year ago, so all of the bills are on me. Thank God for my uncle Thomas and the money that he gave me from Tiffany's life insurance. If it weren't for that, I would probably be broke and homeless. I never told Scott about it because he would probably drink it all away. I couldn't believe that it's been two years since my cousin was killed. Starr and I visit her grave and talk to her often. I've been coping with it one day at a time, but it's still hard.

"Get your ass up," I yelled as I kicked Scott's legs. He was sprawled out on the living room floor with an empty Jack Daniel's bottle right next to him. I wanted his ass to get out of my house so bad, but I made a stupid mistake and put him on my lease. His mother has been paying his half of the rent since he's been out of work, but that's still not enough.

"What?" He asked groggily barely able to stand to his feet. I don't know what the hell made me even go there with him. If my mother had something to say about Dominic, who was damn near perfect, she would die if she sees what I'm dealing with now. I missed my mother so much that it often brings tears to my eyes. She was given a ten-year sentence for the many charges that they had on her. She probably would have gotten more if my uncle Thomas hadn't paid for her an attorney. I hate that she has to see her one and only grandchild from behind the prison walls.

"Get up and help me clean up this mess that you made. You need to find your ass a job because your time here is running out. I'm not putting you back on my lease when it's time for renewal," I fussed.

"Bitch you should be happy that I'm still here. It's not like you're a catch or nothing. We don't fuck, so it's not like I'm missing some anything. Shit, I see why Dominic left your ass for his new wife," he slurred. He's always throwing the fact that Dominic left me for Brooklyn in my face.

"And that's why he beat your ass for telling me about it. Your nose is still crooked from that beat down," I laughed.

He had looked at me with fire in his eyes before he staggered upstairs. He hates when I remind him of the time that Dominic broke his nose. Just thinking about Dominic had me missing how things use to be with us. I never had to worry about anything when we were together. All of my bills were paid, and I had money for whatever I wanted. Now, I barely have fifty dollars to spare after paying all of the bills and making sure Starr is straight.

Lately, I've been thinking that it's time for me to find another sponsor. I need a new man with money, so I don't have to spend my own. Of course, I can't do anything until my broke ass baby daddy is gone. I can't wait until it's time for me to renew my lease so I can take his name off it. Unfortunately, I have five more months of hell to live in before that time comes.

DOMINIC

"Alright Brooklyn, work it bitch," Co-Co
yelled through the bullhorn that he was holding.
We're all seated up front cheering for Brooklyn as
she received her degree. We have the first three
rows of the auditorium on lock with all of her
family and friends. It took Brooklyn two weeks of
begging her classmates to be able to get enough
tickets for everybody who wanted to attend. Even
DJ was standing in the chair screaming when he
saw his mama walking across the stage. He used to
be my shadow when he was younger, but he's a
straight up mama's boy now. He still hangs out with
me all the time, but he loves Brooklyn to death.
Dominique clings to both of us, but she's more of a
daddy's girl. DJ is four and Dominique is two, and
they're both spoiled rotten. I told my wife that I'm
ready for another one, but she's not having it.

"Cordell sit your ass down somewhere before
these people escort us out of here," Co-Co's father
yelled.

"Do y'all hear somebody talking?" He asked in
his usual dramatic tone. "I don't see anybody here
named Cordell."

"Boy, sit down and shut up with that damn
bullhorn," Mrs. Pam fussed.

I swear there is never a dull moment whenever
our families get together. It's definitely going down
later on tonight at Brooklyn's graduation party. I
rented a hall and paid somebody to cater the food
and decorate it for us. Our kids are going to be with
my parents for the weekend, and I'm ready to turn
up with my wife.

After the graduation, we stood in the front of the auditorium waiting for Brooklyn to come out. They have a beautiful waterfall out front, and Brooklyn's mother wanted us all to take pictures in front of it.

"Girl sit down and stop waving that cheap ass ring around," Co-Co yelled as he pushed Taylor away from him.

She's so excited that Bryce finally popped the question. It happened over four months ago, but she's always flashing her ring in somebody's face. Since Bryce's shop burned down he had it rebuilt bigger than it was before. He had the stylists and barbers downstairs while he and the other artists worked upstairs. Business is so good that he had to hire some more people.

David and I are also doing our thing. Since signing with the other construction company, we've signed on with two more this past year. I told Brooklyn that even though she has her degree she doesn't have to work if she doesn't want to. She's always wanted to be an elementary school teacher, so she's not trying to hear that.

Surprisingly, Candace and David are still going strong too, but they aren't ready to make any commitments. It's probably because they break up every other week. She hasn't been home in over a year, but she still swears that they don't live together. Even Dwight and Co-Co are hanging in there. I just feel so bad for Dwight for having to put up with that drama king every day of his life. Co-Co is always embarrassing him, but he doesn't seem to mind.

"Look at my mommy," DJ said as he took off running in Brook's direction. Dominique wiggled out of arms and took off running after him. She picked our daughter up and walked over to us.

"Congratulations!" Everybody yelled. She's smiling hard from ear to ear, and so am I. It took a lot for us to get to where we are, but it's all been worth it.

"Thanks, everybody," she said as she came stood next to me.

Mrs. Pam is dying to take some more pictures, so we spent the next hour doing just that. Once we finished, we all went out to eat before going home to get ready for Brooklyn's party. We have a few more hours to chill before we go to the hall. I looked over at my wife and smiled. She returned the smile, but she doesn't know that I'm smiling for a reason. I can't wait until she gets home and sees her surprise in the driveway. She still has her Audi, but I got her a brand new silver Mercedes Benz SUV as a graduation gift. I had Tiana to wrap a red bow around it before we came home.

"I know you're tired of hearing me say this, but I'm so proud of you baby," I said as I grabbed Brooklyn's hand.

"I'll never get tired of hearing you say that. I'm…" she started to say until we pulled up to our house.

"Ahhh! Dominic I know you didn't!" She screamed as she jumped out of my truck. She didn't care that the car was still rolling when she did. I parked and got the kids out while Brooklyn ran around her new truck like a kid. I tossed her the keys and watched as her, and the kids climbed inside. I laughed as they played around with all the features like it was a new toy.

"You like it?" I asked even though I already knew the answer.

"Yes, I love it. You already know that I'm driving this to my party tonight. Thank you, baby," she smiled as she gave me a big kiss.

Seeing her smile is all the thanks I need. Unlike Kennedi, Brooklyn never asks for anything. That only makes me want to give her the world and everything in it. I always tell her that she's not perfect, but she's perfect for me. She's not only the mother of my kids, but she's also my wife. It's kind of hard to believe that she started out as being just my little secret.